Murder on the Way

A Camino de Santiago Mystery

P. T. Shaw

Copyright© 2024 by Peter Shaw

All rights reserved. No part of this book maybe reproduced or transmitted in any form or by any means, electronic or mechanical, including photocopying, recording, or any information storage and retrieval system, without written permission from the author.

This book is a work of fiction. Any references to historical events, institutions, real people, or real places are used fictitiously. Other names, characters, places, and events are products of the author's imagination, and any resemblance to actual events, places, or persons, real or dead, is entirely coincidental.

*To Mary, my wife and inspiration,
and to my family, both relatives
and all those who walk the Camino.*

Contents

Prologue	1
1. Chapter One Naples	3
2. Chapter Two South Philly	11
3. Chapter Three Where's the Cash?	26
4. Chapter Four The Hunt is On	39
5. Chapter Five It's All Uphill From Here	50
6. Chapter Six Raging Bulls and Wizard Squirrels	77
7. Chapter Seven Emilio Estevez Ruined My Life	100

8. Chapter Eight Santiago Matamoros	120
9. Chapter Nine Banditos and Cutthroats	143
10. Chapter Ten Another Family	154
11. Chapter Eleven Max the Hero	175
12. Chapter Twelve The Holy Grail	199
13. Chapter Thirteen The Iron Cross	216
14. Chapter Fourteen Only a Priest Can Say Mass	227
15. Chapter Fifteen Santiago de Compostela	254
16. Chapter Sixteen The End of the World	273
Epilogue	282
Glossary	284
Acknowledgements	288
About the author	290

Prologue

For more than a millennium, people from across Europe and the globe have made the pilgrimage that bears my name. Some of them know little or nothing of me or of my evangelical works on the Iberian Peninsula. They make their pilgrimages both in my name and for various other reasons. They are from all walks of life and have different levels of piousness. Some profess to have no belief at all. I see and welcome them all. Mostly, they have come of their own free will, but that has not always been the case. The meaning and outcome of each person's pilgrimage are unique to that individual. Some will find their way, some will not. That is "The Way of St. James."

Chapter One

Naples

The bright morning sunshine provided a stark contrast to the shadowed corners of the ancient city. A statuesque figure loomed in the darkness, his arms relaxed and his right hand behind his thigh as he clenched the handle of a stiletto. He focused on the man admiring the life-size marble figure of Eumachia. He heard only the internal beat of his symphony of rage. He saw only the sweet spot on his target's back. On a warm spring day in 2015, Max was ready to kill.

Max started the day the way he started every day for the past week. He followed the target from his house to his office and waited for him to leave for his daily jaunt around the city. He followed him around the streets of Naples, visiting cafes, restaurants, and many of the city's tourist sights. This guy spent most of his time goofing off, drinking coffee, and stuffing his face with pastries and gelato, all at the taxpayer's expense. The only thing close to work that he ever did was to gab to a reporter about the garbage strike occasionally and blame others for it, mostly Max's employers and their associates. The big-mouthed bureaucrat never did anything to resolve the issue, which was actually his job.

One day, the fat cat must have been bored with roaming through Naples, so he decided to drive to nearby Pompeii.

The target drove to Pompeii. He parked his city vehicle in a reserved government spot and strutted right through the gates of the ancient city as if he were Caesar himself. Max parked his car at the end of the lot, near the exit. He strolled to the gate, paid for his ticket, and entered through the turnstile into old Pompeii.

Max kept his distance. He stalked the target through the ruins of the ancient Roman city that lies at the base of Mount Vesuvius. As he passed by the skeletons of lavish villas and buildings which dated back to the fourth century BC, the crunch of the gravel underfoot provided a soft cadence to his pursuit. When they reached the house of Triptolemus, Max intensified his focus on the target. He planned to rid the world of this pest, finishing in time for some morning coffee and biscotti. Max stared at the target's back, reached back to grasp his stiletto, and made one last check for witnesses. Some early-bird tourists entered the area, causing him to put his plan on hold for the moment. Max didn't want to wait too long because more tourists would arrive as the day grew later. He wanted to complete this project today because he was tired of watching this waste of tax payers euros run through the seven deadly sins on a daily basis.

The target strolled around the streets and pathways of Pompeii, enjoying the sights with little concern for the duties of his position. He had no idea he was being watched, and certainly no idea what the day might entail. He reached the Temple of Apollo and admired the Etruscan architecture with its Greek and Roman enhancements. The target moved onto the Forum. A few other tourists were around, but fewer and fewer as Max and the target ventured into the city ruins. Eventually, they entered the large, open courtyard in the building of Eumachia. It was surrounded by a long, mostly intact exterior wall, and there were no other tourists. Good cover for Max, who got close to the target without being noticed. The aura of death was strong in this place where so many had lost their lives so long ago. The target stopped to view the statue of Eumachia and had the entire area to himself; at least he thought he did.

Max scanned the area. No one in sight. The target stood in a secluded spot.

This place was Sin City, right? Think of all the debauchery and brothels. Before the eruption, of course. It's a fitting place for this gluttonous pig to die.

His heart was pounding, and all his senses focused on his task. Max crept silently to within striking distance and plunged the stiletto between the target's ribs, just to the right of his spine, penetrating a lung and his heart. The target released a hushed gurgle and fell to the ground next to the statue of Eumachia. A stiletto in the lung is a quiet termination technique. He withdrew his knife as the body fell and wiped it clean on the dead man's shirt. He placed the knife back in a sheath under his shirt, adjusted his sunglasses, and strolled through the ruins. He was now just another well-built, handsome Italian man with his olive skin, dark hair, and fashionable clothes, enjoying the warm spring morning and blending in with tourists. As he made his way toward the exit, Max noticed a turtle on its back with legs flailing, trying to right itself. Max stepped over the rope barrier and flipped the turtle back onto its feet.

Time for coffee and biscotti.

The corpse would lay there and bleed out, baking in the morning sun, until some lucky tourist came upon it in this maze of the ancient Pompeii ruins. This body was a confirmation; it was a message meant to be found. The target was a loud-mouthed government bureaucrat who was constantly sounding off to the newspapers and television stations, blaming Max's employers and their associates for the ongoing garbage problems that had plagued Naples for the past decade. If this wasn't bad enough, European Union officials had seen one of his television interviews, and decided to get involved. He had to be silenced.

Once assigned a termination task, Max followed a rigid process. He went incognito, cutting off communications with all associates and even his mother. He followed and studied his targets long enough to learn their habits and soon knew what they would do next better than they knew it themselves. He had never had an issue, and nothing ever came back to him or his bosses. This made Max a valuable asset to his capo, Carlo Marino.

The job was done; it was clean, and Max went to Carlo to report his results. "Everything went well. We won't be hearing anything from that chiacchierone anymore."

Carlo Marino was the top capo in Naples and controlled not only the underworld and streets but also held substantial influence in the local government. As Max stood in front of Carlo, a man at the top of his world, Max couldn't help but notice how worn out he looked.

Carlo is only in his fifties, but his face is filled with cracks and crevices. He has sunken eyes, and he looks much older than a man of his years. He seems fit, but he smokes those guinea stogies and you can see the stress and strain of being a capo. He forces a smile sometimes, but not often. This is a rough life.

Carlo glanced around the room, not paying as much attention to Max as he normally would during the debriefing of a big job like the one that Max just completed. He cleared his throat and looked at Max, but not directly into his face.

"Carlo, what's going on? You seem distracted. The job went well."

"That's good, Max. I can always depend on you. But I have some sad news. You see, your mother died while she was attending mass on Sunday."

"Oh my God, what happened?"

"It was just her time."

"You should go see the priest. He has been taking care of her until your return."

Max went pale. He looked down at the ground for several seconds and then back at Carlo. His eyes were glassy, and his hands slightly trembled.

"Okay, Carlo, I need to go."

"You go and do whatever you need to do. Let me know if I can help."

"Grazie, Carlo."

Max slowly turned and walked away. He wore a blank face with distant eyes, not knowing where he was in the world. He never imagined not having his mother with him. She was his only living blood relative, and she was the only person on earth he really cared about. He was a street soldier, and his associates were called family, but they were not blood, at least not his blood, and he did not love them. Max was now alone in the world.

After burying his mother, Max's heart was empty. He roamed the streets of Naples, his eyes sunken and distant. Max's mother had always been there for him. She had raised him by herself and always defended him, no matter the situation. She fed him, put clothes on his back, and put a roof over his head all by herself since the day his father was killed. With his mother gone, Max was lost in a sea of doubt and despair. His confident stride was replaced by a hapless meandering. He no longer greeted acquaintances with his usual charm. His sharp mind was clouded with sorrow and uncertainty.

Spring turned to summer and summer to autumn, and the garbage was still piled high as ever. With no hope of a resolution in sight for this interminable problem, life seemed futile. It didn't matter to Max.

Life is trash, just like this city. I need to get out of this line of work.

Max ventured out into the world less and less. On the rare or necessary occasions when Max did go out, he trudged from one street to the next, not taking notice of the lively cafes and restaurants and ignoring the beautiful churches spread throughout the city. He barely acknowledged anyone who wished him well or offered him condolences for his mother's passing. Many of them were friends of his friends and their associates. He didn't think of how he had enjoyed cafes and restaurants, but only of his last target and how he gorged himself during the work day. Max now ate little, and when he did, it was just to live. His primary source of caloric intake was in the form of wine. The only somewhat normal part of his life was that he continued to go to the cinema. He had loved movies since he was a child; it was his escape, and he could sit in the dark and not talk to or see anyone. After his father's death, his mother took him to a special showing of *The Wizard of Oz*. The film allowed Max to be happy, at least for a short time. Best of all, he didn't have to interact with anyone while in the theater. Other than the occasional trips to the theater, he no longer lived the life of a Neapolitan. Especially one in Max's line of work.

Max avoided Carlo and had no interest in returning to work. People were beginning to talk—people who worked in the System and would demand action to correct the situation. A System street soldier who would not leave his house was not a good look. Something would have to be done.

Chapter Two

South Philly

About the time Max lost his mother, Joey Conti sat in a bar on Passyunk Avenue in South Philadelphia. The early summer evening began just like most of his other evenings. Joey sat alone in his usual booth in the back corner of Angelo's Bar, under ceiling tiles colored amber by decades of cigarette smoke and indifference, trying to figure out how to make the changes that would make his life bearable. His elbows were on the table and his head down as he stared at his plate, picked at his mushroom tortelloni in marinara sauce, and sipped on a glass of dago red. The benches with cracked maroon vinyl over worn-out pads and flattened springs were just uncomfortable enough to remind the occupant that this place was real. The neon beer signs that adorned the walls hummed and flickered sporadically, adding a sense of nonchalance. In Angelo's, simmering sauces and grilling meats flavored the air in the room. This all helped to make Angelo's what it was: a hangout for the people who grew up in the neighborhood, both local working-class and mob wannabes. Good Italian food at local bar prices and old crooner songs on the jukebox made the place more like the mid-twentieth century than fifteen years into the twenty-first century. Angelo's lets people escape from the neighborhood's ongoing gentrification.

The new folks in the neighborhood had become a royal pain in the ass, causing more parking problems in an area already known for parking problems by using their garages for storage instead of cars but insisting that no one park in front of their driveways. They also wanted to control the local little league and most everything else. They didn't go to Angelo's because it wasn't bistro enough for their taste, coupled with the general vibe of hostility they got if they happened to wander in. That was fine with Joey and the rest of Angelo's patrons. No yuppies need apply.

Joey, a skinny loner in his mid-thirties who lived with his mother, had sad brown eyes and a big, hooked nose. He blended in with the decor in Angelo's and pretty much went unnoticed. While Joey slowly sipped his wine and ate his meal, he was engaged in his favorite social activity of eavesdropping on his fellow diners.

Man, this is sad. I've got to get out of here and do something to get my life right. There's no way that I want to be doing this until the day that I die. This isn't me, and I need to do something to change.

This night, opportunity knocked, and Joey was ready to answer. He overheard a conversation between two brothers who sat in the adjacent booth, Rocco and Louie Rizzo. Rocco, who had classic Mediterranean looks, was a hair under six feet tall and built solidly with a subcutaneous layer of insulation that many with his lifestyle had obtained over the years. Louie had cropped, curly black hair, was younger, a couple of inches taller, and about eighty pounds heavier. Oblivious to Joey's presence, they discussed in detail a foul-up from earlier that day.

Joey listened intently to Rocco and Louie's description of the debacle that resulted when they double-crossed a couple of drug dealers from the projects.

Rocco and Louie had asked their boss, local capo Enzo Marino, an old-school, third-generation made man who liked to keep up appearances and keep control of his neighborhood, for the go-ahead to launder some money for these drug dealers.

Enzo was a big man, both in height and weight. He had a good head of pepper gray hair for a man nearing sixty, and when he spoke, it was with a booming voice. He had hands the size of baseball mitts, and he never hesitated to put them to use when necessary.

Earlier that day, Rocco and Louie entered the back door of Enzo's office at Hank's Hoagie Palace. The dimly lit room had file cabinets topped with meat-slicing machines, large cans of Marzano tomatoes, jars of peppers, and pickles. On the wall behind Enzo's large metal government surplus desk hung a poster of a Frank Sinatra mugshot, a particular favorite among those in Enzo's line of work. The aroma from the kitchen in the next room was the only pleasant feature of this place.

"Boss, we got a chance to make some easy money laundering some cash," Rocco said.

"For who?"

"Nobody, just a couple of melanzane dope dealers."

"Why do they want us to do it?"

"I don't know. I think they're new to the business."

Enzo gave them the go-ahead. "Do not foul this up. There is word that the feds are in the neighborhood, and I don't know why."

Rocco and Louie drove over to the projects in their new Cadillac Escalade and discussed their plan of action if things went as they expected. Once they arrived, they walked over to an empty section on the ground floor of a high-rise apartment building and entered a utility room, where they met their new business acquaintances, Philly Phil and T-bone, as arranged.

Philly Phil and T-bone showed all the signs of young men from the projects with newfound wealth. They were decked out in loads of gold jewelry. They also donned ball caps with the stickers still on them and, of course, Air Jordans.

"You guys need to find a better place to conduct your business. These fluorescent lights are nasty," Rocco said.

"That noisy boiler don't help neither," Louie added.

"You guys are soft. That's just life in the projects," Philly Phil said.

"Besides, that noise keeps anybody outside from hearin' what we doin'," T-Bone said.

Rocco smiled, nodded his head, and said, "That's a good point. How you doin'?"

"We're doing just fine," Philly Phil said.

"Let's get down to business. I don't like leaving my car around here. What do you need from us?" Rocco said.

T-bone and Philly Phil opened two large duffel bags filled with rolls of cash. "We need this clean. It's too hard to make any legit large purchases with cash, and I want to get me one of those Escalades like you got."

"Why can't your own people do this for you?" Rocco said.

"We're a couple of independent entrepreneurs," T-bone answered. "We don't have no people, and we don't need no people."

Rocco and Louie looked at each other, grinned, and nodded. This confirmed what they suspected all along: these guys were not connected. Rocco and Louie each pulled out a .22-caliber snubbie.

The dope dealers laughed. "What are you going to do with those?" Philly Phil asked.

Rocco laughed and said, "I'll show you."

Rocco and Louie each fired bullets into the eyeballs of their new business acquaintances. The bullets rattled around inside their skulls, and they were dead in an instant. The partnership was dissolved. The snubbie is a no-muss, no-fuss weapon. Hold it close to the target and pull. Little sound, little blood, big results—the money now belonged to Rocco and Louie, minus Enzo's cut, of course.

"Maybe we shouldda asked them how much was in there before we offed them," Louie said.

"It don't matter. We gotta count it anyway, so let's get goin'," Rocco said.

The two drug dealers lay silently on the floor with blood running out of their eyes. Rocco and Louie made their hasty exit and headed straight to their car. That's when things started to go sideways. The Drug Enforcement Agency and local cops had the drug dealers on their radar, and when they spotted a couple of mooks with duffel bags leaving the projects where these drug dealers were known to hang out, the police decided to follow them.

As Rocco pulled out onto the street, a brown sedan halfway down the block also pulled out. Rocco and Louie were concerned with what Enzo might do now that they had killed two people without getting the go-ahead, so they drove around with no particular destination in mind. They made their way to Columbus Boulevard and were headed toward the Ben Franklin Bridge when Rocco noticed that the same car had been behind them for some time.

"Louie, do you see that brown car back there?"

"Yeah, it could be a cop."

"Keep an eye on it."

After a few more blocks, it was still there.

"I think they're following us," Louie said.

"Let's see if they are," Rocco answered.

Rocco took the on-ramp to the Ben Franklin Bridge, and the sedan followed. He made a U-turn in the middle of the bridge and headed straight for the Vine Street Expressway.

"If they follow us now, we'll know they're cops because only a moron would make that turn," Rocco said.

"Yeah, I know," Louie said.

The brown sedan made the same dangerous U-turn and followed them to the expressway. Traffic was heavy, and Rocco was swerving from lane to lane with horns blaring, brakes screeching, and the sedan trying to match every move, but the volume of cars and chaos caused by Rocco's reckless driving made it difficult. The chase vehicle flashed its reds and blues and blared its siren in an attempt to gain ground on the Escalade. This had the opposite effect, as some vehicles pulled over and blocked the shoulder lane, while others tried to avoid the chase but kept driving in the traffic lanes. Rocco and Louie got to the exit for the art museum and took it. They no longer saw the brown sedan, and the sound of the siren faded away.

"We gotta find a place to stash this cash in case we get pulled over on the way back," Rocco said.

They drove down a side road that paralleled the railroad track and pulled behind a rickety equipment garage in an old and seldom-used playground to keep out of sight and think. There was a faint rumbling of a slow-moving freight train off in the distance.

"We're not too far from the Alamo. That'd be a great place to stash it," Rocco said.

"Yeah, you're right. It would be a good place to stash it, but we're really not that close. It would be a long walk," Louie said.

"You're just lazy, and besides, don't you hear the train? We can ride in style like in the old days," Rocco said.

So they walked over to the edge of the park, went down the slope to the tracks, tossed their bags on a flatcar, hopped on, and rode the mile or so down the tracks, just like when they were kids.

When they reached the Alamo, an old concrete dock between the railroad tracks and the Schuylkill River, they tossed their bags of cash onto the dock and hopped off the train, falling and rolling away from the tracks and into a weed-filled gully.

"It didn't use to be that hard to get on and off these trains," Louie said.

"You weren't such a fat-ass back then," Rocco replied.

"You didn't look so good yourself."

"Just go get the bags. We gotta find a good place to hide them."

They looked around the abandoned, dilapidated dock, trying to find a place to put the bags of cash. They needed a spot where the bags would be invisible, even to any wanderer who might stumble past.

"You know, Roc, we had a lot of good parties here."

"Yeah, but that's not what we're here for now. This place kinda smells, and there's chest-high weeds growing all over the place, but that's good. That's probably why nobody comes here anymore. Let's hide these bags and get outta here," Rocco said.

"But it was a great place in its day. Now, we just hide the cash, get it later, and keep Enzo off our backs," Louie said.

The Alamo was once a place to have keg parties where they could make all the noise they wanted, with no one around to hear it and call the cops. Over the years, most people had forgotten about the Alamo, and the younger crowd never even knew about it. No one ever went there any longer.

"Louie, throw these guns into the river, and make sure you throw them far. We don't want nobody finding them."

"Look, we can go down beneath the dock over by the edge and toss the bags under it behind some weeds," Louie said.

"All right, you go first, and I'll hand the bags down to you," Rocco said.

Louie walked over to the side of the concrete dock, stepped onto the sloped riverbank, and slid down to the edge of the water on his backside. It was not a graceful act.

Rocco laughed and called out, "Yo, Fall-Guy, don't drown."

"Just shut up and pass me the bags. There's a cave here that I can put them in, and nobody will be able to see them."

Louie put the bags in the cave and made repeated attempts to get back up the muddy bank. "Give me a hand. This shit is slippery."

Rocco pulled him up, and they made the long walk back up the tracks to their car.

When they got back to the neighborhood, they stopped by Angelo's to get their story straight before seeing Enzo. They didn't even know how much money they had. They were in such a hurry to get away from the cops and hide it that they never even counted it. Some wine, cheese, and, of course, gabagool, at Angelo's would help them figure things out.

Joey sat quietly and continued listening to these two numb-nuts talk about their screw-up.

"Roc, do you think that the money is safe just sittin' in that cave like that?" Louie said.

"Yeah, nobody ever goes to the Alamo anymore, and besides, we're gonna get it in a day or two as soon as the coast is clear," Rocco answered.

"I hope you're right. Enzo will be pissed if we lose it."

"Don't worry, I know what I'm doin'."

After listening to Rocco and Louie's tale, Joey finished his meal and casually walked out the door, unnoticed as usual. These two goons, who had tormented him throughout high school, had just provided Joey with what he needed to make the changes to live his life as he wanted to live it. He would never have to deal with assholes like these two again.

Joey left Angelo's at dusk, stopped by his house to pick up his car and a flashlight, and was off to the Alamo. Joey drove up to Twenty-Third Street and looked for a place to park. He couldn't drive all the way to the Alamo because it was a fifteen-minute walk from the nearest city street. He parked in an abandoned lot and made his way through broken glass, old appliances, mattresses, tires, and other debris that people threw there to avoid a trip to the dump. He then made the quarter-mile trek up the tracks to reach the Alamo. Once he got there, he looked around; it was much smaller than he remembered. He walked over to the edge of the dock overlooking the river; it still looked steep. This brought back a bad memory that etched the Alamo and its location in his mind.

Back in high school, Joey was a frail, unsure kid with a big nose that made him subject to much ridicule. He didn't have any brothers or friends who could handle themselves in a neighborhood where that was almost a requirement. He was bullied, especially by Rocco and Louie, who, to no one's surprise, grew up to be mob wannabe thugs. So Joey kept to himself. He liked to read, and he attended church with his parents on a regular basis. He always said that his mother was his best friend.

But one sunny day in the summer after Joey's senior year, school had just let out, and as was done at that time, a keg party was planned to be held at the Alamo. Joey, along with many of the others from their South Philly neighborhood, were invited, or more accurately, heard about it and showed up. That's how it worked in those days. Joey was in good spirits.

I'm finally done with high school. I don't have to worry about dealing with all the crap that comes with that. This party should be great—just a bunch of us having a good time. No more punks bothering me to act cool in front of their friends.

Things were better at first, with everyone there drinking and singing songs like "Saturday Night's Alright for Fighting" at the top of their lungs. Good times were being had by all. Then, as the night went on and the beer kept flowing, Rocco and Louie got drunk and rambunctious and decided to focus their attention on Joey. Tormenting him was one of their favorite pastimes.

"Yo, Toucan Sam, who invited you?" Rocco called out to Joey.

"Real funny, Rocco; you're such a wit," Joey said.

"What did you say?" Rocco said.

"Let's get him, Roc," Louie said.

The two Rizzo boys then grabbed Joey by the arms and legs, carried him as he struggled to try to break free to the edge of the dock, and tossed him into the dank, polluted Schuylkill River. Joey sank but quickly surfaced, slapping at the water as he gasped for air. He flailed his arms, kicked his legs erratically, used the strokes of a non-swimmer, and barely made it to the bank. He came up next to a cave just under the concrete slab that was the Alamo. He made his way ashore, sat by the cave, and gathered himself. He then climbed up to the dock and sloshed straight past everyone, most of whom were still laughing. Soaked wet with shoulders slumped, he plodded the five miles home alone.

Will this torment never end?

Little did he know that this experience would lead to his chance for revenge and redemption, and over the years, everyone pretty much forgot about Joey. This poor soul will have his day.

The sun had long been down when Joey arrived at the Alamo after his trek up the tracks, but the moonlight was bright enough for him to look around and eye a spot where he could climb down the bank to get under the concrete deck and into the cave. The trampled high grass and fresh skid marks indicated where someone had recently slipped down the bank. This was the right place. He entered the shallow cave and shined his light; the bags were there. Joey grabbed the two duffel bags, unzipped them, and looked inside them. The money was there.

Thanks, Rocco and Louie; this is mine now. You dumb asses.

He scrambled up the bank as well as any mountain goat. Life was good.

Then, a faint rustling came from the bushes across the tracks.

What was that? Shit, is somebody there? Did they see me? Back in the day, a lot of gay guys used to come here to hook up. Maybe they still do?

Joey started to run down the tracks and fell flat on his face, and the bags flew off into the darkness. A train whistle blew in the distance.

That's all I need.

He got up and looked at his bloody, greasy hands. The jagged rocks around the railroad tracks were not forgiving. He wiped his hands on his pants and saw one of the bags just ahead on his left, but he couldn't see the other bag. He searched, looking all around. He darted in short bursts in every direction. He then spotted the other bag in the bushes, a little further up and next to a pile of stones. He picked it up and hurried down the tracks.

I can't get stuck behind this train; sometimes they are miles long. I gotta get out of here.

Joey rushed down the track towards the lot where he parked, but this time taking care to place his footsteps properly. The train came up right behind him and blew its horn. Joey jumped over into the lot where he was parked.

Two young thugs came from behind the bushes and yelled, "Yo, whaddaya got in those bags? C'mere."

"None of your business, you little punks." Joey yelled back, still panting from his escape from the train.

The two teens rushed towards him. He swung one of the bags and knocked the first thug to the ground. The thug, who was still standing, rushed towards Joey, and Joey kicked him in the chest and knocked him on his backside.

"What's your problem, mister?"

The young thugs were not expecting this and were shaking and looking around as if they were complete innocents who had been wronged.

Joey took the opportunity to run to his car. The teens hurled rocks and insults at him as he ran.

"You better run, you creep," the first teen yelled.

"Run, pussy, run," the second teen yelled.

"Yeah, Forrest Gump, run," the first teen added.

The teens half-heartedly ran after Joey as he traversed through the debris, banging the bags on almost everything that he passed. It was not a graceful departure.

Where did that burst of bravery and strength come from? I guess my life is already changing for the better.

He made it to his car, tore out of the lot, and headed towards home.

I need to find someplace to hide this money. I can't bring these bags into the house; my mother spends every day cleaning it from top to bottom. She would surely see them, and those nosey neighbors might also spot me bringing them into the house. I need to find some place to hide these until I can make my plans, get out of town, and change my life.

He pulled into a Wawa parking lot on Columbus Boulevard and put the bags in his trunk. He went in and grabbed a coke and a soft pretzel, and when back in his car, contemplated what he needed to do next.

The first thing that I need to do is go home and get cleaned up.

He was washing up in the bathroom, and his mother walked by and saw him.

"What happened to you, Joey? You are bleeding."

"I just fell; I'm fine."

"Okay, good night."

"Good night, Mom."

What am I going to do with this money until I can get things going? I know. My aunt and uncle have a shore house down in Wildwood Crest; I can store it there.

My relatives only go there in the summer. I have been there so many times when I was growing up; I know where they hide the keys. I can go there alone and hide the bags of cash, my clothes, and anything else that I need to get out of this place. The Crest is dead in the off-season, but even if somebody does see me, nobody would give a second thought to someone carrying baggage into a vacation home.

The next morning, Joey packed his car, drove down the shore, dropped off his bags, and was back home that evening with no one the wiser.

Chapter Three

Where's the Cash?

The day after the job, Enzo called Rocco and Louie into his office to get his cut of the money.

"Where's the cash?" Enzo said.

"We hid it so the cops wouldn't catch us wit it," Rocco said.

"What cops?"

"We kinda got chased."

"Whadda you mean, you got chased?"

"We were drivin' around and noticed that a suspicious lookin' car was behind us ever since we left the projects, so we headed to the bridge and did a U-turn to see if it followed us, and it did. Then we knew it was the cops. So we hightailed it down the expressway and lost them by the art museum. Since we were there, we decided to stash the cash at the Alamo in case we got pulled over on the way back to the neighborhood."

"It was good thinkin', don't ya think?" Louie said.

"Yeah, you're a couple of geniuses; now go get that money and make sure that you're not followed. Then bring it to me."

"OK, boss, we're on our way," Rocco said.

Rocco and Louie left Enzo's office through the back door of Hank's Hoagie Palace, and Louie asked, "Do ya think we shouldda told Enzo about what we did to T-bone and Philly Phil?"

"Whatta you stupid? We got enough trouble wit him as it is. Besides, if he does hear about it, we can play dumb and say we don't know nuffin' about it."

Louie snickered and said, "Yeah, we're good at that."

Rocco and Louie drove to the Twenty-Third Street lot this time to get to the Alamo. It was closer than the playground, and they couldn't count on another freight train happening by. They tramped their way up the tracks to the Alamo and over to the edge by the cave.

"Go down there and toss the bags up to me," Rocco said.

Louie climbed down the slope, sliding half the way, and came to an abrupt stop at the bottom.

He looked in and saw nothing. "They're not in here."

"Get in there and look."

"I am lookin'; it's not that deep."

Rocco climbed down himself and looked into the shallow cave, and there was nothing.

"Where the hell are they?" Rocco yelled.

"I don't know. Look around; they're not here," Louie yelled back.

Rocco and Louie searched the embankment for fifty yards in each direction. They also looked all around the top of Alamo. They found nothing.

"Oh shit, Enzo's gonna kill us," Rocco said.

"Whatta we gonna do?" Louie asked.

"We gotta tell him," Rocco answered.

"Man-oh-man, we ain't never gonna get straightened out," Louie said.

"Straightened out, we'll be lucky if we don't get whacked," Rocco said.

"Enzo won't do that," Louie gasped.

Rocco looked down, shook his head, and sighed. "I hope not."

Rocco and Louie brought the bad news back to Enzo and got the royal ass chewing that they deserved, but he didn't shoot them on the spot, so it didn't go as bad as it could have.

"Go find that money," Enzo commanded.

"Yes, boss, we will, we will," Rocco said.

"Get outta here, you stunads."

Rocco and Louie left Enzo's office, and when outside, Louie asked Rocco, "How we gonna find the money?"

"I don't know, but we better think of something."

"I don't wanna think about it," Louie said.

"You just don't wanna think at all."

Joey spent the next few days surfing the web, reading magazine articles, and making plans for his new life. Then one morning, while he was online looking at travel information for Europe, there was a knock at the door.

"Joey, please get the door; I'm cleaning the bathroom," his mother said.

He closed his laptop and went downstairs to the front door. Joey opened the door of his South Philly row home, and there was a man standing on the front step who showed him a badge, and another was standing on the sidewalk.

The two men stood there, looking just like a couple of feds from the movies. Smith, the senior agent, was a black man in his forties, and Jones was a white man in his late twenties. They wore the proverbial trench coats, cheap suits, Oxford shoes, and Walmart socks.

"I am Agent Smith, and this is Agent Jones; we're with the Drug Enforcement Agency (DEA). We would like to speak with Joseph Conti."

"Really, Smith and Jones?"

"Yes, really," Smith said.

"We get that a lot," Jones added.

Joey crossed his arms and said, "I'm Joey Conti; what do you want to talk to me about?"

"The local police noted, on the night of the incident, that a vehicle registered in your name was parked in a remote lot on Twenty-Third Street, near where the suspect vehicle was last seen.

What were you doing in such a desolate area several miles from home that late at night?" Smith asked.

With a slight hesitation and in his mousy voice, Joey tugged at his collar and said, "I just went for a walk by the river to clear my head; I'm out of work and don't know what I want to do. I do it all the time; there's nothing wrong with that."

Joey waved at his neighbor as she peeked out of her door from across the street. "Hello, Mrs. Pasamonte, nothing for you to see here." The neighbor closed her door. Shortly later, her window curtain was pushed slightly aside. "The neighbors here keep an eye on everything but never see anything."

"Did you see anyone else or any other occupied vehicles there?" Smith asked.

"No, I didn't see anything."

"Just like the neighbors," Smith said.

"Yep," Joey answered.

"That's a known meeting place for homosexuals looking for casual encounters; is that why you were there?" Jones said.

"No. I was just taking a walk. We're done talking," Joey snapped back.

"Your hands are cut up; what happened?" Smith said.

"I had a little too much to drink and fell on my way home the other night."

"Good night." Joey tried to shut the door, but Agent Smith blocked it with his foot.

The agents didn't believe that he had given them the whole story, but at the time, they had nothing else to suggest that he was involved. For the time being, they gave him the benefit of the doubt; he did seem pathetic to them. "That's all for now, but we may have some additional questions in the future," Smith said.

Smith removed his foot; Joey closed the door, bowed his head, and sighed.

I need to get things going soon.

"I could tell that he was lying when he folded his arms as soon as we started to question him," Jones said.

"He was lying alright, but that just means that he was trying to comfort himself, which is normal for anyone who is not a criminal and is getting questioned by the authorities. The tell that he was lying was when he pulled on his collar, trying to ventilate himself. That's a pretty good indication that he wasn't being totally truthful. But keep paying attention; you're learning, kid," Smith said.

Since nothing went on in the neighborhood without Enzo getting word of it, he found out that law enforcement had questioned Joey. This could not be a coincidence. Enzo decided that he would talk to Joey.

The DEA also had sources in the neighborhood, and they found out that Enzo had an interest in Joey. This was not good for their case, so they had the local police pick him up for additional questioning.

Joey sat by himself with folded arms in a metal chair behind a metal desk with a vinyl top in a small rectangular room with pale green walls on three sides and a two-way mirror for the fourth wall.

"It's been about an hour; he should be ready to talk by now," Agent Smith said.

The two DEA agents entered the room.

"Hello Joey," Agent Smith said.

"What do you guys want? I told you that I don't know anything," Joey said.

"We think that you know more than you're telling us," Agent Smith said.

"I don't know anything."

This back and forth went on for another couple of hours, and Joey gave them no additional information.

The DEA agents left the room and went into the office of Captain Jumbo O'Hara.

"Hello, Captain," Agent Smith said.

"What can I do for you, gentlemen?" Captain O'Hara asked.

"Joey Conti is the only potential witness that we have to a string of drug deals and two homicides, but we have nothing to hold him on. I'm afraid that if we let him out on the street, he could end up dead, and then we'll have nothing," Agent Smith said.

"Is that all?" Captain O'Hara said while grinning.

"Is that all? No judge will give us a warrant to hold him without any evidence," Agent Smith said.

"No problem; we can just 'Take a Mulligan,'" Captain O'Hara said.

"What are you talking about?"

Captain O'Hara, who never let the law get in his way, explained that "Take a Mulligan" had an entirely different meaning around the courthouses and police precincts in Philadelphia than it did on the golf course. Judge John Mulligan, known as Irish John to his friends, was put into office with the backing of a corrupt union boss. Irish John was also as corrupt as they came and had to do pretty much whatever the cops and crooked union bosses wanted him to do to keep himself out of jail.

So the warrant was issued and Joey was charged as a suspect and taken into custody.

The police carted Joey off to jail and kept him in a sort of protective custody with white-collar and non-violent offenders who were awaiting release. There were no connected inmates in this section, and none of the others there paid much attention to Joey.

Rocco had a brilliant idea and burst into Enzo's office. "Boss, it's been over a week and Joey's still in jail; why don't we get someone inside to lean on him to find out what he knows?"

"Like I didn't think of that, they won't let anybody with the slightest connection to us or our people in that minimum security section of the jail. If you got OC stamped on your file, you're a marked man inside. But I'm going to get that SOB when the time comes," Enzo said.

"What about getting someone who's not associated with our crew and is already in there to talk to him?" Rocco said.

"We can't go around telling just anyone about this. If he does have the money and they find out where it is, we might never get to see it."

"That makes sense. But they can't keep him in there forever."

"That's what I'm counting on. As soon as he gets out, we get him and find out where the money is and if anybody else was involved."

Two more weeks went by, and Joey remained in custody. They questioned him every day about the killings and drug deals. Every day he was questioned, and every day he told them nothing. It wasn't too difficult, as the only thing that he knew about any of the crimes was that Rocco and Louie screwed over some drug dealers and hid the money. He didn't know anything about the drug deals, and he didn't witness the shootings. All he had was hearsay and cash, and he wasn't about to give up his newly found cash.

Then one morning, an opportunity presented itself when the Philadelphia Mayor and District Attorney decided that they wanted to reduce the number of inmates. A majority of those selected to take part in this mass release were housed with Joey. On release day, Joey blended in with them and walked right out of the door. There was an advantage to no one ever paying you much attention. He then headed straight to the bus terminal and down to the shore to pick up his clothes and cash and start his new life.

When they got word of Joey's escape, the DEA agents chose to yell and scream at Captain O'Hara. He just sat back in his cushioned desk chair with his elbows on the padded arms and his fingers interlocked, resting comfortably on his beach-ball-sized belly; he couldn't care less what they thought. He just smiled and nodded contently, waiting for them to leave.

As time moved on and the DEA had other priorities to address, Joey's file was moved to the bottom of the pile. Enzo was not so inclined.

When Enzo found out about Joey's escape, it confirmed that he did have the money and must be found. Enzo was not to be denied, even though Rocco and Louie would have liked the whole thing forgotten.

"Why are you so worried about it, boss? The money isn't out of our pockets," Rocco said.

Enzo stood up from behind his desk and roared. "Because for over a century now, since our grandparents came to America with nothing but the clothes on their backs and the determination to build a better life for themselves and their children, Italian Americans have been the hardest-working, most productive people, doing everything from building the cities and railways to teaching the medigan how and what to eat. We have enriched the culture and the economy. That and it is our money, and nobody steals from us!"

Enzo then sent Rocco and Louie to break into Joey's mother's house while she was at church to see what they could find. They searched the entire house, including the basement, and found nothing that even resembled large amounts of cash. They searched his room and found nothing really out of the ordinary, just a laptop and some library books. The only thing that looked out of place was a magazine, folded open to an article listing the top European plastic surgery centers. They took it back to Enzo.

"Here, boss, that anteater had this magazine on plastic surgery centers in Europe," Rocco said.

Louie chuckled and said, "That ugly prick could use some work."

"That stugotz is spending our money on a nose job," Enzo said.

"That might make it harder to find him," Louie said.

Enzo threw up his arms and said, "I'm surrounded by stunods here."

"Did he have anything else?" Enzo asked.

"He had a couple of weird library books," Rocco said.

"What were they?"

"Some chemistry book, and a book about the pilgrims by some Paulo guy, and another book about off-roading. There was nothing worth taking and nothing that looked like it could hold all that money."

"Alright, I know what to do," Enzo said.

Enzo decided that he had to try a new approach to get information on Joey's whereabouts. He enlisted his mother and aunt to cozy up to Joey's mother to see what they could find out.

They didn't know what was going on but knew enough not to ask any questions, plus they loved to gossip, so it wasn't anything out of the ordinary for them. Rocco and Louie wanted to lean on Joey's mother, but Enzo was old-school and would not allow any harm or intimidation to come to a good woman, a civilian, especially one who was friends with his own mother.

Enzo's mother, Sofia, saw Joey's mother, Marie, outside of Biagi's butcher shop. "Hello Marie. How have you been?"

"My house was broken into, and I'm frightened; nothing was taken, so I'm afraid that they might come back," Marie said.

"That's terrible. How about Joey?"

"I haven't heard a word from him."

"I'm so sorry to hear that; don't worry. I'll tell Enzo, and he will take care of it."

"God bless you, Sofia; you are a true friend," Marie said.

Sofia told this to Enzo and told him that he should help her get her door fixed because in this neighborhood, they took care of their own. Enzo had Rocco and Louie, two nice Italian boys, go over and repair the damage.

Rocco and Louie asked Marie if anything was taken, and she said, "Nothing, as far as I can tell," as they well knew.

She thanked them, gave them some pizzelles and pignoli cookies, and told them that they were "Gooda boys." For the locals, the police were little more than a nuisance in the neighborhood; they took care of their own.

The police had also continued to question Joey's mother about his disappearance but had finally come to the conclusion that she knew nothing of his whereabouts, which was true. She hadn't heard from Joey for months and had nothing to report to the police or to Sofia except her worry for him. The question on everyone's mind was, "Where had Joey gone?"

Chapter Four

The Hunt is On

It had been several months since the death of Max's mother, and he was now spending most of his time at home. When he did venture out, he would get drunk at local dive bars or attend an occasional film. The streets were filled with rumors of weakness and behavior not fitting for a member of their organization. Word got back to Carlo that the other families considered Max an embarrassment. Carlo knew that he had to do something about it. He knew what was expected of him. He just didn't want to do it, and he didn't like being told what to do. He liked Max, valued his past work, and didn't want to cause him any harm. But Max was not the Max of old. Carlo had to call him in for a meeting.

After months of praying for Joey's safety and that he may someday return home, Marie's prayers were finally answered when a letter from Joey arrived. It had no return address, but did have international postage markings. His mother read the letter, held her hand to her mouth, and gasped—her son was alive and well. Joey wrote that he was making the changes in his life that he needed and that he had never been happier or felt better. He wrote that ever since he read 'The Alchemist' and 'The Pilgrimage', by Paulo Coelho, and 'Off the Road', by Jack Hitt, he has wanted to walk the Camino de Santiago. He loved the idea of getting in touch with himself and meeting new people from around the world. He planned to continue his new life by making this pilgrimage to St. James in an attempt to make peace with his dead father, James. He explained to his mother that by making his pilgrimage on the Camino de Santiago, he could make amends for the worry that he had caused his mother and especially his father. He wrote that he knew that he had not always been easy to get along with, and he regrets how he treated his parents, who were the only people in the world who truly loved him. He planned to start his pilgrimage on the birthday that his mother shares with the blessed mother Mary, for whom she is named. Her heart fluttered, and a sudden flush of heat came over her. She was overjoyed and couldn't wait to tell her friends, Sofia and Millie, the news. She hurried to Sofia's house and blurted out, "Joey wrote me from France; he is going to make a pilgrimage through France and Spain. He wrote that St. Augustine said, 'The world is a book, and if you do not travel, you only read one page.' He is so smart and such a good boy."

"That's good to hear, Marie; I'm so happy for you," Sofia said.

Marie didn't realize that she had put her beloved Joey in danger. Enzo and the boys had a lead.

Enzo, Big Tony, and the Rizzo brothers got together to discuss what should come next.

"The first thing we need to do is find out what the hell he means by a pilgrimage to St. James," Enzo said.

And then Louie said, "Yeah, and when the birthday of the Blessed Mother is."

This annoyed Enzo since they all grew up Catholic, and he was proud that he won the religion award in the sixth grade. Enzo turned his palms up and talked while he waved his hands. "It's September 8, you moron. Don't you remember anything from Catholic school?"

Big Tony, who was not only Enzo's right-hand man but also his best friend since childhood and quite a bit brighter than the other two, said, "Don't worry, I can do a search on the internet to find out what we need to know."

"You do that. At least somebody's got some brains around here," Enzo said.

It didn't take Tony long to learn that a pilgrimage to St. James was actually one of the three main pilgrimages in Christianity and was commonly referred to as the Camino de Santiago. He walked into Enzo's office and said, "There is more than one route, but the most popular route is called the Camino Francés, and it starts in the French Pyrenees mountains in a town called Saint Jean Pied de Port. People backpack across a 500-mile trail, mostly through northern Spain, to a town in the west called Santiago de Compestela. There lie the remains of the apostle St. James the Greater in a shrine beneath the altar of the cathedral built in his honor. Joey's mother said that he was going to go to France and Spain, so the Camino Francés is probably where he will be."

"So why would anybody in their right mind want to do that in this day and age? That's like walking through four or five states," Rocco said.

"People do it for many different reasons: some still for religious purposes; some for spiritual; others for the physical challenge; some just want to get out of their comfort zones and face their fears; some want to get away from stress; and others want to get in touch with their inner selves and reflect," Tony said.

"And others want to hide out after they steal our money," Louie said.

"OK, Colombo, so what else do we know about this Camino thing?" Enzo asked.

"There's a movie about it with Martin Sheen," Tony answered.

"The Apocalypse Now guy? Marone, what's this involve?"

"We need to watch the movie and find out."

"What's the movie called?" Enzo said.

"The Way," Tony said.

"What Way?" Enzo spoke in a sharp tone as he hit the table with his meaty right hand.

"No, just The Way," Tony said.

So they got a copy on DVD, watched it to find out what they needed to do, and decided two things. First of all, they were city boys; none of them were outdoor types, and after years of pizza, pasta, and sausages, they were in no shape to go hiking up and down mountains halfway across Europe. Second, they needed someone who would blend in with the pilgrims.

Joey needed to be identified; he would most likely have a new look since they believed he had had plastic surgery, and why wouldn't he with that nose? They also needed to find out where the money was now located. Whoever does it needs to gain the confidence of the people he is questioning without raising any suspicions. They didn't want to blow it before they could get the cash back, and they also wanted to know if anyone else was in on it. After that, they could off him. They decided that the best approach was to get someone from the old country for the job. They were already over there, anyway.

Enzo called his cousin Carlo in Naples and explained the situation to him.

"We need a fit young man who has knowledge of the Catholic faith," Enzo said.

"Why do you need that?" Carlo asked.

"It could come in handy to blend in and make conversation with these pilgrims. Joey is also religious because he lived with his mother, who is a real churchgoer. She is the kind of old lady who goes to confession just to tell the priest how good she is. And besides, nobody these days is going to think a wise guy is gonna be talking religion."

They also decided that a working knowledge of English, Italian, and a little Spanish would be useful. He should be able to blend in with the international crowd of pilgrims. Enzo knew that the job could take some time, so he told Carlo that whoever was selected needed to be expendable for a potentially long period.

Carlo, reluctant to give up one of his people for this job when no one was even sure exactly how much money was involved, wanted to say no, but Enzo was blood. There were two large duffel bags, but how much was in them and how much was left? Then Max came to mind; his mother died months ago, and he had been in a funk ever since. Carlo had to do something to correct Max's behavior, but Max's mother was the only person that he cared about on the entire planet. He was a good son, having dinner with her almost every Sunday. He kept her apartment well furnished and in good working order. He made sure that she never wanted for anything. And in turn, she loved her little boy and always told him to be careful. She wanted him to find a nice girl to settle down with, so that she could take care of him when his mother was no longer around. Whenever she said this to him, Max just embraced her and said, "Don't talk like that, Mama; you are the only girl for me." That's part of the reason she said it so often.

This was just what Carlo needed to get Max out of town and give him the chance to redeem himself. He might not have to eliminate him after all. Max was in his late twenties, fit—rock hard, actually—and six feet tall. He knew how to handle himself, but he was no longer pulling his weight. In the past, when he had to think for himself, he had always made smart decisions; he spoke English well, which he was forced to learn by the priests in reform school; and an Italian can figure out Spanish well enough when needed. Before his mother died, he was a reliable and good soldier, and on holy days, he even went to church with his mother.

His mother was the only real family he had, since he saw his father killed in front of his own eyes when he was just five years old. Max's only memory of the whole ordeal made him shiver in fear when the killer gave him an instantaneous glance with his cold, steel-black eyes, that were deep pools of nothing. It was as if Max was staring into hell and into the eyes of the devil himself. Max's mother quickly embraced him, holding him tightly, and Max was in the only place where he would ever feel safe again. His mother never told him why it happened, nor did anyone else, for that matter. The once happy and playful child became emotionally rigid and would not trust anyone but his mother for much of the remainder of his life. His mother bought him a pet mouse to cheer him up. She wanted him to relate to someone or something other than her. Max played with the mouse and cared for it; it kept him occupied, but he continued his quiet ways and avoided others. Then the mouse died.

Does everything I care about die?

Max's mother bought him another mouse. Shortly after she gave it to him, he held it in his hand, and it bit him, so he crushed it. When Max's mother saw this, she wept. She took the mouse from his hand, wiped it clean, and put the mouse in the trash. She hugged him and felt his heart pounding, his heavy breath on her neck, and his chest heaving. She then looked at his face and saw his intense and distant stare. Her little boy was still in a dark place.

Max and his mother lived in Scampia, the toughest neighborhood in Naples. Throughout his life, his family was involved with the local mob. His father was a respected figure in the organization, and Max grew up surrounded by whispers of power and secrecy. As he entered his teen years, he ran the streets, was in and out of trouble with the police, and even spent time in reform school. His life in crime was pretty much predetermined by these factors. His whole life, he was groomed to take his place in the organization. After Max's father was killed, his father's friend Carlo would occasionally visit Max and his mother, bringing them gifts of food, toys for Max, and sometimes household items that may have fallen off of a truck at some point. As Max grew older, Carlo would give him little jobs, such as washing cars and running errands. It kept Max in pocket money and helped to put food on the table and pay the rent. Max matured into a fine specimen of a young man who was even taller and more well-built than his father, who was a man that no one would dare look at without a smile and a nod of respect. Carlo continued to employ Max and moved him to more physically demanding roles with increased responsibilities. He started collecting from the street vendors and enforcing Carlo's law on the streets of Naples. Max became one of Carlo's most valuable and trusted soldiers. He eventually became the go-to guy for the most important removal tasks. This was all dwindling away with the death of Max's mother.

Carlo called Max in to talk. He wanted the old Max back and really didn't want to get rid of him, but his moping and lack of focus made him more of a liability than an asset. Carlo was old school in his own way: 'You screw up, you're gone,' and not to a retirement home. Getting away and focused on a solo task might be just what Max needed; he'd come back and be useful once again.

Max trudged his way through the backstreets of Naples; every step made was with apprehension. In the past, getting called in by Carlo was no big deal. Max was one of his best soldiers. This time was different. Max had not been of any use to Carlo since the death of his mother. Max entered through the side door of the Bocce Club, where Carlo kept an office. Max stared at the floor, hesitant to look into Carlo's eyes. It could be their last meeting.

"Max, I don't like what I've been hearing about you lately. The manner in which you conduct yourself has a reflection on me," Carlo said.

Max lowered his eyes and swallowed hard, even though his throat was dry. It was more a reflex of guilt and shame. "Carlo, you know how people like to talk. It doesn't mean anything."

"It does mean something, and not just to me, but to the memory of your father and your mother. They would be ashamed of you."

"You're right, Carlo, but I'm not sure what I can do."

"I know what you can do. You're going on a trip. You need to get a backpack and some hiking shoes."

"What are you talking about?"

"You've got to go to the mountains in France and find someone for my primo in America."

"France, I don't want to go to France. I can't even speak the language."

"It doesn't matter what you want, and you probably will only need to be in France one night. Then you will go to Spain, and you should be able to figure out enough Spanish to get by."

Max grimaced and opened his mouth again to say something, but then cut himself off.

"What?" Carlo said.

"Nothing," Max answered.

"You can't let your grief consume you; you need to use it to fuel your internal drive. Your mother raised you better than this; she taught you to be strong. Don't dishonor her memory with weak behavior."

"You're right, Carlo."

"If you don't straighten out and do this job right, you can no longer work for us. And you can't work for anyone else."

"I know Carlo."

"Now go out and get your gear while the stores are still open, and then come back tonight. I'll fill you in on all of the details. You don't have much time before you need to leave, so get on it."

That night, Carlo filled Max in on the job, gave him a picture of Joey and some cash, and gave him the details of how he must proceed.

"Keep a low profile; you don't want to get involved with any police over there. I don't have the right connections in those countries and might not be able to get you out of any situations. Also, the target might not look like this picture anymore. My primo thinks that he used some of the money that he stole to get some work done."

Carlo handed Max a photo of Joey.

"As you can see, he has a huge nose."

He told Max that he must mingle with the pilgrims and chat them up to try to identify the target.

"I don't know how to talk to these people; I don't like talking to strangers."

"I've got two things to say to that. I don't care, and you better learn fast. You need to get your ass to France by September 7 and be ready to start hiking early the next morning. You need to find this guy and the money."

"Okay, Carlo, you're the boss."

"That's right, now get moving."

"I am Carlo; I'm on my way."

I could use a break from all of this bullshit, anyway; being told what to do all the time; kill or be killed by people you don't even know; what kind of life is this? I'm surely not getting rich. Maybe this is just what I need. My mother's gone now. What do I have around here?

Chapter Five

It's All Uphill From Here

Max's trip to Saint Jean Pied de Port began on the first of three buses required to get there. It would be a grueling twenty-two-hour journey, as anyone who has traveled long distances by bus would attest. He traveled by bus and carried no phone in an effort to stay off the grid. His intention was to leave no documentation trail that could be used to place him in any particular place at any particular time. Working in a foreign country was new to him. He would use pay phones to keep in touch with Carlo as he made his way. Max's usual job was as a street soldier, an enforcer, but when his Capo needed a clean hit, Max was the man. He always kept his head, made the effort to do it right, and his work was never traced back to him or his boss.

During his long ride from the south of Italy to the mountains that separated the Iberian Peninsula from the rest of Europe, Max had plenty of time to think, and think he did.

I like being able to plan out a job properly; I always study my targets and get to know their habits better than they know them themselves. When I had to take out that scumbag senator, I watched him for weeks. Every morning, he sat at the same table at the same cafe. It was easy to swap out the cocoa shaker that he always used on his morning cappuccino before he went to his office. With his heart condition, no one even gave a second thought to the digitalis in his system. And that sleazy magistrate—I just jogged behind him for a few days, and when the opportunity presented itself, I cracked him on the head, took his wallet and watch, and it was just a mugging gone wrong. I even took my time with that fat pig bureaucrat touring around the city every day of the week instead of working. But with this guy, I know nothing of his habits or even what he really looks like. This is just stupid.

On the third and final bus of this intrepid journey, Max picked up a pamphlet that was lying on the floor with information on Saint Jean Pied de Port in several languages.

I can do a little research on the town that I'm starting out in, even if I can't do much on the target.

The pamphlet read as follows: Saint Jean Pied de Port is a walled city in the Pyrenees mountains that dates from the 12th century. It once had a castle, but now a citadel stands in its place. It served as a guardian post for the Kingdom of Navarra. It was first a fortified town, guarding the northern approach to the Kingdom of Navarra and serving, as it does today, as a way station for travelers and pilgrims crossing the Pyrenees. In the Religious Wars, or Guerres de Religion, in the 16th century, it was the scene of a bloody struggle between Catholics and Protestants. It has survived both a revolution and religious wars and, at various times, has come under the control of both Spanish and French kingdoms. Today, in addition to being one of the primary starting points of the Camino de Santiago, Saint Jean is a major tourist center in the modern département of Pyrénées-Atlantiques, which takes in the whole of the French Basque Country and part of Gascony.

Max arrived in Saint Jean Pied de Port late in the afternoon on September 7.

Now what?

He looked around, trying to find someone who could point him in the right direction, whatever that was. He followed the other passengers down the dark street, sizing them up to decide to whom he would speak. There was a middle-aged woman walking with a confident stride, indicative of a woman who knew where she was going. Max approached her and looked into her face.

"Allo," she said.

Mistaking this for the English "hello," Max replied, "You speak English?"

"Well, yes, I do."

"I am here to walk the Camino de Santiago. Do you know how I can get any information on how to go about this?"

She smiled, nodded her head and said, "I bet that you are new to backpacking, aren't you?"

"Yes, how did you know?"

"Your denim pants and new, stiff hiking boots gave you away. Continue down this street for about five minutes to the rue de la

Citadelle, where you will find the pilgrim's office. Go in, and they will help you with everything that you need. They stay open until 2200, so you have ample time to visit them tonight."

"Grazie."

"Buen Camino," the woman said.

Max, with a blank look on his face, nodded and went on his way.

Max didn't take note of the cobblestone streets with shuttered stone and whitewashed shops and houses as he passed them. He focused on his task and hastily made his way to the pilgrim's office. He went in and found three people sitting behind a long table. The walls had posters, maps, and signs related to the Camino. Max looked around, and then one of the men behind the table waved him over.

"Can I help you?" the man said.

"I would like to walk the Camino de Santiago; can you help me?"

"Yes. Welcome; you have come to the right place."

The man went over some of the basics of the Camino pilgrimage, explaining to him the many stages and other details. He then set him up with a Camino passport, his credential, and told him to get it stamped at every town where he stayed during his pilgrimage. The man then stamped and dated his Camino passport with its first stamp and handed it to him. "You are now officially a pilgrim, Ultreia."

"I don't understand," Max said.

"Ultreia is a traditional greeting that we like to say to pilgrims here in France; it just means to go further. The more common greeting used today along the Spanish sections of the Camino Francés is 'Buen Camino' meaning Good Way."

Max nodded in a gesture of thanks and said, "I understand."

"You will need to show your credential along with your EU identification card when you check in each night to prove that you are a pilgrim. You will also obtain a stamp each time, so by the time you are in Santiago de Compostela, you will have a completed passport."

"I see," Max said.

So much for staying incognito; I will just have to make sure that I don't draw any attention to myself.

The man then added, "Be sure that you pay attention to your body, especially your feet; they are your engine, and you must keep them in good condition in order to complete the journey. Drink plenty of water and rest before you become overly tired. Remembering these things will increase your chances of completing your Camino."

"Thank you; I will."

The man finished by saying, "The first day is the most difficult of the entire Camino. You must climb and descend a mountain; don't let it discourage you."

"I will not. Thank you for your help."

He then directed Max to a nearby gîte, a pilgrim's hostel, where he would spend the night with other pilgrims.

Max was tired after the long bus rides and made his way along the street, each step an effort.

I am not looking forward to climbing mountains tomorrow on this pazzo quest.

He arrived at the gîte, checked in, and was directed to the sleeping area. "Great," he grunted.

Bunk beds in dormitories, just like in reform school.

Max put away his gear, got out his shower kit and fresh clothes, and got cleaned up. After his shower, he lay in his bunk, waiting, staring at the wall, and formulating his plan. He didn't know it yet, but this would be his routine for the next several weeks. He would have dinner in the gîte and listen to the conversations of the other pilgrims to see what he could learn. The chatter in the background of the dorm room was a mix of several different languages and often intermingled with English. He needed to try to get an idea of how he could identify his target. All that he knew was that Joey was an Italian American man who was thin and in his mid-thirties. Besides English, the target spoke Italian well and also a little Spanish, but he was known to be generally quiet and keep to himself. Max had a picture of Joey but was told that it may no longer look like him as it is believed that he'd had plastic surgery.

How am I going to find this guy?

One good thing was already coming out of this trip, as he no longer dwelled on his mother's death and the feeling of aloneness that came with it. He knew that he faced a difficult challenge, and his bosses didn't take failure very well. This and the fact that he had never been out of Italy or done anything like a long backpacking trip before and had no idea of what to expect made him less than enthusiastic about the task that lay ahead.

Max entered the dining room and first looked for an open spot to sit. The room was austere, with a brown wood motif, and then Max took notice of the one big exception. The wall just to his right had a large map painted on it. It was the route of the Camino Francés, with many of the major towns and cities shown along with depictions of typical points of interest, such as cathedrals, castles, vineyards, and other things that were waiting to greet the pilgrims on their way. Max looked over the map and then at the pilgrims already seated. It was communal seating, just like the sleeping arrangements.

At least I'm dressed right; there's not much fancy about this place.

He saw an empty seat in the corner at the far end of a large table. He went to the seat, mumbled, "Mi scusi," and sat down, not making eye contact with anyone. His arms and back stiffened as he leaned his elbows on the table and looked down. Max did not enjoy being in social situations with strangers.

The man next to him, who was from France, said, "Italiano, Benvenuto."

The man who was seated across from him, who was from Germany, said, "Happy you've joined us."

Max forced a smile, nodded to the men, and said, "Grazie."

The Frenchman asked Max, "Is this your first Camino?"

"Yes, it is."

"It is my fourth time on the Camino Francés. I have also walked the Camino Finisterre and Camino Portuguese," the Frenchman replied.

Max continued to look at the spot where he wanted his dinner to appear and softly said, "You must really like it."

The Frenchman said, "I guess I do."

The German interjected that it was his first Camino and that he was on a mandated break from work and was there because he didn't know what to do with himself and needed time to think.

"A mandated break—that must be nice," the Frenchman said.

"Not really; I had just started a new job at a kindergarten, and they were not happy with my methods. I might not have a job when I return. I think they are being unreasonable. I did nothing wrong."

"What are they upset about?" asked the Frenchman.

"When the children would get into fist fights, I let them fight. They need to learn to fight. And when I told them how animals were butchered to get meat, the parents got upset and complained and said they were too young to learn that."

The German then asked Max, "What do you think about that?"

Max didn't know how to respond and didn't care, so he said, "You don't look anything like I thought a German would."

"That's because I am originally from Turkey."

Max remained silent and stroked his chin with his thumb and forefinger.

The more people I speak with and conversations I overhear, the more countries are represented. It's like the Tower of Babel, but in reverse: people whose native languages are all different but who are communicating with each other.

As if he knew what Max was thinking, the Frenchman told them that it was the same in gîtes throughout St. Jean; people from around the world were meeting and getting ready to start their Caminos. Max asked the Frenchman, "How do I find and follow the way?"

"It's just like "The Wizard of Oz," except that you follow yellow arrows instead of yellow bricks."

"I can do that," Max said.

As the meal progressed, Max overheard some of the other pilgrims talking about walking together, even though they had just met. This was a good sign. He would look for a group that had American men and join them.

I can move from group to group to find some likely candidates. It will not be easy, but it can be done.

The plan was set.

After dinner, Max collapsed into bed, in need of a good night's sleep and an early start. As he lay there, a disjointed chorus of snorers rang through the room.

Are you kidding me? I feel like shoving socks down their throats.

He was tired and normally wouldn't let it go, but he needed to keep his cool and blend in, just as he was told. A man on the bunk across from him noticed as Max fidgeted and turned, trying to cover his ears with his pillow. The man had pity on him and handed him a pair of earplugs. Max nodded in thanks. The ear plugs helped some, and Max eventually got to sleep as he was exhausted from his arduous journey and the effort of talking to people.

The next morning, Max picked up an espresso to go and stepped out into the cool and foggy morning air. Even though the visibility wasn't great, Max had a good night's sleep and took notice of the small French town that he had hurried through the previous night. He followed several other pilgrims down the Rue de la Citadelle, all traveling south. He started out by mixing among them and looking for groups with members who fit his target's profile. When he saw a possible target, he would get next to him, introduce himself, and ask him some questions to determine if he understood English and from which country he came. Max struggled to talk to these strangers, but he knew what was expected of him and was a good soldier with a job to do.

The cool mountain air had a moist taste that he had not experienced since he was a child. It reminded him of a time when his mother and father had taken him to a mountain lake resort for a vacation. It was the last vacation that he ever went on. This memory helped to buoy his spirit and gave him a lift that made talking to these strangers a little less difficult.

As he approached the end of the street, he passed the "Our Lady at the End of the Bridge" Gothic-style church. On his way out of town, he went under the clock tower archway and then crossed a bridge over the River Nive, following the other pilgrims through the Porte d'Espagne. He marched on, following the direction of the other pilgrims. He came to and climbed a steep dirt trail that ran between large dew-covered fields. He could see sheep dotting the landscape as far as the fog would permit. He kept on task and talked with every pilgrim he came upon, but he did not find anyone who met the profile of his target.

This is nonsense; there are no Americans or even Italians that could be this stronzo. I need to find him and be done with all of this climbing.

There were many pilgrims from several different countries, and most of them knew little about the other pilgrims who were walking at this time. A nun dressed in her habit with a pack slung over one shoulder was sauntering down the trail, admiring the giant chestnut trees that towered to the sky, like she didn't have a care in the world.

I guess they always dress like that; I never really thought about it. She seems much happier than most other nuns I have seen.

Like Max, Joey was taking on the mountains between St. Jean and Roncesvalles on the first day of his Camino. Unlike Max, he was not talking to anyone. The dampness of the low-lying fog fit Joey's mood as he quickly glanced around at the woods and at the other pilgrims, trying not to make eye contact as he took in his surroundings.

I really did it, and now I am living my new life. I am all alone in a forest in a foreign land, and it's a little creepy. Am I excited or terrified? A little of both, I guess.

As Max reached Orisson, a rest stop for most and an overnight stop for those who do not wish to wear themselves out on their first day, the fog lifted and the view was clear. The trail was also paved in this area, making the footing more sound. With the fog gone, the most plentiful residents of the Pyrenees, sheep and wild horses, were populating the luscious green fields as far as the eye could see. Max took the opportunity to sit at a picnic bench outside of the inn and have some water and a bag of salty chips as a snack. He knew from the hot summer days of Naples that the body needed salt as well as fluids to maintain stamina. He pulled out his chips and was surprised to see that the bag was inflated like a balloon.

I guess that I really have climbed a mountain today.

Around midday, Max, back on the dirt trail, slipped as he descended a steep, damp section. A young blonde woman called to him.

"Be careful; it's slippery here, and those boots of yours still look new and stiff; you will have trouble with them until you have broken them in."

"I realize that now. Thank you for caring about what happens to me," Max said.

"It's in my nature; I'm a physician back in Germany. I am Eva; may I walk with you?"

"Please do; you can tell me all that you know about the Camino de Santiago, Eva."

"Okay, that sounds great."

This pleasant, petite German smiled as she bounced along the trail, exuding her good spirit. She told Max about the people she had met in her gîte and along the trail so far. She told him other pilgrims' names, where they came from, and other tidbits of information that could help with his effort. Her gregarious personality made her worth speaking with, even though she was obviously not the target. In an attempt to reciprocate the small talk, and since she was a physician, Max said to her, "Your services might be in great demand out in this wilderness, away from other medical care."

"It is easier to find physicians and medical specialists here on the Camino than it is to get to see one anywhere in the EU. Many physicians choose to walk the Camino de Santiago to get a prolonged break where they won't be contacted or at least not be called back into work for an emergency," Eva said.

She's impressive. She already knew so much about other pilgrims on the first morning, plus she's a natural gossip. She will be a good resource. She is well-spoken and pretty. I can make use of her.

"What do you do for a living?" Eva asked.

"I'm here to try and not think about work. I hope that you don't mind, but we should walk together during some of this Camino. We can meet some others along the way as well," Max said.

"I understand, and that sounds great; we can talk more at the albergue tonight. You should remember the Camino saying, "You will see people today who you will meet tomorrow," Eva said.

"That sounds good, but what is an albergue?"

"That's the Spanish name for a gîte. They also call them refugios, or hostels; they're all pretty much the same, just places to spend the night."

"Okay, thanks. I'll see you there."

Max then hurried his pace and was off in search of his quarry. He constantly adjusted his stride, moving from pilgrim to pilgrim. He was fit, but this would wear him out if he kept at this pace. It was almost all uphill, and the pilgrims were spread out thinly along the trail. He also noticed that most of the other pilgrims had smaller packs than his.

I'm going to have to lighten this pack before it wears me out.

And as if on cue, Max approached a solo pilgrim, who nodded to him.

"That's one heck of a pack you have there, mate," he said in an English accent.

"It is getting to feel quite heavy," Max said.

"On day one out of St. Jean, the long and continuous climb followed by the steep descent really tests your mettle and your knees," the man said.

"You might want to go through your things at the albergue tonight and remove what you don't really need; there will be plenty of other pilgrims there who can help you sort it out. You can leave the things that you don't need in the share bin; those jeans that you are wearing are definitely not a good idea. Remember that cotton kills," the Englishman said.

Max grinned as he found this statement amusing and then, just to be thorough, asked, "So, what brings you to this Camino?"

"Well, you see, after twenty years of marriage, the passion is gone, and I have been having an affair for the past two years. I am walking to see if I want to try and save my marriage or if I should end it in divorce," the Englishman said.

I can't believe this guy just told me all this; I don't even know him. Back in Naples, no one would even tell their friends or family something like this. These people are so open about telling strangers their very private details on this Camino de Santiago. Max stared at the ground as he walked, contemplated how to reply, and just said, "I hope things work out for you."

"The Camino will help me to clear my mind and make the right decision."

"How so?" Max asked.

"When you spend so much time walking and thinking with nothing to consider but making it to the next town, you find that you truly get in touch with your inner thoughts and feelings. You know what they say here on the Camino: 'Solvitur ambulando. It is solved by walking'."

"Let's hope that is so," Max said, then wished the Englishman well, quickened his pace, and was off to find the next candidate.

Maybe it won't be too difficult to identify the target once I find him if everyone opens up like this guy on this Camino de Santiago.

Max next came upon a young couple relaxing in front of a large blue-and-white statue of the Virgin Mary and Baby Jesus. As he looked up at it from the trail, and the backdrop of a blue and white sky served to enhance its majesty, his mind wandered for a moment. Then he quickly got back on task.

Joey could be walking with a woman; I will talk with them.

"Buen Camino, that is a beautiful statue," Max said.

Max held his head upright, shoulders high, and wore a smile proud of his newly learned lingo; he was fitting in as instructed.

"Buen Camino," they said in unison.

"Yes, it's the Vierg d' Orisson. It was brought here from Lourdes to watch over the pilgrims and it is one of the most iconic sites on the Camino Francés. How are you making out on this first day?" The man said.

"It's been challenging, but I'll survive," Max said.

Max got right to work and asked, "So what brings you to the Camino de Santiago?"

The man said, "This is our second Camino, and I don't know why we're here; we just need to be."

"Yeah, it was just calling us back. We were going about our mundane lives and constantly referring to the great time that we had when we were on the Camino last year, so we decided, why not? Let's go. So here we are again," the woman said.

"That sounds great," Max said.

This is Joey's first Camino, and this guy looks too young, and they definitely seem like a couple who have been together for some time. It's time to move on.

"Arrivederci, I'm on my way." Max, not wanting to waste time, hurried on to the next pilgrims within his sight.

When Max reached them, they were an older Italian couple. He decided to chat with them anyway, since they were the first fellow countrymen that he encountered. The man told him that he was a baseball coach and that his wife was a baker. They were nice but only spoke Italian, appeared to be content with their own company, and were walking at a slow pace.

"Have you met many other Italians or Italian Americans on this trip?" Max asked them.

"No, you are the first person that we have met on this Camino who speaks Italian, but I'm sure that we will meet some before long. I believe that only Spaniards outnumber Italians on the Camino de Santiago. Will you take one word of advice from an older countryman?"

"Of course," Max said.

"Take your time to enjoy your Camino. Right over there, do you see those ruins?" The old man pointed to large piles of stones that were the remnants of fallen walls.

"Yes, I see them," Max said.

"That was once a castle, the Chateau Pigńon. You just need to use your imagination and you will be taken back in time," the old man said.

"Grazie, I will try. Arrivederci." Max was then on his way to find more candidates and identify his target.

Joey worked his way uphill; he was conscious of every step and the effort required to lift his legs. He took off his jacket and stuffed it in his pack.

Thank God for the cool weather. It's a strange set of circumstances that has put me here on my own in a foreign country. It all started when I overheard two brutes blabbering in Angelo's. They say that there's no such thing as a coincidence. Is this my destiny, my maktub, like in The Alchemist? Will I ever find my Personal Legend?

Max continued moving from group to group and from pilgrim to pilgrim, meeting people from Europe, Australia, and even South Korea. There were pilgrims from all over the world, but he needed to find Americans.

Max sees a man on his own and walks towards him to see if he might be the target. "Buen Camino," the man said to Max.

"Buen Camino, how is your first day going?" Max asked.

"This is not my first day; I have been walking since Le Puy. Many French people start there."

"So you are French," Max said.

"Yes, so how is your day going?"

"Good so far, but I didn't bring enough water and am getting thirsty again, even though it isn't very hot," Max replied.

"You only need to look over there. It's the Fontaine de Roland. You see, the Camino provides. Just fill your bottle, and you will have enough water to make it all the way to Roncesvalles."

"Thank you; I will do that." Max went to the fountain named in honor of Roland, nephew of Charlemagne, and filled his water bottle.

"Why is there a fountain named after this Roland person?" Max asked the Frenchman.

"He is a legendary hero in this part of the world. He battled and defeated Farragut the giant, who is a descendant of none other than Goliath of biblical fame."

"Well, I guess naming a fountain after him is the least that they could do," Max said with a grin.

The Frenchman continued on, and with a full water bottle, Max was also back on his way.

Max soon reached the point on the trail that was marked as the border between France and Spain. He took a pause from his mission and reflected.

I had never been outside of Italy before this trip, and now I'm meeting people from all over the world and walking from one new country to another. I don't know if I will even be able to find this target. I don't need this, and it's for some asshole American goombas that I don't even know. They're lucky that Carlo has zero tolerance for failure.

As Max continued on, he couldn't help but notice the sheep and horses in the fields and valleys between the forests and towns. This scenery, along with the scents of the pines and eucalyptus trees, wildflowers, and even the smells from the farm animals, caressed his senses and transported him into a more calm and serene state of mind.

Max then took notice of a small structure. A stone building with a tiled roof. Acting on the advice of his elder countryman, he walked over to investigate. It was an emergency shelter for pilgrims who might get caught in the severe weather so common to the Pyrenees.

It seems that they look out for the pilgrims even when they are not present.

He left the shelter and noticed a unique-looking hiker on the trail ahead. He was wearing a beret and carrying a large wooden staff but no pack, looking more like a shepherd of old than a pilgrim. Max reached the man and greeted him, "Buen Camino."

"Buen Camino Peregrino," the man said.

"Are you a pilgrim?" Max said.

"No, I am Basque."

"So you are not on pilgrimage."

"No, I am on a quest to find the Basajuan," he said with a smile.

"What is a Basajuan?"

"Since you are in the forests of the Basque country, you must know the legend of the Basajuan."

"I don't."

"Then I will tell you." The Basque man proceeded to tell the legend of the Basajuan, or the Lord of the Woods, as he is known in English.

"The Basajuan are the original shepherds of these woods; they are large, powerful, very hairy, and intelligent beings. In ancient times, they kept watch over their flocks of sheep and taught humans how to tend sheep and farm. They also taught them how to make tools to help with these efforts. The Basajuan protected the sheep by scaring off the wolves, and they warned the shepherds and farmers of any impending storms, which is very important here in the Pyrenees. They are not so common today, but have been seen on rare occasions as recently as the 1990s. I intend to meet one; at least I will try until I reach my home for tonight in Zubiri."

Max grinned and continued on his way.

Well, that was a nice break from reality, but now I need to get back to looking for the target.

The road turned to a steep decline and was unrelenting for many kilometers, amplifying and transferring every step through his already tired legs, hips, and back. By the time he neared Roncesvalles, Max was trudging along, mumbling profanities to himself and panting from the heavy load and altitude changes. He had not met any Americans and was already sick of talking to people. He then gazed out into the valleys, and the fog was rolling down the ravines as if it were racing the pilgrims down the hills. This caused this city boy to pause and take a breath of appreciation for this new land in which he was immersed. After traveling a little further along the trail, he could see the tiny town of Roncesvalles in the distance—the place that he was told was the first traditional stop on the Camino Francés, the Camino route he had been forced to follow.

I've been in some rough scraps in my day, but this was the most physically and mentally taxing thing that I have ever done.

For the first time in his life, he may not successfully complete a job. "This is bullshit!" Max grumbled as he made his final steps into the village.

"Don't fear, my son, all stages are not so demanding," a voice from the shadows said to Max. A priest emerged and approached Max.

"Hello, Father," Max said.

"You have made it through a difficult mountain pass and can now enjoy the comforts of the albergue," the priest said.

"I'm glad that it happened to be built here," Max said.

"The location of the historic monastery in Roncesvalles is not a result of mere chance. Roncesvalles is in a mountain pass between what is today Spain and France, which at the time of its construction were Navarre and the Frankish Empire. Many people and commodities passed through the area at that time, and Roncesvalles was an ideal location to control them. Charlemagne was also interested in expanding Christianity, and the monastery would do well to serve that purpose. The pilgrims of the Camino de Santiago needed a place for rest and rejuvenation after crossing over the Pyrenees, and the monastery has continued to serve this purpose into the 21st century," the priest said.

"It is a convenient and serene place," Max said.

"That wasn't always the case. Throughout history, waves of invaders, including Romans, Celts, Barbarians, and Goths, have passed this way, taking advantage of the relative ease with which the mountains can be crossed. In their footsteps came hordes of pilgrims, making Roncesvalles an important and symbolic Camino landmark at the gateway to Spain. Since its creation, the monastery of Nuestra Señora de Roncesvalles has always been heavily influenced by French religious orders and belonged for a time to the monastery of Sainte-Foy de Conques, which is on the Chemin du Puy. In medieval times, pilgrims could stay for three days in bad weather in order to give them time to recover from the hardships of the Pyrenees. While here, they could avail of services such as beard trimming, foot washing, and, if they were feeling plush, a bath," the priest said.

"I'm not sure that I will be taking advantage of all of those services, but a shower, meal and bed will certainly be welcome," Max said.

"And don't forget the pilgrim's mass, I will be there with some other priests."

"Thank you, father, I hope to be there."

With the monastery in clear sight, Max followed the priest across a small footbridge on his final approach for the day. Max checked into the albergue. When he got into the dormitory, he talked with a pilgrim who occupied a bunk near his, and learned that almost all pilgrims in Roncesvalles would be staying in that albergue, as it was basically the only open choice besides a four-star hotel. He flopped into a chair, leaned back, and exhaled loudly.

I might still be able to do this after all.

He set up his bunk, took a long, hot shower, and proceeded to meet fellow pilgrims. He worked at it before, during, and after dinner. He even attended the pilgrim's mass in the old monastery. Joey was said to be religious; he might spot him there and be done with it. The middle-aged Italian couple, a young Italian man, a couple of Americans and Spaniards among them, and some locals were also at the mass. The mass itself was much grander than Max had expected for such a small village. There were five priests conducting the service, and at the end of mass, they called up the pilgrims for a blessing, which was given in several different languages, including Spanish, Italian, French, German, and English.

Max had done his due diligence and was rewarded with his first potential candidates. Max attended the mass to see what he could learn, and he noticed that a high percentage of the Italians, relative to the other pilgrims, along with some Americans, attended mass. Max decided that he would continue attending mass throughout the pilgrimage to follow along as he was blending in, and this had proven to provide the best results for his efforts so far.

After mass, Max approached the two American men, who looked to be in their thirties and could very well be Italian Americans.

"Hello, nice mass and blessing," Max said.

"Yes, they have been blessing pilgrims here for hundreds of years," said the taller, well-built, rugged-looking man.

"I am Dean, and this is my new friend Vinny."

Vinny, who was of average height and had the olive skin, dark hair, and features of an Italian tradesman, nodded hello.

"So, you are new friends?"

"Yes, we just met today, and as two fellow Americans, we decided to walk together," Dean said.

"Just the two of you?"

"No, there are a couple of others back in the albergue who will join us. You are welcome as well. No one needs to be alone on the Camino unless they wish to be."

"That is good. I also have a new friend in the albergue, a young doctor."

"We can all meet and talk when we get back there," Dean said.

This is starting to work out; I have two potential targets, and there may be more among their group.

He got back to the albergue and found Eva. "We have a couple more people to hike with. We are all getting together in the common area."

"Great, let's go," Eva said.

"Max, are those boots the only footwear that you have with you?" Eva asked.

"Yes, why do you ask?"

"They look new and not broken in very well; they are also heavy to wear all of the time. You should buy a pair of light slip-on sandals when we reach Pamplona. Your feet are very important for making the Camino, and you need to take care of them. You want to give them a rest when you are not hiking."

"OK, I will, grazie."

Max and Eva joined Dean and Vinny, who introduced Mattia, a slightly built Italian man with a short ponytail sticking out of the top back part of his head. Mattia looked to be in his twenties or thirties, and he was also at the mass. He next introduced Gina, a tall, thin, dark-haired, olive-skinned American woman who looked to be in her thirties and who might have been at the mass; Max wasn't sure. Vinny introduced Sun Hee, a petite South Korean woman who liked to be called Sunni and looked to be anywhere from twenty to forty. There were also two Spaniards, Ramon, or Ray, as he liked to be called, a scholarly middle-aged patriarch, and his son Pablo, a compact version of his father who wore the scowl of teenaged angst. Max introduced Eva to them, and Eva introduced a young Irish woman with auburn hair, ivory skin, and sparkling green eyes that she met in the afternoon and invited to join her, who was named Orla.

Vinny smiled and put his hand out to Orla. "Hi, I'm Vinny."

"I'm sure that you are," Orla retorted, and ignored his attempt at a handshake.

Hot, but a bit of an attitude. Vinny pulled his hand back and placed both hands in his front pants pockets.

The new group was now getting acquainted and discussing the journey ahead when a peppered-haired, middle-aged Australian man who was listening in asked if he could join the group.

"May I join your group? I am on my own," the man said in an Aussie accent.

"Sure, the more, the merrier," Dean said, and the group was formed.

"By the way, I'm Grant," the Australian man replied.

"Welcome, Grant," Eva said.

"I'm sure that I will be a great addition to this group with my Outback experience," Grant said.

"If we run into any kangaroos, you can take the lead," Orla scoffed.

"That I will, my dear. That I will," Grant said with a smile.

"On that note, good night; I'm going to bed. I never get very much sleep at this albergue, even after the rough climb and descent from Saint Jean Pied de Port. There is so much snoring all in one place here in Roncesvalles," Mattia said.

"I hope not; I don't care much for snorers," Max said.

With plans set, the newly formed group retired to their bunks. Max lay in his bunk and contemplated his situation.

It could be any of these three guys, either of the Americans or even Mattia. Joey is said to be fluent in Italian, and Mattia's accent sounds strange. I can focus my efforts on these pilgrims until I find the target or rule them out. I should be able to wrap this up quickly and get back to Naples.

Chapter Six

Raging Bulls and Wizard Squirrels

Max's newly formed group of pilgrims embraced the cool morning air, donning their packs and their smiles, as they embarked on the road towards the next planned stop in Zubiri. Even with sore muscles and burgeoning hot spots soon to become blisters, they chattered and welcomed the upcoming walk in good spirits, as the hardest day on the Camino was behind them. The group left the albergue together, and the first thing that they saw was a sign that read, Santiago de Compestela, 790 kilometers.

"Oh boy, there's still a long way to go," Vinny said.

The others nodded and murmured in agreement.

The pilgrims left the road, entered the forested section, and meandered along the trail. They gradually spread out into smaller groups, coming upon and mixing with others. This is the communal nature of the Camino de Santiago. While the others enjoyed the camaraderie of the pilgrimage, along with the natural beauty of the forest, the cool breezes, and the rustling leaves, Max focused on how to find and identify the target. He looked over every other pilgrim they came upon to determine if anyone fit the profile. Eva came up from behind and said, "A pfennig for your thoughts."

Startled out of his concentration, Max said, "I didn't catch that."

"Nothing; it's just an old expression. What do you think about this section so far? It is a bit hilly, but the beautiful trees and golden fields make the walk pleasant."

"Yes, and it is much easier on the back and legs than yesterday's mountains. The steep downhills were just as or more difficult than the uphill climbs," Max said.

"I agree you with there; the Navarre countryside is beautiful and as easy on the joints as it is on the eyes," Eva said.

The first town that pilgrims reached after leaving Roncesvalles was Burguete, which gained some notoriety due to a couple of interesting but very different events in its history. The first being that they burned witches there in the times when such things were done, and the later in the 20th century because Ernest Hemingway would stay there to go fishing and write after partaking in the running of the bulls at the festival of San Fermin in Pamplona.

As the pilgrims encountered locals on their walk through town, they were greeted with a smile and a "Buen Camino" by most people they passed, especially the older folks. This occurred in most of the small towns and villages they visited.

"Being greeted and welcomed by the locals really makes you feel like a pilgrim," Eva said.

"It puts you in a Camino frame of mind and is one of the reasons that so many pilgrims choose to return," Mattia said.

Much of the trail in Navarre was through woodlands, where the pilgrims walked under canopies of trees that acted as gateways into other worlds. The lush greens and vivid browns painted a warm and welcoming ambiance, followed by grand openings where fog-covered mountains appear in the distance and rolling fields lie at your feet. When walking through these woods, the pilgrim not only communes with nature but also with the many pilgrims who have come this way through the centuries. On the way to Zubiri, upon reaching a broad field with a grand view, Mattia shed his pack and ran through the dew-covered field like he was in a scene from 'The Sound of Music.' Max stopped and looked over at him.

Mattia is one strange Italian; no one from Scampia would ever do that. And that manny-bun wouldn't go over very well either.

The next misty field had farmers baling hay and a mare and colt grazing while the clanging of a cow bell rang through the cool mountain air. This part of the Camino de Santiago was what everyone hoped it would be.

As they moved along, Max got to work and chatted up Vinny, but he was constantly interrupted by Grant.

"You seem like a tough guy, not a pilgrim. What are you doing on this Camino?" Grant asked Max.

Max just stared at him and didn't say a word. He was not accustomed to being confronted like this. Back in Naples, it would not happen to him. He couldn't do what he'd like as he was blending in, but there was something about this Australian that rubbed Max the wrong way.

Grant then proclaimed to all in earshot, "I don't need to do the Camino for vacation or stay in albergues. I'm very successful; I'm from Down Under, but I own property not only in Australia but in Ireland and California as well."

"Then why are you here?" Mattia asked.

"I don't know why I'm here; I'm here to figure that out," Grant answered.

Max mumbled to himself, "I don't care what you own or why you are here; just get away from me." But he was keeping his cool and his cover, so he just decided to let it go. Grant was oblivious to Max's internal fury and continued to babble on. Grant then asked Max what he did for a living.

Max clenched his jaw and managed to open his mouth just enough to utter the words, "I'm not here to talk about work."

Grant continued, "I don't see the problem; I just want to know something about you."

"I don't want to talk about work; let it drop."

Keep annoying me, and I just might have to show you.

It became apparent early on that this one pilgrim might become a thorn in the side of not only Max but the rest of the group as well.

I need to find the target soon. I need to get back to Naples and tell Carlo that the job is done. I can't have this pain-in-the-ass cause me any problems or delays.

"I guess you get one in every group," Vinny said.

"Maybe he'll get lost," Max said.

"We can always hope," Vinny replied.

After not getting much feedback from Max and Vinny, the Australian moved on to one of the other pilgrims. Max walked along quietly, fists clenched, and stared at the ground to calm down before he got back to work. After all, it was early, and he didn't want to make this job any more difficult than it needed to be. As some time passed, Max once again approached Vinny as he walked nearby, but separately from the others. Max resumed his investigation.

"So, how did you end up on this Camino de Santiago so far from home?" Max asked Vinny.

"I needed to think about whether I wanted to continue in the job that I was working or to move on to something else," Vinny said.

"Why were you considering not staying in your job? Did you come into some money?" Max asked.

"No, I wish. I had been working as a plumber for the past couple of years for a small home remodeling company. I had some trade school training, but I was still learning and buying tools as I went along. All totaled, I purchased a few thousand dollars worth of tools before and during the time that I worked for the builder, and one night they were all stolen out of my truck. I called the police, and they sent an officer to take my statement. I was already sick of my job, and then this happened.

"So I assume that you didn't get your tools back," Max said.

"After he took my statement, the officer looked at the houses near mine and noticed that one of the neighbors had video cameras on the outside of their house. He went to their door and asked them if they had any video from the previous night. They searched their files and found that they did capture the thieves pulling up in their jeep and loading my tools into it. The neighbor provided the video to the police, and the next day I got a call from the police department. I was given the number of a detective to call to get information on the progress of the case. I called the detective after a couple days, just like they told me to do, and the detective said that he didn't have a chance to look at the video and that I should call back another time. I called him a week later and asked him if he got the license plate number of the thieves' jeep from the video. The detective gave me a lame excuse that it could have been a rental car or a stolen car, so there was no way to find the thieves because he wasn't technical. It was obvious that the detective was lying and didn't even look at the video. I tried one more time a few days later, but nothing; this issue was a non-starter as far as the detective was concerned.

"By this time, my boss was pissed that I didn't have the tools that I needed to do my work, and I didn't even know if I wanted to be a plumber anymore. I didn't fit in with the crew; they all liked to drink a lot, and most of them also smoked. The boss was an older Irish guy who was always razzing me about being Italian and a lightweight drinker. Sometimes I thought that he thought that my name was Eedjit, because that's what he called me half of the time. It was not my ideal job situation. One thing is for sure:

I didn't feel like spending all that money buying more tools that could end up being stolen again. That's when I decided to use what savings I had and walk the Camino."

"How did you know about the Camino?" Max asked.

"I once dated a free-spirited girl who had done the Camino and told me all about it. I didn't think much of it at that time, but when my tools were stolen, I thought that it was just what I needed."

"The police in America sound as useful as the police in Italy." They both chuckled.

It is one heck of a story, but I can't rule him out just yet.

Max and Vinny once again walked quietly along, admiring the scenery and sinking into the Camino state of mind.

Further down the trail, they saw Grant chatting up Sunni, and she looked like she wanted no part of him. Max and Vinny couldn't hear their conversation, but they could hear the hammering of Sunni's walking sticks, and the sound grew louder and more rapid as Grant continued to talk to her.

"You should put end caps on those poles; the constant pounding sounds on the hard surface are annoying," Grant said.

"I didn't bring them with me, but I will buy a new set when I get to Pamplona," Sunni replied.

Talk about annoying; you seem to be an expert.

"I guess he's pestering Sunni now," Vinny said.

By lunchtime, it had warmed much more than the previous day in the mountains. Max and most of the others had reached a small village where the homes had flowers planted along the walls with boots and gardening shoes left by the doors, and they decided that it would be a nice place for a rest and lunch. There was a grocery store and a bar that provided the women with a chance to use the restroom in comfort—everything that the wandering pilgrim needed. Mattia suggested that they purchase some baguettes, meats, cheese, and fruit to make a picnic in the small park across the road. With their groceries in hand, they entered the park through a gate that read "No se permiten perros," which means "No dogs allowed." They spread their food out on a picnic table and prepared their sandwiches.

"I wish I had some mustard for this ham and cheese sandwich," Vinny said.

"Put some potato chips on it. They make any sandwich better," Gina said.

"It's salty enough. I'll eat it dry."

They were all eating when the uninvited but welcome guests arrived. You see, when eating al fresco in the small villages of northern Spain, you rarely have to dine alone. A local cat or kitten will usually join you. The pilgrims shared some of their meat with the cats, and a nice, relaxing lunch was enjoyed by all. They reasoned that the cats came there so they didn't have to deal with the perros since they were not permitted. As lunch was finished and they prepared to leave, an older local gentleman, accompanied by his own pack of dogs, kicked open the gate and walked right in, followed by his four-legged companions. The dogs barked, the cats scattered, break time was over, and all were back on the trail once again after a filling lunch and a fulfilling rest. So much for signs.

To enter the aptly named Zubiri, Basque for both bridge and pueblo, the pilgrim crosses the river Arga via the medieval Puente de la Rabia, so-called because in times past locals would walk their animals around the bridge's central pillar to prevent them from contracting rabies.

When Max's group of pilgrims reached Zubiri, their planned stop for the night, they chose a small, privately owned albergue that was just the right size to hold their group and no more. They could even make their own meals since it had a well-equipped and partially stocked kitchen for their use. Each of the pilgrims selected their sleeping spot for the night. When Grant reached his, he threw his hat onto his bunk. Max said, "Careful; it is bad luck to put your hat on the bed."

"I don't believe in such nonsense," Grant replied.

Max grinned and said, "OK, but remember that I warned you."

After they were all settled in, they needed to go to the grocery store to make the purchases for the evening meal. Mattia and Dean asked Grant if he wanted to go with them to pick up supplies for the meal.

Grant chuckled and said, "I'm not so good on grocery runs. Once, when I was a boy, my mother sent me to the market to pick up some marinara sauce for a lasagne that she was going to make. At the store, I didn't remember the name of the sauce correctly and asked for marijuana sauce. The grocer and his wife both laughed at me, and he said, 'I guess we'll all be flying high tonight.' After that, they called me Fly Boy every time I went into that store."

"I'll go in his place. I do all of the shopping at home," Ray said.

The three of them returned with enough antipasto to be worthy of any Italian feast, quite an accomplishment for a small town in the Spanish countryside. They also had bread, pasta, tomatoes, and seasonings for red sauce, along with bottles of red wine and a local specialty called Patxaran, a hybrid of wine and liquor. The group was set for a relaxing and enjoyable evening. Mattia suggested that the Italians be put in charge of the meal prep, as he has tasted Spanish attempts at Italian food in tourist restaurants and deemed that it was not good. "That is not a good representation of Spanish cooking of any type, but I agree that the Italians will do the best job preparing this meal," Ray said.

"I'm already tired of all of this bread and pasta that I've had since I've been over here. I don't like it, and I can afford better," Grant said.

"You had your chance to buy some of the groceries, and besides, we have a long way to go, and many of us don't have an unlimited budget while on this Camino, and pasta and bread are good and inexpensive. Besides that, we need carbohydrates to fuel us and provide the energy that we need to continue day after day," Mattia said.

"If you say so, but we don't normally eat like that where back where I live."

Orla then asked Grant, "Where did you say you came from?"

"From a place where we don't end sentences with a preposition," Grant answered.

"I'm sorry. Where did you say you came from, arsehole?" Orla replied.

Everyone laughed; the mood was lighter, and Grant decided that he would tell a story of his own.

"When I was a boy, I was at my friend Vito's house, and his mother was making what she called pasta with gravy for dinner. The gravy was actually spaghetti sauce. She asked me if I liked spaghetti, and I told her that I did, but I only liked Ragu sauce from a jar because that is what my mother used. Vito said that he would only eat his mother's red sauce and that he would never eat sauce from a jar. His mother invited me to have dinner with them that night, and I did. To my surprise, I did like it. She asked me how I liked it. I told her, Yeah, it is good; it tastes just like Ragu. I was never invited back for dinner; I don't know why."

"What a gaguzz," Vinny said.

They all laughed. Grant then sat with his chin held high and a gleam in his eye, basking in the glory of his story-telling abilities, not realizing they were laughing at the fact that he was still unaware of the insult that he levied upon this woman who welcomed him into her home so many years ago.

The sweet aroma of the garlic sautéing in the olive oil and the tomatoes simmering in the pot enhanced both the appetites and the anticipation of the feast to come. "These wonderful smells remind me of my mother's Sunday sauce. She would spend the entire day cooking and getting everything ready for the relatives to come over. My job was to stir the gravy for what seemed like hours. I didn't mind; it all made us so hungry that we attacked the table like a pack of wolves. That's love," Vinny said.

"I can't argue with that," Dean said.

"It makes me a little homesick, but I still love being on Camino," Mattia said.

Vinny gazed at Orla across the table in the dim light and got lost in the moment when she snapped him out of it by bellowing, "What are you looking at?"

"Nothing."

"You better not be," she added with a sideways grin.

Two other pilgrims joined the group for the meal; they were a French couple traveling rough. The albergue owner allowed them to use the showers, even though they weren't staying there. A couple of the group members had met them earlier in the day, so they invited them for dinner. They contributed their version of banana flambé, complete with brandy and flames. It turned out to be a classic Camino meal. Max, sitting satiated and content, contemplated: *I've had worse jobs than this one.*

Gina, with a subtle grin, leaned in towards the others and said, "I was afraid that I might be lonely or unsafe coming on Camino by myself. I also worried that I might not fit in or be a real pilgrim, but after meeting all of you, I'm not worried about that at all."

"Many people start the Camino not knowing or believing that they are pilgrims, but do come to this realization while they are on the Camino. They start with a problem and then discover what they need to do, and this discovery comes from within. They also find that they have in common with other pilgrims that they have left the familiarity of their homes to come to a new place and experience the Camino," Mattia said.

"Yes, I too had concerns, but it seems that even though the Camino goes through France and Spain, the language of the Camino is English. It allows pilgrims from all over the world to communicate with each other," Sunni said.

"This group is proof of that," Mattia added.

"On the Camino, you are on two journeys, one physical and one spiritual. Most people have not prepared for both, but you experience pain from both, and they are joined together," Dean said.

"We can now all take these journeys together," Eva said.

Max decided that he would try to learn a little more about this Camino and posed a question to the others: "I noticed that many of you, as well as other pilgrims, had scallop shells with crosses on them attached to their packs; why is that?"

"It's tradition," Mattia answered.

"Actually, it's more than that; in the early days of the Camino, it was used as proof that the pilgrim made it all the way to the Atlantic Ocean. They would collect a shell there to show to the people in their home towns as proof that they had completed the entire Camino," Ray said.

"Don't the compostelas prove that?" Max asked.

"They didn't always have them; the Cathedral in Santiago first started issuing them in the 12th century. Before that, the scallop shells were the proof," Ray said.

"Some say that the ridges of the scallop shell all converging into a single point are representative of all of the different Camino routes converging in Santiago," Eva said.

"That too makes sense. Maybe it was God's or Saint James' hand that directed the early pilgrims to select the scallop shell over other available choices," Dean said.

After an evening of good food, good wine, and good company, they were all ready for a good night's rest. They would sleep well this night as the albergue was small, and the pilgrims slept in rooms of two or four beds each; it was quiet relative to the large bunkhouse-style albergues in St. Jean and Roncesvalles. The albergue owner left out coffee and a light breakfast for them to eat in the morning. And they were once again on their way.

The pilgrims continued their trek through this section of small Spanish villages and on to the next, over the cobblestone streets alongside the quaint houses adorned with the reds, blues, and yellows of their window boxes full of flowers. There were even occasional family crests majestically marking these modest but historical homes. The distant sounds of the church bells and the smells from the local bakeries invited the pilgrim to reminisce about times gone by. The welcoming smiles and greetings of Ultreia and Buen Camino from the locals only helped to add to this wonder and to make memories that would last forever.

As the pilgrims entered Larrasoaña and strolled down the Calle San Nicholas, Eva remarked, "Look at these beautiful, tall homes."

"They are typical Basque homes, and you are correct; they are beautiful. This village is developed in the pueblo calle style, which focuses economic activity in the center of the town. We are also approaching their church, the Iglesia San Nicholas de Bari, built in the Baroque style," Ray said.

As they were leaving Larrasoaña, Ray said to the group, "Take a last look back at the Pyrenees Mountain that you climbed for the last two days."

After they walked for another hour, they were strung out along the trail, as tended to happen with larger groups of pilgrims. Max noticed a solo male hiker who wasn't with his group and who might fit the bill. He approached him and got to work questioning him.

"Buen Camino," Max said.

"Buen Camino," the pilgrim replied.

"Are you enjoying your Camino?" Max asked.

"Yes, it is beautiful and just what the doctor ordered," he said. Then he paused and said, "Well, not exactly."

Max stared at him with a raised head and a slight squint, so the man explained.

"I had a heart attack about a year ago, and my doctor put me on strong medication and a strict diet and exercise program. No alcohol, no cigarettes, no fatty foods, and worst of all, the medicine made me impotent. I didn't mind the exercise so much, mostly long walks, as that is all that I could really handle, but everything else just made me think, 'If this was my new life, why prolong it? I'm miserable.'

"Then one day, a few months ago, while at a christening of a friend's baby in my hometown in California, I couldn't help but notice how unique and beautiful the altarpiece was in the church. I had never seen anything like it in any church in California. It was as high as the church, with elaborate designs covered in gold on a blue marble background. The sole human-like figure was Jesus, on the crucifix in the center. The term breath-taking does not do it justice.

"After the ceremony was over, pictures were being taken, and everyone was chatting, so I asked the priest about the altarpiece. As it turned out, he was a French priest who told me that it was called a retablé and that he found it stored in an old church hall not in use while he was walking the Camino de Santiago in Spain. He made inquiries, eventually purchased it, had it restored in a specialty guild hall in Madrid, and had it sent back to California to be the central piece in the new church that his parish was building. I then asked him about the Camino de Santiago, as I had never heard of it. He smiled, perked up, and explained it to me. It sounded like a good idea and was just what I needed. I figured that since I've already been walking a lot, why don't I head on over there, chuck all the medicine, have some good food and wine along the way, and let life play out? So far, so good. Maybe I'll get to Santiago; maybe I won't, but I'm enjoying life once again and am already losing weight."

"Have you found a woman?" Max asked.

"It's not really that kind of place, but you do meet many nice people, and the scenery is magnificent," the man answered.

Not wanting to spend any more time with someone who wasn't the target, moved on without bothering to get his name. He may or may not ever see him again, and that too is the way of the Camino.

After his first few days on the Camino, Joey became more comfortable interacting with other pilgrims. He didn't shed his loner mentality, but he was learning to appreciate his fellow pilgrims' company.

It's nice to meet people from different countries and get to use my Italian and Spanish. At least I did a little training for this; it's still really difficult, and my feet and most other parts of my body are killing me. I chose to do it, and I'm sticking with it.

The pilgrims reached the outskirts of Pamplona and walked along the bank of a small river, the Rio Arga, until they came to an old stone footbridge, the Puente de la Magdalena. They crossed the bridge, slowly ascended a cobblestone road, and passed under a large stone arch, the Portal de Francia. This brought them to the old town section of Pamplona. They were soon immersed in a sea of humanity that was in stark contrast to the first few days of mountain roads, forest paths, and small villages. The muffled hum of the crowd and occasional jolts of sound confirmed this reality.

The Roman city of Pompaelo was founded on the site of a Basque village called Iruña in 74 BC by General Pompey (Pompeyo Magno). The Romans had good relations with the native Basques and introduced progressive urban planning and agricultural techniques to the region. Their successors, the Visigoths, found relations with the natives more difficult when they arrived in the fourth century, but nevertheless ruled over the city until the early eighth century, when it came under Muslim rule for about fifty years, until this was interrupted by the arrival of Charlemagne, who laid siege to the city and placed it under the control of his allies. Pamplona's location on an important access route to Iberia and on the fault line between several ethnic groups led to it being divided into walled neighborhoods known as burgos (boroughs), in which each group was confined to its own area with contact between them mostly limited to commerce. The Navarrería district, around the cathedral, was the Basque area; other areas were set apart for Franks and Jews. These divisions lasted until King Carlos III (el Noble / the Noble) abolished the boroughs and had the walls separating them torn down. In the 19th century, the old city's southern walls were demolished, and work began on the construction of the modern city center to the south. Today, Pamplona is a prosperous city and the capital of the autonomous community of Navarra.

The pilgrims made their way through the old city to the large wooden doors of the Saints Peter and Paul municipal albergue, adorned with a gold-colored scallop shell that was a full one meter in diameter. They checked in, set up their bunks, and got cleaned up. This albergue did not offer meals, so they planned to go out and enjoy what Pamplona had to offer. Mattia said to the group, "Why don't we be ready to go out together by 1800, so we have time for dinner and drinks before we have to be back for lockdown?"

Everyone liked the idea, except for Grant. He commented, "I don't need Mattia making plans for me."

The others told Grant that Mattia was a professional tour guide; it was in his nature to organize, and they were lucky to have him to help the group function smoothly. Grant clenched his jaw and lips and did not reply.

Pamplona's biggest festival is San Fermin, with its running of the bulls. But it wasn't exactly a sleepy village the rest of the year, at least not in the Old City. This was where the locals and tourists honed their partying skills whenever the weather was good, and this was where Max and the other pilgrims planned to spend that first Camino big city night.

The group strolled along and soaked in the ambiance of their surroundings. With the sounds of crowds chattering and music emanating from the bars, along with the aromas from the restaurants filling the air.

"This is more like Naples than the rest of the Camino has been so far," Max said.

There is also a better chance of finding the target with so many people.

The group came to a cafe with an outdoor patio and a large table available, so they chose to start their evening there. Soon their table was topped with pitchers of beer, sangria, and pintxos, local appetizers very popular with those out for an evening of drinking and exploring the night scene. As they sat around the table and enjoyed their refreshments, the conversation turned to the bumps, bruises, and blisters they had acquired during their first couple of days of walking. Pablo, the Spanish teenager, complained, "I don't think that I will be able to continue on much longer; my blisters are too sore."

Eva said, "Take off your shoes and show me. I'm sure that they're not too bad; I can fix them for you right here." Eva then got out her first aid kit and tended to Pablo's tender feet.

As this was happening, Dean nodded towards a table across from them. "Look over there; he doesn't seem to be complaining." Among the pilgrims sitting at the table across from them was a man with one leg. Dean waved to the man and asked him, "How is your Camino going?"

The man smiled and said, "Great, so far, no IEDs."

Dean got up, walked over to the man, and talked with him. When he returned, he told the group that the one-legged man was a veteran of one of the conflicts in the Middle East who had a bad encounter with an improvised explosive device (IED), and he was now walking the Camino with a prosthetic leg. It gave them all a bit of perspective. "I guess a couple of blisters aren't all that bad," Dean said.

Pablo, with a reddened face, shook his head in agreement and sat quietly as Eva finished tending to his feet.

The group next decided to explore the town and came upon a small bar where there was a ukulele group having a get-together. They went in, had a couple drinks, listened to a few tunes, and when the REM song "Losing My Religion" was played, Orla barked, "I hate this song; my ex always played it, and he wasn't even religious."

Vinny said, "We should find someplace else before it gets too late."

The group made for the exit. There was no shortage of nightlife in Pamplona that night, and as they walked to find the next venue, Dean explained that the term "Losing My Religion" had nothing to do with faith. It is an expression used in the southern United States for someone who is losing their mental faculties.

"Thanks for mansplaining it, but it still annoys me," Orla said.

There was a sound of lively music coming from just ahead, so the group moved towards it. It was a discotheque, so they went in to give it a try. The preponderance of bass was vibrating windows, and the floor was bouncing from the dancing patrons. It was loud and jam-packed with local young people. The pilgrims were standing around and looking at each other, some with their hands in their pockets; none of them were dancing. This scene was not fitting with their Camino state of mind. In addition, Grant started acting strangely, telling the male pilgrims that he wanted them to get him a woman and saying that the place was filled with Nazis. He tried to make advances on Gina, but she wanted nothing to do with him.

Orla said to the group, "I think that Grant is losing his religion."

"Either that or he has taken some kind of drug," Vinny said.

Max got right next to Grant and whispered something in his ear. Grant's head and shoulders stiffened, and his eyes got big. He then walked away from Gina and into the crowd on the dance floor.

"What did you say to him?" Mattia asked.

"I just told him that he was being rude, and that was no way for a gentleman to act."

If I told you what I really said, you might not think of me as a pilgrim.

"Do you want to leave?" Max asked the others.

They all nodded yes; none of them felt like staying any longer, and besides, they needed to get back to the albergue before the doors were locked at 2200.

"We need to get back before the Albergue doors are locked; we don't want to cut it too close," Mattia said.

They decided to leave and not bother telling Grant. He had quickly become "that guy." They made their way through the music-filled, festive streets of Pamplona to the peaceful area of Old Town and got back to the albergue by 2130. They were glad to be back in a quiet environment. 2200 came and went without any sign of Grant; he was locked out for the night.

The next morning, the group left the albergue early and was once again back in the world of the Camino. They hoped they had now seen and heard the last from Grant on their journey, but the Camino didn't always work that way.

The pilgrims passed through the old town and across the Citadel grounds on the way out of town. The Citadel in Pamplona is a star-shaped fortress that King Felipe II ordered built to protect the city and keep it loyal back in the time when Pamplona was the capital of Navarre. He commissioned Italian engineer Giacomo Palearo to erect the structure, and its construction started in 1571. It was modeled after a similar structure in Belgium. In modern times, it serves as a 300,000 m2 city park.

Pamplona is a pleasant walk when the streets aren't filled with raging bulls doing their best to gore you. As they reached the outskirts of town, the pilgrims passed through a city park with large evergreen trees and a community of furry red squirrels. This park was their turf, and the pilgrim does not pass without contest. As the group strolled down this comfortable path in blissful ignorance, admiring the easy footing and pleasant surroundings with birds chirping and cool pine-scented breezes blowing, one of these tiny but brave creatures stood in the middle of the path on its hind legs with arms raised, akin to Gandalf in "The Lord of the Rings," and commanded, "You shall not pass." At least not until you cough up a nut, a raisin, or something else to appease this formidable beast. Fortunately, Gina had some trail mix that did the trick, so the trip was saved and the group was able to continue. Just another peril to overcome along the way.

Chapter Seven

Emilio Estevez Ruined My Life

After the big city experience of Pamplona, the pilgrims cross the river and follow a bidegorri, a red man-made path made to support both pedestrians and cyclists, back to the serene world of towns with Basque-style homes and churches that have stood in their places for hundreds of years. In addition to these typical sights, in Cizur Menor, the pilgrims encounter their first frontón.

"Look at that; it's a giant handball court. We would love that back in my old neighborhood," Vinny said.

"It's a frontón, and it is used to play pelota. It is a very popular game here in the Basque part of Spain. Sometimes the hand is used to play, but usually a Chistera, a curved woven racket, or a Pala, a wooden racquet, are used. Nearly every Basque town has a frontón," Ray said.

By midmorning, they had arrived in another small Basque village, and the pleasant aroma of baking bread called them into a bakery where they would purchase baguettes for use in making the day's lunch. Inside, there was a solo pilgrim who asked if there was any day-old bread for sale as he was traveling on limited means. The bakery shop owner gave him a loaf of bread and told him there was no charge. Max was taken aback by the kindness of the people in these small villages; they had so little but were so generous to total strangers; it didn't make sense to his big city-hardened mind. When they were outside, they spoke with the pilgrim, and he told them that he was sleeping rough to save money. He also said that in one town he asked if there was a place where he could pitch his tent where he would not be forced to move, and a local man told him not to pitch his tent but to set up his sleeping bag under the overhang on the side of the church and no one would bother him there. Later that evening, the same man brought him food for dinner and even some small cans of tuna to use for other meals. The people of the small towns and villages along the Camino are very generous and caring toward the pilgrims. They are commonly referred to as "Camino angels."

After hearing this account of kindness, Sunni said, "All people have it in them to be friendly; you just have to give them the opportunity."

Vinnie added his own version of rock-n-roll philosophy and offered, "The Rolling Stones must have been thinking about the Camino when they sang, 'You can't always get what you want, but if you try some time, you just might find, you get what you need.'"

Dean laughed and said, "You are a modern-day Yogi Berra."

The group continued onward in search of the next challenge along the way.

When Joey passed by the bakery and inhaled the aromas of the freshly baked breads and pastries, they reached deep into his memory.

My father made homemade bread every Easter. I miss those days and I now also miss my mother. I understand how Santiago felt in 'The Alchemist', traveling in a foreign land when the smells of freshly baked bread and the odors of sheep reminded him of his home. Will I ever be able to go home again?

On the steep climb to Alto de Perdon, young Pablo was griping and whining the entire time he was ascending the hill. Pablo said to his father, "I don't want to be here; this is hard; I'm in pain; and it's all your fault." His constant tantrums and stopping and starting were making his climb much more difficult than it should have been. When Pablo lagged behind, Ray chose to give him his space and let him walk by himself for a while.

We may be climbing the Alto de Perdon, "The Height of Forgiveness," but Pablo has no forgiveness in his heart for me.

Max, who was trailing far enough behind to give them a sense of privacy but not so far that he didn't hear Pablo's loud complaining, used the opportunity to walk with Pablo.

Max made his way up to Pablo and said, "You seem to be having a tough time today."

"This is a steep hill, and I really don't want to be here," Pablo said.

"It's just part of being a pilgrim," Max said.

"You don't seem like a pilgrim to me. What are you doing here?" Pablo said.

"I'm here for the same reasons as everyone else. I do think that you're being hard on your father; someday you might regret it. My father was killed when I was only five years old. It happened right in front of me. I miss him, and now my mother has also died. I have no one left in the world."

Talking about this memory slowed Max's pace and had him looking down as he climbed the steep hill. Pablo shrugged his shoulders as if he didn't care what Max had to say, but it did give him something to think about. He just wasn't ready to admit it. Ray was all that Pablo had left. Ray and Pablo's mother divorced a few years prior, and Pablo blamed his father and had never forgiven him. He would not visit him and barely spoke to him when Ray visited him at Pablo's mother's apartment. His mother had de facto sole custody. Then she passed away suddenly from a ruptured brain aneurysm. Ray now had custody of Pablo, at least for the next few years. Ray tried to improve his relationship with his son, but Pablo resisted. That's how they ended up on the Camino de Santiago. Ray had hoped that it might bring them closer together. He was at his wit's end and didn't know what else to try.

Max worked his way up to commiserate with Ray. "You put up with so much backtalk from Pablo."

"Yes, I know; you see, besides his mother's passing, there is another reason. Pablo was born with a large cancerous tumor on his spine. He had to have it surgically removed when he was only a few days old, but they could not get it all since it was on his spine and the risk of paralysis was too great. This meant that he also had to have chemotherapy—a particularly strong type of chemotherapy. He was scheduled to receive five cycles to try and kill what cancer cells remained. After the second cycle, his lungs stopped functioning properly; they could no longer draw oxygen from the air to oxygenate his blood. He was going to die. His only hope was a very dangerous procedure, and only half of the people who received it survived. He had to be put on an extracorporeal membrane oxygenation (ECMO) machine, and none of the doctors at the hospital were comfortable performing this surgery on someone so young. Dr. Russo, a renowned Italian pediatric cardiothoracic surgeon, was brought in and performed the surgery. The staff at the hospital seemed to be both in awe of Dr. Russo and a little bit afraid of him. He was a stylish man who wore white silk suits and Italian loafers and drove a high-end Jaguar. His swagger, along with his kind and gentle demeanor when dealing with the parents of his patients, instilled a confidence that allowed parents to be at ease with this man performing highly dangerous surgeries on their newborn infants. He spoke and smiled in a way that showed concern, confidence, and hope.

"After the surgery, Pablo was on the ECMO machine for three days with round-the-clock care and survived. He spent the next year in and out of the hospital, struggling to survive, until we could finally keep him at home. That is the reason that he is so much smaller than me. So naturally, his mother was very overprotective of him his entire life. I, too, am guilty of leniency when it comes to his discipline, such as when he is mouthing off to me. I see the baby in the incubator with tubes going in and out of his body and have a hard time being cross with him."

"I understand," Max said.

On the ascent of the Alto de Perdon, windmills dominate the sky and continue to grow larger as the pilgrims approach them. "Where's Don Quixote when you need him?" Vinny shouted in an attempt to overcome the noise from the wind and the turbines.

"They are an assault on the skyline," Mattia said.

"And on the birds too, from what I hear," Vinny added.

At the peak of Alto de Perdon, the pilgrims were welcomed and rewarded by the life-size flat metal sculptures of pilgrims past and present, one of the iconic sights along the way of St. James.

"That was an extremely difficult climb, and that wind didn't help," Mattia said.

"I sweated like a farm animal even with that strong breeze," Eva added.

Mattia smiled and said, "Animals sweat; men perspire; and women glisten."

"You are a smoothy, Mr. Mattia," Eva said with a glistening smile.

Gina then joined the conversation, adding, "When I'm climbing these hills, I'm not only struggling physically but also emotionally. I know that I have things to work out, but I'm wondering if it is all worth it. Do I want to continue? Will it really help me?"

"The struggle to continue on the Camino is both a physical and emotional struggle. Continuing and meeting these challenges on the Camino will help you meet and defeat your challenges in life," Mattia said.

"I told you he was a smoothy," Eva said, grinning.

After a pause to look around and admire the sculptures and the views of the countryside below, it was time for the descent. Even though it was shorter, the steep and rocky trail proved to be more difficult than the ascent. In a way, this was representative of Ray's struggle with Pablo. Whenever he thought that he saw a sign of progress, another dose of his rocky relationship with his son would arise.

After conquering the Alto de Perdon and its treacherous descent, the group passed through Uterga and proceeded to the town of Muruzábal. Upon entering Muruzábal, they came upon a sign with details of Santa Maria de Eunate. It is said that this church is modeled after the Holy Sepulchre in Jerusalem, with its octagonal shape and ring of arches. It is considered one of the jewels of the Camino and may have an affiliation with the Knights Templar.

"Are we up for the extra five kilometers to visit this jewel?" Dean asked.

"I think that we have earned it," answered Mattia. So off they went, and when they arrived at the church, its unique architecture of eight faces and thirty-three arches did not disappoint.

"My guidebook tells of a tradition that if you take off your shoes and walk around the church three times, you will have a successful Camino," Sunni said.

"I might have heard a rumor about that, but I am not sure of it," Ray said.

"I'm going to do it, anyway; it will feel good to get out of my boots for a little while," Sunni said.

Some of the others joined her.

After the side trip to Eunate, the group of pilgrims made it back to the Camino Francés at the town of Obanos, which has a unique legend as part of its history.

When they entered the town of Obanos, Sunni smiled and took out her guidebook and said to the others, "Obanos is another town that I have read about in my guidebook. It is the setting of an interesting Camino legend dating from the 14th century. At that time, the daughter of the king and queen of Aquitaine, Felica, decided to follow the family tradition of going on pilgrimage to Santiago. She returned from her journey so filled with piousness and religious fervor that she was unable to settle back into the life of idleness and privilege that befitted one of her station and instead, leaving it all behind, set off to live an anonymous life of service to others. Needless to say, her family was outraged and sent her brother Guillén to track her down. He found her after much searching in Obanos, and when his efforts to persuade her to return to their family home proved to be for nought, he flew into a rage and killed her with his dagger. Having killed his sister, Guillén was racked with guilt and, as penance, decided to follow in her footsteps to Santiago. While there, he, in his turn, saw the light and decided to dedicate the remainder of his life to poverty and charity. On his return to Obanos, he built a hermitage on a nearby peak called Arnotegui, where he lived out his days as a hermit dedicated to prayer and helping passing pilgrims. The hermitage at Arnotegui is still there on a hilltop about 3 km south-west of the village; the road up is signposted from the main road."

"Thank for that story Sunni, it was sad but still very interesting," Ray said.

Up next for the group was a nice stroll down a country lane towards Puente La Reina, or Gares in Basque, a town named for its bridge, where the pilgrims follow in the footsteps of millions of pilgrims who have come before them.

Ray, proud of his knowledge of the history of the Camino as well as his knowledge of Spanish history, told the others, "Puente La Reina is mentioned in the opening lines of Book Five of the Codex Calixtinus, the first guide to the Camino de Santiago by Pope Callixtus II: There are four ways that lead to Holy St. James, and they become one near Puente La Reina, in Spain."

When the pilgrims entered Puente La Reina, they came upon the Iglesia del Crucifijo, or Church of the Crucifix, as it is known in English.

"This church was built back in the 12th century by the Knights Templar. The church is now named for a Y-shaped crucifix that was carried here by German pilgrims in the 14th century," Ray informed the others.

They continued through the town, and as they neared the bridge at the edge of the town, Ray once again donned his Camino guide cap.

"In this church, the Iglesia de San Pedro Apóstol, is the statue of the Virgin of Puy, known locally as Txori, which has a legend associated with it. Txori is Basque for bird, and back during the times of the Carlist wars, a bird would routinely clean the face of the statue, which at that time was in a small chapel on the bridge."

They exited the town by crossing the 110 meter long Romanesque bridge for which the town is named and continued towards and then through the winding streets of Mañeru. They travel on dusty roads through vineyards on the way uphill towards Cirauqui.

On the ascent to Cirauqui, the pilgrims got their first glimpse of the town, which is perched atop a hill. They climbed to the edge of town, traveled under Gothic arches on narrow streets, and reached the Town's oldest buildings near the top. They came to the church of San Roman, a medieval, although substantially modified, structure that is a fusion of Muslim, Romanesque, and Cistercian architecture. After admiring the exterior of the church, Ray said, "Our night's lodging is just over here.

The evening's lodging was at an albergue situated next to the Iglesia San Roman. It is known for its ample and delicious communal meals with excellent wine, of course. At this albergue, each evening at the end of the meal, the hosts ask each of the pilgrims to stand and tell their names, where they are from, and why they are walking the Camino. Most of the pilgrims, both from Max's group and the others who were there this evening, gave fairly generic statements; they gave their names, countries, and brief reasons such as to get away, to clear their heads, etc. Max didn't really want to talk but was called upon, got up, and said that he was Max from Italy, and to his own surprise, said that he was walking the Camino to try to get over the death of his mother. He didn't know why he had said this; he was usually very private about his feelings, and that really wasn't his purpose for being there. Max stopped talking abruptly and sat down quickly, not very happy with himself. Gina put her hand on his arm and told him that she could sense that he had a troubled soul and that he was doing the right thing to heal.

Next, an American man traveling on his own who looked to be in his fifties got up and said something strange. He gave his name, said he was from the United States, and said he was walking the Camino de Santiago because Emilio Estevez had ruined his life.

Since most of the pilgrims there knew of Emilio Estevez, maker of arguably the most popular film ever made about the Camino de Santiago, their interest peaked, and questions followed.

"Do you know Emilio?"

"No, I have never met him."

"Then how did he ruin your life?"

"This is how: One evening my wife and I were looking for something to watch, paging through endless lists of movies available for streaming, and we came upon a film titled "The Way," starring Martin Sheen and written and directed by Emilio Estevez. Its description was about a man hiking through Spain after losing his son. We liked to watch films based in Europe because we love to travel and also enjoy hiking. We watched it and loved it. I had two upcoming business trips in Europe and decided that I could fit in some time on the Camino if I made it one trip with the Camino sandwiched in between. I finished my work in Gibraltar and took a bus and a couple of trains to Pamplona. My goal was to get to Saint Jean Pied de Port and start there. There was a problem: it was November, and there was no bus to Saint Jean Pied de Port from Pamplona; I could only go as far as Roncesvalles. I met two other pilgrims in the bus station and asked them if they would like to share a cab to Saint Jean. They told me that it was winter and that it was too difficult. Since they were both quite a bit younger and more fit than me and I had no other choice, I decided that it would be wiser to join with them and to start in Roncesvalles. The plan was to walk for a few days, make my way to Lisbon, and then fly to the Azores to complete my business trip. I would then return with my wife and pick up where I left off. This worked out because she did not want any part of the Pyrenees mountains. Things sort of went according to plan except that during this, my first Camino, I became addicted to it. I cannot get over the call to return, and I have done so several times. After spending all of my vacations walking the Camino, my wife was tolerant at first, but is now sick of it. We were discussing what to do for our 30th wedding anniversary trip, and I said that I wanted to go on the Camino again. She told me to "just go!" So here I am on the Camino by myself. I'll tell you how terrible I am. I can't understand why she got angry with me. Some fun, huh? I will be thinking about how to be a better husband. Well, you know, after I get to Santiago."

There were a couple of the pilgrims who understood his obsession, at least to some degree. Sunni then asked, "Have you always made bad choices in life?"

He replied, "On the contrary, my life choices usually serve me quite well. I have worked my way through school to get an engineering degree, which in turn allowed me to move out of the depressed area of the city where I grew up. I accepted a job right out of college that was not providing me with the real-world engineering experience that a new graduate required in order to grow professionally, so after a few months I found a new position that did allow me to grow my technical skills as well as provide me the opportunity to travel the world while doing so. This eventually led me to lead a number of large and successful international programs. It also gave me the opportunity to obtain patents, publish technical papers, and lecture and work on six of the seven continents. I have even represented my country on a dais at a European technical conference, sitting and answering questions on state-of-the-art technologies with industry leaders from some of the top companies in the world. With all of that said, the best choice that I have ever made was to marry my wife. Without her love and support, I don't believe that I would have had nearly the success that I did. So you see why I need to make things right when I get home?"

With that, they wished each other a good night, settled in, and prepared for the next morning's walk.

The Camino, after Cirauqui, follows an ancient road built by the Romans. Ray told Max this, and Max said, "See, it is still good; Italian craftsmanship lasts."

Ray laughed and said, "Yes, yes, it does."

The pilgrims continued on their way and towards Estella, and as they neared the edge of the town, they were stopped in their tracks. "My God, look at that doorway; it is a masterpiece," Mattia exclaimed.

"It is the Iglesia del Santo Sepulcro, the Church of the Holy Sepulchre. Its doorway is a perfect marriage of Romanesque and Gothic styles," Ray said.

"Look at those statues, the crucifixion, Las Tres Marias, the three Marys at the sepulchre, the rescue of the innocents, and the moment when Mary Magdalene recognized Jesus after his resurrection. Then you have the last supper above the door, and on the sides are the twelve apostles, with St. James and St. Martin of Tour closest to the door. It is inspirational," Mattia said.

The group continued on the Calle Curtidores and next came upon the Iglesia de San Pedro, a Romanesque church with arches and a cloister that is built on the site of an old fortress. Across from the church of St. Peter is the Palacio de los Reyes de Navarra, the palace of the monarchs of Navarre, with exterior walls adorned with great armorial crests validating the historical importance of this palace.

Estella is another town that owes much of its development to the Camino. In fact, before it was founded around 1090 by Sancho Ramírez, then king of Aragon, the Camino used to go from Villatuerta to Irache more or less in a straight line. To attract Frankish settlers, Sancho Ramírez granted them the right to sell to passing pilgrims. Soon the town was thriving with Camino-related commerce, attracting many more settlers from among those who passed through. Like in Pamplona, it developed distinct, walled ethnic neighborhoods for its Navarran, Jewish, and Frankish populations. Occitan, a medieval language spoken in France and Northern Spain and the primary language of troubadours, was still spoken here until the 14th century. Estella receives a gushing review in the Codex Calixtinus, where bread is good, wine excellent, and meat and fish abundant, and which overflows with all delights.

The pilgrims departed Estella by crossing the river Ega via an unassuming bridge and made their way towards the small town of Ayegui. Ayegui, like many of the small towns in Spain, has its own folk hero.

There has been a monastery in Ayegui since 958, and the first pilgrim hospital opened in 1050. According to a local legend, San Veremundo, when still a young boy and in the employ of the monastery, used to sneak food hidden under his robes to pilgrims who were staying there in order to supplement the meager offerings given to them by the monks. Once, when he was challenged by the abbot about what he was hiding under his robes, he replied firewood, and when made to reveal what it was, the food miraculously turned into firewood.

The group left the town of Ayegui and headed for the Bodegas Irache Wine Fountain. This is a popular stop on the Camino Francés that provides a fountain with free wine and water for pilgrims.

The pilgrims entered through the ornate iron gates into the courtyard, which is home to the fountain. In the middle of a stone wall is the majestically decorated stainless steel fountain with its two spigots, one for water and one for wine. Pilgrims line up to take their turn.

Mattia read the inscription on the fountain: "Peregrino, si quieres llegar a Santiago con fuerza y vitalidad de este gran vino, echa un trago y brinda por la felicidad!"

"What does it mean?" asked Sunni.

"It means, Pilgrim, if you want to arrive in Santiago with strength and vitality, drink a mouthful of this great wine and overflow with happiness," Ray said.

They then each took their turn; some filled small empty water bottles for later, and others used their scallop shells to take a small drink. Max took a sip and said, "This is a nice welcome, and the wine is not too bad either."

Ray said to him, "Spanish hospitality is legendary."

Max said, "Yes, yes, it is." They both laughed.

The pilgrims left the fountain and plodded along the paved path through suburbia until they reached a small forest of oak trees. After a stretch, they climbed once again, this time with vineyards on both sides. On the steep hill before they entered Villamayor de Monjardin, they passed the Fuente de Moros, or Moors' Spring, a restored Gothic cistern whose cool waters were too much for the weary group to resist. So they gave their feet a soothing, refreshing dunk while taking a well-earned rest.

"This is a nice treat left to us by our friends, the Moors, from hundreds of years ago," Ray said.

"They picked a good spot to put it," Mattia said.

After their break ended, the pilgrims worked their way to the top of the Monjardín hill. It was there that they encountered the castle of San Esteban de Deyo, which was originally a Muslim fortress until it was captured by King Sancho Garcés III, who is buried there.

The group next traversed three hours of open space before coming to the next town, Los Arcos. Los Arcos today retains some of the splendor of its heyday in its narrow streets and squares, surrounded by arched arcades. At one time it had a massive defensive wall, but only the Arco de Filipe, Philip's Arch, facing on to the bridge, remains.

The pilgrims marveled at the Iglesia de Santa María, or Church of the Virgin Mary, which was built in various stages between the 12th and the 18th centuries.

"That church has a little bit of everything," Gina said.

"You have a good eye for architecture. Its exterior features a plethora of the different architectural styles seen in the churches throughout Spain. Take notice of the peak of the entrance. That statue of the Virgin Mary is in shadow all year except the late evenings of April 23 and August 16. On those dates only, its face is illuminated by the sun," Ray said.

"This area is also where the common but easily misunderstood Spanish saying 'Wander more than Saint Gregory's head' has its origin," Ray said.

"That is a strange saying. What does it mean?" Mattia said.

"I'm glad that you asked," Ray said, and then told the story to his fellow pilgrims.

"During a time of great despair in this region, the Pope sent San Gregorio Ostiense to help the people. He was tasked with ridding the area of plagues of locusts that were devouring their crops. He arrived from Rome and conducted a preliminary investigation. San Gregorio concluded that the plagues were a punishment from God for the poor morals of the local people and their lack of devotion (i.e., donations) to the Mother Church. A clampdown on deviant behavior was ordered, and in due course, the plagues stopped. As an unforeseen consequence, San Gregorio became so beloved by the locals that they wouldn't hear of him leaving, and he was obliged to live out his days in Logroño until his death in 1044. After his death, a vicious row erupted between the bishops of Nájera and Pamplona over his earthly remains. The King of Navarra, hearing of this, intervened and decreed that his remains should lie in a purpose-built basilica on neutral territory. Another version of this story claims that in order to settle the dispute between the two bishops, San Gregorio's remains were tied to the back of a donkey, which was set loose with the intention that the place where the donkey died should be the place where the holy man would be buried. After much wandering and several false alarms, the unfortunate donkey died at the summit of a hill called Piñalba. San Gregorio was duly buried there. His basilica is still visible to the right of the Camino between Los Arcos and Sansol. This legend gave the Spanish language the expression, Andar más que la cabeza de San Gregorio, Wander more than Saint Gregory's head."

"If you know enough history, you can make sense out of anything," Mattia said.

As the group made their way through the narrow streets and squares, they passed by a bank, a pharmacy, shops, several restaurants, and cafés. One café had a sign advertising pizza; when Max saw it, he sighed.

I've got to get out of this tourist mode. I'm not making any progress. This is not good.

On the way out of Los Arcos is a cemetery with an inscription above the entrance that reads: Yo que fui lo que tu eres, tu seras lo que yo soi; I once was what you are; you will be what I am. Max read the inscription and looked at the ground. *I don't need to hear that now.*

The pilgrims continued past Sansol and down to Torres del Rio, where they intended to spend the night.

"That church looks just like the one in Eunate that we walked all those extra kilometers to see. We could have just waited to see it here," Pablo said.

"What would be the fun in that?" Ray smiled and said to his son.

The church of Santo Sepulcro in Torres del Rio is, like Eunate, octagonal in shape and, also like Eunate, something of a mystery. It is known to date from the 12th century, and its architecture is mostly Romanesque, but its domed roof supported by stone beams that intersect to form an eight-pointed star at its highest point betrays some Mozarabic influences. It may also have originally been intended as a funeral chapel, as it has a space for a beacon light on its roof.

After the long day's hike, Joey reached around to the side compartment of his pack and took out the small bottle that contained the wine he saved from the Irache fountain. He unscrewed the lid and had a sip. It reminded him of home. *This tastes like the table red that I've had so many times at Angelo's. That's one thing from the old neighborhood that I still miss.*

Several hours after the group had moved on from Irache, a lone Australian pilgrim reached the fountain, only to find that the wine was finished for the day.

This trip stinks; first I got ditched by my group, and now the wine is all gone. Wait until I find those guys.

Chapter Eight

Santiago Matamoros

The many hills and valleys that make up the long stretch of uninhabited area between Torres del Rio and Viana wear on the pilgrims' bodies and minds. The monotonous trek numbs the senses until something happens to wake them up.

"Look at that; it's about a hundred fuzzy brown caterpillars walking head to tail like they are connected. I've never seen anything like that before," Vinny said.

"They are an invasive plague here in Spain. Don't ever touch one; they can cause health problems," Ray said.

"What exactly are they?" Vinny asked.

"They are called processionary caterpillars, and you can become very sick if you touch one. Some people have developed symptoms similar to a heart attack from merely having them fall on them from trees," Ray said.

"Well, I guess I won't touch one then," Vinny said.

The pilgrims entered the beautiful hilltop fortress town of Viana, which was founded in the year 1219 by the indomitable King Sancho the Strong to guard the frontiers of Navarra. It has prospered, like other Camino towns, thanks to passing pilgrims and inward migration. The townspeople commemorate the founding of the town each year on the first of February. After casually taking in the sights of Viana, the pilgrims moved on, leaving the province of Navarre, into the community of La Rioja, and towards the next larger city on the Camino, Logroño.

On the way into Logroño is a plaque commemorating the assassination in 1937 of 27 people, victims of fascist repression. The inscription reads: Los pueblos que olvidan su historia están condenados a repetirla. A people that forgets its history is condemned to repeat it. "That's a lesson that we must all remember, not just here in Spain, but everywhere," Ray said.

Before entering Logroño, pilgrims cross the mighty Ebro River, one of Spain's longest. It flows all the way to the Mediterranean. This is also where the Camino del Ebro, which follows the Ebro from the Mediterranean coast, joins the Camino Francés.

Logroño is a great place for wine and tapas, but during a festival, it is something special. It is the capital of the world-famous wine-producing region of La Rioja. Through pure luck, the group happened upon Logroño during this year's wine harvest festival. They enjoyed the ample wine, food, and entertainment, along with many other pilgrims and even more locals. While savoring this good regional food and award-winning wine, they conversed on many subjects. Max, Vinny, Dean, and Mattia were all in a fine state and listened to the wine-assisted chatter of peregrinas from other groups of pilgrims. One of them mentioned that she was a vegan and was finding it difficult to get vegan or even vegetarian meals while walking the Camino. Max couldn't help but notice that some of these women who were chiming in and agreeing on the subject were not what one might call slim. Max leaned over and whispered to Mattia, "I didn't realize that vegetables were so fattening."

Mattia laughed and said, "I don't think they are."

Upon hearing the laughter, one of the women looked at the food on the plates of Max and the other men, which largely consisted of roast pork, sausages, and beef steak, and remarked to them, "You should have some salad with lettuce and other greens instead of all of that meat."

"Lettuce and greens aren't food; they are what food eats," Vinny replied.

The men have a small chuckle. If the women only knew what they were just whispering.

One of the peregrinas, who was not only on the slim side but also a very attractive blonde Polish girl, was paying particular attention to Dean. When the opportunity presented itself, she moved to the seat next to him and introduced herself. "I am Susie, and how are you called?"

"I'm Dean."

Vinny and Mattia smiled and winked at Dean. Dean exchanged the usual pleasantries and worked into the conversation that he was a Roman Catholic priest. This did not deter Susie; she told him that she was Catholic, and she liked priests. "They are usually so nice; I think that they should be able to marry."

She then rubbed her hand down his forearm and embraced his wrist. Dean turned red, developed goose pimples, and looked down.

"I believe that God is testing me."

"Behave," Mattia said with a sly grin.

Vinny and Mattia laughed and shook their heads in mockery, and Vinny said, "Remember that blondes have more fun."

"Blondes are more fun," Susie added.

Susie had had enough fun and decided to take pity on Dean and move back to her friends.

"Have a Buen Camino," she said as she looked back on the way to her table with a walk that highlighted her shapely proportions.

It was a meal filled with laughter and pleasant conversation—a memorable night that they may or may not remember. After a couple more bottles of wine were consumed, Mattia said, "This drink seems chewy."

To that, Ray said, "That makes it time to stop drinking. We should call it a night."

The others contently agreed.

The next morning, before leaving Logroño, the group visited the Iglesia de Santiago Real, which contains one of the statues of Saint James in the form known as Santiago Matamoros, Saint James the Moor Slayer. This depiction of Saint James arises from a legend born in a ninth century battle between the Catholic King

Ramiro I of Asturias and the Moor emir of Cordova, which is said to have occurred in Clavijo, south of Logroño.

"This statue is inspired by a great story that depicts the love that Saint James has for the people of Spain and how he helped to overcome the occupying forces in order to allow Spain to once again be ruled by Spaniards," Ray pronounced to his fellow pilgrims.

He then told them the story of the men of Asturias, who were greatly outnumbered and suffered heavy losses during the battle. The prospect of a victory was dim until, out of the sky, on a white horse, rode Saint James, who proceeded to slaughter all of the emir's soldiers. This legend spread throughout the kingdoms of Spain, gave them hope and courage, and eventually spurred on the other Spanish armies until they vanquished the moors from their land, and once again, the kingdoms of Spain were under the control of the Spanish. Many people point out that Saint James had been dead for hundreds of years before this battle occurred, but that is part of the legend, even if it is not accepted as history. The outcome is history—Spanish history.

It was time to move on, and Eva decided that she would take this opportunity to talk with Pablo. He was younger than the others and was not enjoying himself as much as he could. She told him that the Santiago Matamoros legend was not the only one from the Camino. In fact, one of the characters from Harry Potter is real and has been on pilgrimage on the Camino de Santiago. This peaked Pablo's interest, and he asked, "Who is it?"

Eva told him that Nicholas Flamel was a real alchemist who was born in France in 1330. The legend is that he actually did possess the philosopher's stone, which, as told in the Harry Potter books, was said to not only turn all metals into gold but also grant immortality to its possessor. It is said that Nicholas Flamel found the key to finding the Philosopher's Stone on the Camino de Santiago.

Alas, his death is recorded in Paris in 1418, but the legend lives on. Pablo now had a smile on his face and was walking with a little more liveliness, at least for the time being. Once again, the group was on their way.

Max focused his efforts on Dean this morning; after all, he fit the profile. Max needed to get to work and find his target. Max and Dean walked along, making an occasional comment, but mostly staying quiet and enjoying the sounds and smells of nature. The leaves rustling in the breeze, the birds chirping, along with the cuckoos of the cuckoo birds, as well as the sweet smells of the eucalyptus trees, set the tone.

Dean said to Max, "They really do sound like the clocks, don't they?"

"Or vice versa," Max answered.

Dean laughed and said, "That's right."

Once they had gained a little distance from the others, Max asked Dean, "Are you on the Camino for any special reason?"

He did not realize what a cornucopia of thoughts he was opening. Dean said, "Until recently, I was a parish priest in the United States and at one time taught high school religion classes. I started having doubts and difficulty deciding if I wanted to remain a priest. You see, I don't like how the church, including my own bishop, has addressed the numerous church scandals that have come to light. I was also concerned with how the Pope seemed to interpret or sometimes ignore church doctrine as I understood it. Remember that the Gospel says, If gold can rust, what will iron do? For if the priest in whom we trust be rotten, no wonder an ordinary man corrupts."

"My mother had similar concerns. She once joked that she remembered when the question 'Is the Pope Catholic?' was rhetorical," Max said.

Dean was still a believer, but needed to come to grips with this inner turmoil. He then asked Max, "Do you believe in God?"

Marone! Max was not expecting this. He was the one asking the questions. Max's mother, whom he loved more than anyone or anything, was a devout Catholic, but Max had such a hard life seeing so many terrible things that he had a hard time believing. Max just said, "I don't understand why life is so trying."

Dean then said to Max, "When the world seems like it has gotten too overwhelming to tolerate, simplify. One of the best ways that I can think of to do this is to make pilgrimage on the Camino de Santiago."

Max then asked, "So will this cure all of my problems?"

Dean shook his head no and said, "The Camino is not a magical fix for your life's problems, but it does help you gain perspective on them. Just as many of us have been discarding some of the material items that we brought with us on pilgrimage to lighten the weight of our backpacks as we move along the way, we can discard some of our troubles and replace them with new hopes and dreams. It is best to walk the Camino with no expectations; just accept it as it comes. That way, you will realize what you need."

Max had never had anyone speak with him like this; he didn't know what to think. Max then said, "I am completely taken aback by how friendly, helpful, and open the pilgrims and local people are all along the Camino."

Dean smiled and said, "The Camino is God's dream of how people should treat each other."

Max continued his effort to gain insight into Dean and asked him, "So what specifically happened that made you decide to come here and question your role as a priest?"

"You may have heard about some of the scandalous things of which some priests and even bishops have been accused. I tried not to dwell on them, and the priests that I know personally are good men. Then I read an article in the newspaper that was about one of the priests who was at the high school that I attended. The story was told by someone who was accusing this priest of inappropriate behavior. The priest, who had left the church, moved out of state, and married, denied the accusations. The problem that I had with this is that the details of how the man described the incident were very similar to an experience that I had with this same priest when I was in high school. I was more fortunate than this man because I became very suspicious of the priest's behavior, got away from him, and never went near him again. He was transferred out of my school at the end of the year, so someone must have found out something. That is why I am having trouble believing and accepting how the church and superiors are addressing these issues."

"I understand your dilemma," Max said.

Max went quiet and furrowed his brow.

My two best candidates seem so legitimate. I can't give up on them yet, but I'm not feeling so confident in my chances for success at this time.

Max was also now starting to notice the impact walking the Camino de Santiago was having on him. He wasn't there to change himself, but it seemed to be happening. He had always spent more time thinking to himself than talking with others, but the extra time walking and thinking day after day was giving him thoughts he had never had before. Thoughts about himself and how he treated others who crossed his path in his life and on his job.

While making pilgrimage along the Camino de Santiago, pilgrims visit many cathedrals, churches, and small chapels along the way. The big city cathedrals are spectacular, and many of the small chapels are ancient and austere. They each have their own redeeming qualities. Navarrete is a beautiful hill town that has kept its medieval street plan and arched walkways. The town was founded at the behest of King Alfonso VIII of Castile, who wished to establish a fortress here to help defend the frontiers of his kingdom. When the group arrived in Navarrete, Orla mentioned she had read the town had a church worth visiting. They came to the Iglesia Parroquial de la Asuncion de Maria, and luckily it was open, as it is hit or miss in the smaller towns. The beauty and impressiveness of this church were as good as promised. The retablé behind the altar was made up of Bible stories, culminating with the Assumption of Mary at the top. For a small town to have such a magnificent church, it was a very pleasant surprise and a worthy stop along the way for pilgrims or anyone else who happened upon it.

"I believe these churches and cathedrals are so magnificent partly because, at the time they were being built, people were inspired by their faith. They also had fewer distractions, and religion was a greater part of their lives. The closest thing to this today is the Sagrada Familia in Barcelona. There are still artisans there who have traveled far and dedicated their lives to seeing this effort, which has been underway for more than a century, to completion. Pilgrimage is, for many, their small version of such an effort," Dean said.

"That may be true, but on the other side of the coin is the growing number of people who are using the Camino as an inexpensive backpacking holiday. They are not so interested in a religious or spiritual experience as they are a cheap good time. This impacts the pilgrims by using their resources, drives up costs, and sometimes causes animosity from the locals," Ray said.

"That may be true in some cases, but I still find most along the Camino welcoming to pilgrims. I have noticed some of the anti-Hollywood graffiti bashing the film 'The Way', but there's not too much of that," Mattia said.

"People who project hate like that are more unhappy with themselves than with others," Eva said.

The rest the pilgrims had while visiting the church turned out to be a lucky break, as not too long after leaving Navarrete, there was a short but steep climb. On the descent, the pilgrims were in a single file line with other pilgrims on a narrow path that stretched almost the entire length of the hill. Gina and Max were at the rear of the line when a group of cyclists came barreling down the hill and almost ran into them. The shock caused Gina to sway, and the weight of her pack knocked her over. "Idioti!" screamed Max. He then helped Gina to her feet and stared down the cyclists. They did not say a word and then gingerly maneuvered their bicycles past the backpackers.

Max asked Gina, "Are you alright?"

"Yes, I was more startled than anything."

One of the other backpacking pilgrims who was not with the group walked back to Gina and Max and asked if Gina was OK. She then said, "On my last Camino, a woman that I was hiking with had her backpack clipped by a cyclist who was passing her at a high speed, and she fell and broke her arm. It was the end of her Camino."

"I don't know what the hell they are doing on this trail; it is not safe," Max said.

If Joey is on a bike, it will be a greater pleasure to end his Camino permanently.

Gina brushed herself off and said, "I don't understand why anyone would even want to do the Camino by bicycle. When you travel at that speed, you miss so much. It is in direct contrast to the whole reason for going on pilgrimage."

"I don't think that they're really on pilgrimage," Max said.

The pilgrims made it down the hill and were once again on a flat dirt road between vineyards. When they came upon a unique-looking stone structure, Vinny called out and laughed, "Look at that; it's a 10-foot-high beehive made of stone and concrete. You must have some giant bees around here."

Ray laughed and said, "Thankfully, that is not the case. It is just a chozo, an old shed made using the abundant stones that are in this area."

"Well, that's good," Vinny said.

They next made their way to the town of Najera. The Monasterio de Santa María la Real in Najera is built on the spot where, in 1056, King García el de Nájera, while out hunting with his falcon, found a cave containing a carving of the Virgin Mary lit by a lantern with a bowl of lilies nearby. He constructed the monastery and its church to house the carving and placed them under the control of Cluny in 1079.

In the late 10th century, King García Sánchez transferred his royal seat to Najera from Pamplona when that town was destroyed by Abd al Arman, renaming his kingdom Nájera-Pamplona. Nájera was to remain the royal capital for less than a hundred years. The assassination of King Sancho IV by his brother Ramón led to the division of the kingdom and the ceding of Nájera to Castile. Nájera is the location of the legendary battle between Roland and the giant Ferragut. The legend says that the fight was long and bloody and that both men were so evenly matched that they both eventually collapsed from exhaustion. A truce was agreed, and they sat down together to eat and drink. Roland, however, had a plan. Feigning friendship, he plied Ferragut with wine until, in a drunken state, he got him to confess his one weakness: he could only be hurt through his navel. The next day, the battle continued until Roland managed to stab Ferragut in the navel, killing him instantly. The place where the fight is said to have taken place is still known as Poyo Roldán, or Roland's Hill.

The group was making good time this day, and when they reached Santo Domingo de la Calzada, they decided to enter the Cathedral of Santo Domingo. Young Pablo said, "Not another church; they are nice, but they all have the same stuff over and over again."

His father said, "You wait and see; I can guarantee this church has something that you have not seen in any other."

They entered, looked around, and Pablo said, "See, just like all the others."

Ray pointed up in the air behind Pablo's head. Pablo turned around and saw the famous chicken coop. "What is that?" he exclaimed.

Ray then proceeded to tell him the legend of the "Chickens of Santo Domingo, a tale of Treachery Most Fowl."

"A German couple accompanied by their young son were en route to Santiago when they stopped off in Santo Domingo for a couple days of rest. Then, as now, dark-eyed southern ladies had a particular partiality to blue-eyed men from the north, and one of the ladies of the town took a particular shine to this couple's son. Sadly, out of indifference, or possibly a surplus of piousness, he rejected her advances, leaving her in a much-agitated state.

"This scorned woman vowed revenge and slyly slipped an expensive chalice from the church into the boy's luggage. Just as the family was leaving town, she came running after them, raising hell and accusing him of theft. His luggage, when searched, revealed the chalice, and as he was unable to account for its presence there, he was quickly subjected to the travesty that passed for justice in those dim and distant times and hanged in the town square.

"His grief-stricken parents continued on their way and, once in Santiago, prayed to St. James for the soul of their son. Retracing their footsteps home, they arrived once again in Santo Domingo and were surprised to find their son still strung up in the town square. Upon approaching him, they were even more surprised to find that he was alive. They hurried to see the king's representative, and they explained to him what they had seen. He was incredulous, and since he was eating his dinner at the time, he pointed to the two fowl in the pot on his table and said, 'Your son is about as alive as this cock and hen that I was about to eat before you interrupted me.' Whereupon the two birds jumped up and bit him on the nose!"

"So what do you think about that?" Ray said to his son.

"I think that I would like chicken for dinner tonight," Pablo said.

Ray just shook his head and said, "We'll see what we can do."

At least he's calm and talking somewhat normally.

While known for its cathedral and chickens today, Santo Domingo is named after Santo Domingo de la Calzada, who is the patron saint of civil engineers, in recognition of his contribution to the subtle art of road building. He was born not far from the town, in the village of Viloria. As a young man, he tried unsuccessfully to join a monastery but was judged by the abbot to be unsuitable. Determined to lead a religious life, he became a hermit. It was a chance encounter with San Gregorio that caused him to be ordained into the priesthood. In collaboration with San Gregorio and with the support of Alfonso VI, who was keen to bring new Christian settlers into this largely Muslim region, he dedicated himself to works for the benefit of pilgrims, building bridges and albergues, and clearing a path through the dense forest to create a more direct road from Nájera to Burgos. He died in 1109 but lives on in his many works in favor of pilgrims.

On to Belorado and Pablo's chicken dinner.

The most popular dining spot in Belorado for both pilgrims and locals is actually a restaurant in an albergue a few blocks away from the albergue where the pilgrims were staying, the Cuatro Cantones. So the choice for the evening meal was set, and they decided to eat outside of their own albergue so that Pablo could get his roast chicken; actually, it sounded pretty good to the others as well. After he had his chicken dinner, Pablo was feeling good and decided to tell the others about the legend of Nicholas Flamel that Eva told him. They all enjoyed the story, and Ray was happy to see Pablo enjoying himself and grateful to Eva for her part. Ray then said, "The Camino has many legends, and I know of one that I was told as a child."

He then proceeded to tell the legend of "The Long Nap of Saint Virila."

"Virila was the abbot of the Monastery of Leyre, one of the most important monasteries in the Kingdom of Navarre during the Middle Ages. Virila lived at the end of the ninth century, and according to legend, one afternoon, he decided to go for a walk in the majestic forest next to the monastery.

"At one point, when he stopped to rest by a fountain while meditating on eternal life, the abbot heard the song of a nightingale, which caught his attention. He was so struck by the beauty of the bird's song that he fell asleep.

"After waking up from a long nap, Virila returned to the monastery, but when he saw it, it was very different. The Monastery of Leyre was much larger than when he left and had annexed areas that were not there before. Once inside, he did not recognize any of the monks there either, nor did they recognize him.

"The monks began to investigate who this man was who claimed to be the abbot of the monastery, and after a long search in the monastery archives, they found that Virila had been the abbot of Leyre 300 years before, until one day he disappeared in the forest.

"Due to the great commotion caused by this news, all the monks immediately went to pray in the chapel. During this service, the vault of the church was opened, and a divine voice was heard saying, 'Virila, you have spent three hundred years listening raptly to the song of a nightingale, and it seemed to you a brief instant. Imagine what an adventure it will be in heaven, contemplating the glory of the Most High with all your senses, so that you will enjoy eternal bliss with no room for fatigue or weariness.'

"After this, a nightingale flew into the chapel, carrying the abbatial ring in its beak. It placed it on Virila's finger, and he was once again appointed abbot of the Monastery of Leyre, a position he held until his death in 950. His feast day is now celebrated every October 3rd at the Monastery of Leyre."

The stories of lore and tasty chicken dinner motivated the group so much that they decided they would go all the way to Burgos the next morning. It was a lofty goal, as it is a long hike from Belorado, but they wanted to have time before they left Burgos to see the cathedral and explore other sights. Max told them he would still leave Belorado at the regular time and work hard to catch up or forego his afternoon rest time.

"I am feeling a little under the weather and want to get proper rest," Max said.

In actuality, he had to make a prearranged call back to Naples. Once again, Max realized that the Camino was having an impact on him, and he was starting to feel like he was becoming a pilgrim and not just someone who was on a job. Also, many pilgrims, especially solo hikers like Max, tend to rely on the bonds made with other pilgrims to maintain the strength needed to continue, and it therefore becomes natural to try to stay with a group. After a nice dinner, the group walked back to their albergue for the evening, and as they passed two British pilgrims, they overheard one say to the other, "That's the puddle of which I was speaking."

Max said to the group, "Why would two grown men talk about a puddle?"

Eva said, "You need to understand the British, if that's even possible for a non-Brit."

The group chuckled and entered their albergue for the night.

The sun rose right on schedule, and the plan was to make it all the way to Burgos this day, so an early start was in order. Except for Max, he needed time to formulate what he would tell Carlo when he called. He was worried because it was looking less and less like either of his two prime candidates could be the target, and he wasn't ready to abandon this group and start from scratch. He lingered, sipped his espresso, and told his fellow pilgrims that he would see them later in the day. They were off, and Max remained and sat at a small round table outside of a café, grasping his demitasse and fumbling with his spoon.

I won't give up on this group, but I will continue to look at other pilgrims when I come across them.

After the group departed, Max finished his coffee and looked for a public phone with some privacy. He plodded along, half dragging his feet and looking down. He knew that it would not be a pleasant call. Max found a phone and made the call.

"Carlo, it's Max."

"What have you found out?"

"I have a couple of possibilities."

"Turn those possibilities into results; I'm getting tired of your cazzate!"

"I'm not bullshitting you, Carlo. It's just not that easy."

"The next time I hear from you, you better have results. Call me back in three days."

The phone clicked, and the conversation was over. Max did not want to make another call until he had completed the job.

This is getting to be a real problem, and Carlo is pissed. His history of dealing with failure is not pleasant. I miss my mother, but I'm not ready to see her again this soon. My enthusiasm for this job wasn't too great to begin with, and it sure isn't growing. What kind of life is this, anyway? My mother was right; I should have found a wife; at least I would have someone to go home to.

Then, Max gritted his teeth, shook his head, and was in no mood to talk with anyone, but he must endure and get on task.

He hit the trail, walked, and searched for potential targets. He continued for a couple of hours with no luck. "Oi Max," Grant called out to him. The obnoxious Australian was back.

Oh no, not this asshole.

His solitude was definitely gone, and his chances to talk with other pilgrims in peace were also greatly reduced. As Grant hurried towards Max, he called to him, "Where did you all go? You left me."

"You were having such a good time; we didn't want to ruin it for you."

"You just wanted to ditch me."

"You were acting like an ass and being rude to everyone."

"That's no excuse; your mother should have taught you better," Grant said.

How dare that bastardo insult the memory of my sainted mother!

Max walked silently with both his fists and his jaw clenched. He was oblivious to the sights, sounds, and smells of this section of the Camino. He tried his best to control his temper. They continued on together, with Max adding nothing more than grunts or monosyllabic replies while Grant continued running his mouth for the next hour or so. Max grew increasingly annoyed and less tolerant of Grant's incessant blabbering. Max's heart was pumping hard. The veins in his head and neck throbbing; he was at his wit's end, as if in an altered state. The only sound, his pulse in his ears, the only sight, the pack on Grant's back. They climbed higher and higher on the narrow trail and had to proceed single file. To their left was a sharp, cliff-like drop laden with jagged boulders and fallen trees. Max's heart continued to pound harder and harder, and his chest pumped so much that it was visible through his shirt. This wasn't new to Max; this always happened just before a kill. Max was behind Grant and couldn't help himself; he grabbed him by his shoulder and backpack and threw him down the steep slope. Grant tumbled downward and repeatedly knocked his head on the boulders during his descent until he came to a stop somewhere near the bottom and just lay there motionless. Better yet, he was not easily visible from the trail. He could be seen if someone were to look directly at him, but most people would walk right by without noticing. This was good. Max then looked both ways, up and down the trail.

Good, there's no one in either direction.

He had not noticed anyone for quite some time prior to this little mishap. It looked like Max was in the clear. He grinned. *I guess you're down under again, mate.*

Max walked along with a pep in his step and a smile on his face; it was a nice way to release some tension.

Max was getting tired of walking and trying to make it to Burgos early enough to meet the others for dinner. Then he saw the solution to all of his problems. It was a horse, or at least what he thought was a horse, all alone in a field.

I can ride this thing to make up some time and distance. I've seen enough Sergio Leóne films. I should be able to ride it, it doesn't seem too difficult. I don't need a saddle; I am strong like the Red Indian.

Max approached the horse and tried to mount it, but it bucked and swung its head, knocking Max to the ground. Max rolled, snapped back on his feet, and tried to grab the horse once again. The horse, which was actually a mule, tried to bite Max, which caused him to jump back. The mule then lunged at him and knocked him down once again. Max jumped up and ran towards the road; the mule followed him to the edge of the road but veered off and remained in his field. Good mules have a tendency to protect and also keep to their fields.

A young local boy who was watching the entire calamity play out with much glee called out to Max, "Oye peregrino, no es un caballa, es una mula."

Max shook his head in disgust and said, "Thanks. Now you tell me."

Max brushed himself off and once again walked toward Burgos.

Max continued along in relative solitude when, just a few kilometers before reaching Burgos, a field of fiery red poppies appeared that stretched to the edge of the horizon.

This is like the "Wizard of Oz" with yellow arrows, crazy animals, and fields of poppies.

"Buen Camino," a solo peregrina, approached and greeted Max as he was gazing at the flower fields.

"Es muy bonita, no?" said the peregrina.

"Yes, it is," Max said.

The peregrina said," Oh, English. Enjoy this now because the first section of Burgos is not very pleasant for the pilgrim, not until you reach the center of town."

"Oh well, what can we do?" Max said.

The peregrina told him, "You can take the bus from the front of the restaurant on the outskirts of town and get off by the theater; it is much more pleasant than walking through the industrial section of the city."

I wish that I knew this before I tried to ride that mule.

Max joined the peregrina, and they went to the bus stop outside of the restaurant on the edge of the highway. As the bus traveled through the initial section of Burgos, the indicators that this was one of the larger cities on the Camino, with its industry and eventually its high-rise apartment buildings and street-level storefronts replacing the country roads, small shops, and trails, became apparent. He was glad that he met this peregrina.

One of the passengers on the bus was playing a news station on his radio. It was in Spanish, but Max thought that he heard that the police had found a dead body on the Camino and were looking into it. His Spanish wasn't strong enough to be certain, but he now had a reason to be concerned.

Chapter Nine

Banditos and Cutthroats

Max exited the bus in front of the theater in central Burgos, and the peregrina directed him towards the old city. She told him when he reached the walled city that he should go under the arch, go to the left of the cathedral, and make a left once he was up the steps and behind the cathedral. The albergue will be on that street. Max passed under the arch and into the plaza de Santa Maria, where the cathedral came into view. He stopped in his tracks and admired what was in front of him. The grand cathedral, with its impressive size and blend of European styles, presented a uniquely Castilian presence. After taking in the view, he continued on. He made it to the albergue Casa de Perigrinos in Burgos as planned, checked in, and met his fellow pilgrims, his Camino family. He settled in with the others, and they all rested after a long day.

Although a settlement existed in Burgos since before the Romans, it remained a minor provincial center until the ninth century, when it became strategically important to the Castilian kings in their battles with the Muslim invaders. From 1035 until 1492, Burgos was the capital of Castile. After 1492, that honor passed to Valladolid. Burgos' growth continued to be driven by pilgrimage, and by the end of the 15th century, there were more than thirty pilgrim albergues within its walls. Los Reyes Católicos, the Catholic kings, received Christopher Columbus there when he returned bearing news of the 'new world'. Francisco Franco was proclaimed head of state in Burgos in 1936.

Later that evening, at the communal meal, there was chatter that a pilgrim had been found dead somewhere between Villafranca Montes de Oca and San Juan de Ortega. The hospitalero, who was serving the meal, entered the dining room, and Eva asked him if he had heard any news about the pilgrim who was found dead.

"Señor, do you have any details on the pilgrim who was found dead earlier today?"

"I have heard of this tragedy; I will check to see if I can learn any specific details for you."

The hospitalero finished serving the meal and then later returned to the dining room.

"I checked the news station's website, and on it was a brief story reporting that a solo male pilgrim who appeared to have slipped off of the trail at a very steep spot and hit his head during the fall was found dead, but no specific details on his identity were provided."

"We have heard rumors through the Camino grapevine that it was a middle-aged Australian man," Eva said.

"I cannot confirm that, but it is sometimes too dangerous to hike alone. All roads on the Camino are not equal. Each year, pilgrims' lives are lost on the Camino de Santiago in many different ways. Sometimes by falls, other times by weather, and also by being hit by motor vehicles. On rare occasions, it is even darker. In fact, a couple of years ago, during Semana Santa, a woman who was walking alone was diverted off the trail by false markers put there by a man with bad intentions. Sadly, she went missing and was later discovered dead. He had murdered her. Even in this place of such goodness, evil can lurk in the hearts of men," the hospitalero said.

This news brought Grant to the forefront of their thoughts, as did the fact that they left him on his own. A solemn silence came over the group, with each of them staring pensively into the distance as they reflected on how they enjoyed ridding themselves of their obnoxious mate. Except for Max, his expression did not change. They then expressed their feelings of sorrow and worry.

Gina took a deep breath and muttered, "Do you think that it is Grant?"

Pablo said, "My father told me that the area has a history of banditos and cutthroats; maybe it was one of them who got him."

Ray said, "No matter what you think of a person, you shouldn't joke about their death. Besides, they said that his death looked like an accident, not banditos."

Max remained silent.

No, it was definitely a bandito, and I do not feel sorry for him one bit.

"Max, you were far behind us; you could have walked right by him without even knowing it," Orla said.

"I was hurrying along and didn't notice anything," Max said in a terse reply.

I don't need anyone asking me any questions about that fool.

"These tragedies are rare, and even though they give us concern when we are here, especially when one of them happens while we are here, the Camino may be the safest place in the world to walk alone because of the Camino community," Ray said.

"That is true, but I have noticed several makeshift memorials for pilgrims who have met their demise," Mattia said.

"That too is part of the Way of St. James," Ray said.

They cleared the dishes and completed the clean-up. Many of the pilgrims from Max's group, as well as other pilgrims, remained in the dining room.

"It's good that we have each other for company and support during a sad time like this," Sunni said.

"It's part of the role of a Camino family," Mattia said.

"That's true, but what has brought each of us here? I'd had no idea about the Camino family before I arrived," Sunni said.

"I guess that we haven't really talked about it much among ourselves," Vinny said.

Dean submitted to the group, "Why are so many people once again walking the Camino de Santiago?"

"People seek adventure and meaning in their lives. St. James embodied the spirit of adventure when he traveled to the ends of the known world to preach his gospel," Ray said.

Dean added, "I believe that is part of it, but I also believe modern society is erasing religion and God altogether, and it is leaving holes in their hearts and souls. They are seeking something to fill these holes, but they reject God and religion because they have become passé and are looked down upon by a progressive society. Religion is inherently good, but flawed men sometimes use it as a cover for the evil that they perpetrate, and those who are against religion accentuate these acts of men in an attempt to further their cause. These are some of the reasons why I am on the Camino. I am trying to understand my life and my future. As you may know, I am a Roman Catholic priest and have left my position to come to terms with this internal struggle."

"You knew that society was heading in the wrong direction once made-guys started to rat on each other," Vinny said.

This peaked Max's interest.

This could be the guy; the target is a thief, but he is not a rat. The word from America is that the target didn't tell the cops anything during the entire time that they had him in custody. I will have to pay more attention to Vinny.

In a soft voice, Gina said, "Since I have been on Camino, I am now again considering becoming a nun once I have completed my pilgrimage. I used to fantasize about it when I was a kid in church with my parents, and my mind was wandering as the priest rambled on with a homily that he had told a hundred times before."

She then told of something that had happened to her while on this Camino.

"Early one morning, I couldn't sleep, and I wanted to get some time on my own to think about something that has been troubling me, so I started walking by myself. It was dark, and I came upon a large group of young locals who were still out partying from the previous night. I became frightened and felt alone and vulnerable when one of the young men called out to me, 'Buen Camino.' It was such a wonderful moment; I believe that I was walking with God; the Camino is a blessed place."

Mattia smiled and said, "See, there is hope for the world; we just need to get everyone to walk the Camino."

"It's good to walk on your own sometimes to think and reflect. It's part of the reason that you are on Camino and what makes you a pilgrim and not just a tourist," Dean said.

"How do you tell if someone is a true pilgrim? In the film "The Way," Jack from Ireland tries to define it, but the others don't agree with him," Sunni said.

"Don't listen to that Irish asshole from the movie; he doesn't know what he is talking about," Vinny said.

"Quit playing the Ugly American," Orla said.

"If you make the effort to walk the Camino in whatever way you choose to do it, you are a pilgrim," Vinny said.

"Many people walk the Camino just to get a break from their lives; it doesn't have anything to do with God or even if there is a God," Eva said.

A Danish pilgrim named Lars, who was also at the table that evening and couldn't help but overhear the conversation, said, "There is no one on earth who can truly state that there is a God or that there is not a God. You can only believe one way or the other, but as long as you are alive, you can never be sure. I hope that God does exist, and I choose to live my life as if he does. I envy people who are sure that God does exist, but I myself remain unsure but hopeful. Today, so many people are so adamant that there is no God that they turn atheism into a religion itself."

Orla then chimed in with, "Anyone who doubts the existence of God or the devil has obviously never had the love of a good man or flown on Ryan Air with a hangover."

There's a group chuckle, and the mood is lightened temporarily.

Orla continued, "Then again, I thought that I had the love of a good man, but when I told him that I wanted to be married, the arse dumped me. He didn't want me, and I've never felt lower. That is when I decided that I needed to gain a new perspective on my life, and so, here I am."

Ray tried to console the young woman and said to her, "There will always be someone who is prettier, smarter, or able to do things better than you, but that person will never be you."

Pablo said, "Boy, dad, you are really crap at this."

Orla said, "Yes, he is."

Ray looked down with his hand on his forehead.

I just can't get Pablo to see that I'm only interested in what is best for him.

Vinny had become annoyed with Orla; she had been moody for the entire Camino, and he was tired of it.

"He is just trying to help," Vinny scoffed at Orla.

"He shouldn't bother."

"You Irish are all either happy drunks or sober asses."

"I've only known you for a couple weeks, and it would take me a couple years to name all of the things that I hate about you. But now, I have nothing more to say to you," Orla said.

"That's what women always say, and then they just keep on talking."

"Don't you bother trying to walk with me tomorrow," Orla said.

"Don't worry; tomorrow I'm out of here and away from you for good."

"You must remember that all men are part Schweinehund," Eva said, to everyone's surprise. They didn't know exactly what Schweinehund meant, but it didn't sound good.

Things were starting to get out of control, and Max needed to fix them.

I can't have this group split up; I need to keep track of them.

So the hitman became the peacemaker.

"We are now a Camino family, and sometimes families quarrel, but we stay together. Tomorrow, things will seem better, and we can explore the wonders of Burgos as planned."

Orla relaxed her posture and Vinny said, "You're right, Max."

Max's efforts brought some calm to Vinny and Orla, at least for the moment.

They were not unreasonable people, and Vinny just seemed to have some baggage when it came to dealing with Orla.

Vinny stood up and said, "I have to go to the bathroom; where is it?"

An older pilgrim sitting at the table behind them stood up and said, "Follow me; I'm going there myself."

As they were standing side by side at the urinals, Vinny said, "Why do women cause me so much trouble?"

The older pilgrim chuckled and replied, "I think that many of our problems are caused by ourselves, at least by what hangs between our legs, as it controls far too much of our thoughts and actions. When you are young, it wants every woman you see, and when you are old, it wants every toilet you see."

Vinny shook his head and said, "I guess you have a point. I'm not looking forward to part two of this adventure of manhood."

The old man looked at Vinny, smiled, and said, "Just try and enjoy the ride of life; it sure beats the alternative."

"Okay, thanks for the advice," Vinny said.

Back in the dining hall, Max rested his forearms on the table and looked down.

Man, family counseling was not in my plans. Religion, philosophy, and psychology all after the evening meal. The Camino is a thought-provoking journey; I may need to get back to Naples just to relax.

Max got up and said, "I think that I will go to bed."

The others followed and wished each other a good night.

The next morning, they all slept in, as there was no rush. An easy walk through the medieval city to the Plaza Mayor for breakfast on the terrace of one of the local cafes was the first stop of the day. The plan was to relax and get some sightseeing in before leaving town. The talk at the breakfast table was a bit more energetic than recent mornings as they viewed the menu and discussed what to order, with grins and smiles adorning their faces, not usually present this early in the day.

As they enjoyed their coffee and tea with tortilla omelets, pastries, breads, and jams spread across the table, they discussed what they planned on seeing in the cathedral and the day's destination after the visit was complete.

With their stomachs full and agenda set, they were off to the Catedral de Santa Maria to get their credentials stamped and commence their tour.

"When I walked through the arch and entered this plaza, the sheer magnitude of this cathedral stopped me in my tracks," Max said.

"It is very impressive," Dean said.

"It is a fine example of Gothic design from the 13th century on the outside, and wait until you see the inside," Ray said.

The pilgrims first went into the gift shop on the plaza level to get their compostelas stamped, then ascended the stairs to the cathedral entrance. The pilgrims entered the cathedral and arrived at the first chapel.

"That's a beautiful chapel," Gina said.

"Yes, it is Baroque style, which shows that this cathedral, like many in Spain, has been built over many years and incorporates numerous design styles," Ray said.

The group strolled their way around the cathedral, taking in the centuries of art and other treasures. Mattia pointed to a golden stairway and said,

"Now that adds some real style to this beautiful cathedral."

Ray grinned and said, "I see that you recognize Italian Renaissance design when you see it."

The pilgrims continued through the aisles and chapels until they reached the area beneath the Rose window. They first looked up and gasped at the complex display of color and design and then looked down to see the sun's rays create a collage of color and light illuminating the floor.

"That is some light show, and it's all natural," Eva said.

"Yes, it is," Mattia said.

Then there is, of course, the final resting place of the famous Spanish knight El Cid and his wife.

"That's nice—a husband and wife side by side for all eternity," Orla said.

As the pilgrims glanced at each other, they shared a feeling of calm as they were renewed and ready to face the day's journey.

The group was once again making their way towards Santiago, but as they continued on, Vinny and Orla kept their distance from each other, but at least the group was more or less intact.

Chapter Ten

Another Family

After some time walking along in the tranquility of the Camino, they came to another small village, and in this village was a very austere stone chapel, so Max peeked inside to see if he might spot a new potential candidate. Instead, he found an elderly nun sitting next to the altar. She looked at Max and motioned for him to come inside. Max entered. She handed him a small medal of the Blessed Mother and told him in Spanglish that it would protect him. He understood enough to get her meaning. Max thanked her and put it in his pocket, but before he could walk away, she stopped him and motioned to him to tie it to his pack. Max smiled at her, tied the medal to his pack, and said, "I guess that I'm safe now." He then proceeded out of the door and back on his way, which for now is "The Way."

As Max passed an elderly man who was strolling along at a leisurely pace, the man gestured toward Max's new medal dangling from his pack and smiled.

"I see that you are protected," the elderly man said.

Max answered, "Yes, are you?"

He said, "I hope that I am, as I am nearing the end of my days and need to shed a lifetime of material excess. I must ease the journey of life to allow for a peaceful transition to the afterlife. Remember, the true meaning of the parable of the camel and the eye of the needle is that you must shed your excess baggage, both material and spiritual, to obtain a true state of grace in order to enter heaven."

The elderly man continued, "I have met a man who is on his second Camino in two years. After his first Camino, he went home and took an early retirement when he was at the peak of his career. He decided that his professional success and monetary gains had lost their meaning. The simpler life of the Camino is more fulfilling for him. He now lives on, appreciates what he has, and doesn't worry about what he doesn't have. He has simplified and is content. Buen Camino," said the elderly man.

"Buen Camino, Señor." Max picked up his pace and moved on.

Well, you sure don't meet many people just worried about the football scores out here.

For lunch this day, the group stopped at a nice outdoor cafe where several other pilgrims they had not seen before were eating and chatting. Ray struck up a conversation with an attractive middle-aged woman who was sitting near him. "How are you enjoying your Camino?" he asked.

"So far, it is very nice. I have seen so much and met so many friendly people."

"It sounds like you are French," Ray said.

"Close; I'm Belgian."

"How long have you been walking?" Ray asked.

"I spent a few days in Burgos, enjoying the sights and the tapas restaurants, and then started walking my Camino. I started alone, but met the others in my group while walking."

"That's how it usually works out," Ray said.

Pablo stared at Ray with a furrowed brow and a scowl on his face.

"What's wrong, Pablo?" Ray asked.

"Just because mom's dead doesn't mean you should be chasing women."

"I'm just being friendly; you should try it."

Pablo just folded his arms, dropped his head, and stared at the ground.

"I'm sorry if I caused any trouble," the Belgian woman said.

"No, he has been in a bad mood ever since his mother passed."

"I understand."

Some of the others in the group were talking about how much the Camino has meant to them and how much they have learned about themselves. One of the women who identified herself as an educator from the Netherlands said that she didn't think that it was such a big deal and that she hadn't learned much about herself or anything else. Vinny whispered to Max, "Some educator—that must be a term for a teacher without a clue. She has no self-awareness. She reminds me of the older brother of a friend of mine. He was clueless, but somehow thought that he was brilliant with little or no evidence or accomplishments to back it up. He was a legend in his own mind. There was a time when a bunch of us were on a camping trip together, and he walked over with a skillet of fried potatoes with onions and claimed that he had just invented the recipe. We pointed out that home fries have been around for at least a few hundred years, but he insisted that his was different, and he invented it. He couldn't explain how, but neither would he relent. So the only thing to do is to just let it go."

Gina, who was sitting on the other side of Vinny, looked down and said, "Sometimes you can't let it go, even though you may want to; bad teachers stick with you."

Max and Vinny leaned towards her. She elaborated. "In my high school, the guidance counselor's office was located just above the cafeteria. I had a full schedule both before, during, and after school, so I took the opportunity to try and visit the office during my lunch to discuss some internal issues that I was experiencing. I was finishing an ice cream sandwich when I entered the office. A teacher who I didn't even have for a class saw me and came into the office to challenge me for having food outside of the cafeteria. He insisted that I show him the ice cream; I had already swallowed the last bite. When I couldn't produce it, he clamped his thumbs and forefingers on each side of my abdomen and twisted, trying to get me to concede. I didn't say a word; I wasn't going to give that sadistic bastard the satisfaction. He eventually gave up and left. Lunch was over before I could see the guidance counselor. I was left with two blisters filled with blood. It was one of the joys of Catholic school."

"Did you ever get your issue resolved?" Vinny asked.

"I guess I'm doing that now," Gina replied.

"American Catholic schools sound a little like Italian reform schools," Max said.

I've come across all types of people from all different places walking for many different reasons, yet this is just a job for me for which I had little time to prepare, and I may be getting more out of it than many of these actual pilgrims.

"What did your parents say? Did they see your blood blisters?" Vinny asked.

"My mother was upset and wanted to take me to the police, but my father was an emotionally broken man, worn down by life, and didn't care much for people. He avoided them for the most part. He just grunted 'No', and that was the end of it. My relationship with him had never been the same since the time that I wanted to wear this short-sleeveless teal dress to church one summer Sunday. My mother just said no, that it was not proper. My father was very upset and never really forgave me. He was staunchly old-fashioned. Ever since then, I have been much closer with my mother," Gina answered.

"That's understandable," Dean said.

As the pilgrims moved along and formed into their natural spread, Gina took the opportunity to talk with Dean one-on-one. "You said that you were walking to gain some perspective on your inner turmoil; is it working for you?"

"I have had more time to think, and that is helping," Dean said.

"I too have inner turmoil, and walking this Camino is part of my attempt to resolve it," Gina said.

"You are in the right place for that," Dean said.

Off in the distance, there was a strange-looking sight. As the group got closer, it turned out to be a Spanish man who looked to be in his sixties or seventies. He was in well-worn clothes with a red bandanna as a cap and a scallop shell necklace. With him was his donkey, which was carrying his gear while wearing a scallop shell on its head, and riding atop the donkey was a small terrier. They exchanged pleasantries.

"Buen Camino."

"Buen Camino."

"Cómo está usted?" Ray said.

Ray then continued to speak with the man in Spanish. He relayed to the group that the man said he spends all of his days walking different Camino routes; he essentially lives on the Camino de Santiago. He has been doing this ever since his wife passed away several years ago. He is waiting to join her but does not want to sit around while doing it. He was at peace with the world.

The old man then pointed to the top of a very large chimney, and on it was a huge stork's nest. He then said, "The birds bring life." It was another pleasant moment on the Camino.

The pilgrims progressed along, and as they breathed the air deeply into their lungs, Mattia commented, "You don't even need to open your eyes to know that you are on the Camino; the smells of the villages and even the manure fertilizers get into your nose and your soul."

The pilgrims were now well into the Meseta, a long, flat agricultural section of the Camino Francés that lasts for days.

Many pilgrims forgo this section and take public transportation all the way into León, but the pilgrim who wants time for contemplation truly appreciates the Meseta. There are not as many places of respite in the Meseta as there are in other sections of the Camino, but that can enhance the Camino experience. The pilgrim, who needs to make a meal out of whatever they have in their pack because there is nowhere to purchase lunch, feels in touch with the pilgrim from times past.

"I'm hungry, and it is getting late; we should pool our resources and make a meal of it," Mattia said.

"That sounds good to me," said Dean.

The pilgrims emptied the food from their packs, pooled it together, and had a meal of bread stumps, cheeses, power bars, fruit, and nuts.

"I guess the Irishman from the movie wasn't all wrong; this is a true pilgrim experience," Vinny said.

"It's another Camino miracle; Vinny learned something," Orla said with a sideways grin.

After resting and thoroughly enjoying their makeshift meal, the pilgrims moved along.

Dean and Gina were walking together in the heat of the afternoon as flies buzzed around their heads. Gina waved them away from her face and said, "I don't know why God made bugs."

"You never know; an insect can even save your life," Dean said.

"How is that?" Gina asked.

"Did you never hear of the story of David in the Old Testament?"

"You mean when he slayed Goliath?"

"No, another story that happened some time after that. David had gained great stature and fame as a result of that battle. So much so that he even married the daughter of the king, King Saul. King Saul eventually became envious of David's popularity and wanted to have him put to death. He sent his soldiers after David, and David ran. The soldiers pursued him, and while on the run, David found a cave and hid in it. While he was sitting and praying that the soldiers would not find him, he watched a spider spin its web over the entrance. When the soldiers came to the cave, they saw that there was a spider's web, and therefore no one could have entered that cave. So you see, that day, a spider saved David's life."

Gina squinted a smile and said, "That's nice, but I still don't like spiders, flies, or any other bugs, but I don't mind caves."

It was much later in the afternoon than the pilgrims typically ended their day's walk. They dragged themselves into Hontanas, tired and looking for a place for the night. A man wearing a chef's hat and apron motioned to them to come over to the albergue where he was standing. "Buen Camino pilgrims, if you need a place to sleep and eat tonight, I am making paella."

"That sounds great," said Dean, and the others agreed. "Is it a special occasion?"

"Every day on the Camino is a special occasion for me. I made my pilgrimage a few years ago and decided that I would live here. I moved from Barcelona, bought this albergue, and am living the Camino life."

"That is wonderful; what time is dinner?"

"We will eat at 1900 or 7 p.m., as you Americans say."

The group checked in, cleaned up, and got ready for dinner. They were all gathered around the table in the dining room with a few other pilgrims, and their host wheeled in a paella pan that was at least a meter in diameter. No one would go hungry that night. As they ate and talked, their host joined in with them.

"Are you enjoying your Caminos so far?" asked the host.

"So far, so good, and it's nice not having to put on makeup every day," Orla said.

"I'm impressed by the Spanish generosity; there were even bunches of grapes left on the benches in the wine region for pilgrims to snack on," Mattia said.

"I was wondering how this Camino de Santiago got started," Max said.

"That is an ancient and multi-faceted story; I will attempt to do it justice," said their host.

The face of the host lit up, and as he spoke, he used his hands, motioning with them, to enhance his story. "After the crucifixion of Jesus, the apostles decided to spread his teachings throughout the known world. St. James traveled to the Iberian Peninsula for his part of the evangelical mission. After some time there, he returned to Jerusalem and, in the year 44 AD, was sentenced to death by beheading by King Herod. He was the first apostle to be martyred and the only apostle whose martyrdom was recorded in the Bible.

"After his death, some of his followers transported his remains back to Galicia, since that was where he spread the word of God. There, the remains were in relative obscurity until the 9th century, when a local hermit named Pelayo noticed an unusual field of stars that led him to the remains of St. James and two of his followers. Pelayo reported his findings to a local bishop named Theodomir. Theodomir, realizing the importance of this discovery, sent word to the King of Asturias, Alphonso II. In 842 AD, the king himself traveled from his residence in Oviedo to witness this discovery, thus becoming the first Camino de Santiago pilgrim. Upon seeing the remains, he declared that they were those of St. James and ordered that a sepulcher be built so that anyone who wished could worship. This resulted in pilgrims from all over Spain and other parts of Europe making pilgrimages on the Camino de Santiago."

"I don't recall passing through Oviedo, so far," Max said.

"That's because it is on the Camino Primativo, not the Camino Francés. That's a whole different story. There are many more historical figures and events associated with the Camino de Santiago," the host answered.

"What about the people who say that this was a pagan pilgrimage before it was the Camino?" Sunni asked the host.

"I think that is because the early pilgrims used established roads to travel across Spain to reach Santiago de Compostela. It only makes sense; why wouldn't they?"

"That does make sense," Sunni said.

"Gracias," Max said.

"De nada."

It was a relaxing and enriching night in this albergue in the town of Hontanas.

Not long after the pilgrim leaves Hontanas, the Camino road takes a pleasant descent for about an hour and then crosses under the archway of the ruins of the monastery of San Antón. "There is much beauty in this decay; so much of it is still standing. You can sense the monks and pilgrims of past times here," Sunni said.

"Yes, you do, and there is still a small donativo albergue here for the pilgrim who desires a serene and restful night's stay. As long as they don't mind going without electricity," Ray said.

"There is also some medical history associated with St. Anton's," Eva said.

"Why don't you tell us about it, Eva?" Ray said.

"Of course I will. The monks of this monastery specialized in the treatment of Ergotism, also known as Saint Anthony's Fire, because it causes a sensation of internal burning in its victims. This disease, whose symptoms include gangrene, convulsions, hallucinations, spasms, diarrhea, paraesthesia, itching, headaches, nausea, and vomiting, is caused by eating a fungus that infects rye. In the Middle Ages, rye bread was commonly eaten across Northern Europe but was unknown in Spain. For this reason, pilgrims suffering from this disease sometimes found themselves 'miraculously cured' during their journey to Santiago. The monks' treatments included amputations of extremities. Not exactly modern medicine, but what they thought was best. Their unfortunate patients sometimes left wood or wax carvings of the amputated body part in churches to encourage heavenly intervention. Fortunately, we have moved past these types of treatments," Eva said.

Orla grimaced and said, "Thanks for that, Eva. I guess?"

The pilgrims traversed a couple of miles of paved road into the town of Castrojeriz, which is the last town, before many more kilometers, including a steep climb, until reaching the next town. "We should have lunch here; I don't think that there is much else after this for quite a while," Ray said.

"I'm ready to eat," Vinny said.

"That shouldn't be a problem, as Castrojeriz has plenty to offer," Ray said.

When the pilgrims reached the Café Lagar on Calle Cordón, Ray turned to the group and said, "We should eat here; it is a historic café. It was at one time a wine press and also served as the town synagogue."

The group entered the café, and some of the equipment from the time when the building was used as a wine press was still present. There were also skull and cross bones carved into the wall.

"It's certainly one of the more unique lunch stops that we have come across," Vinny said.

They finished a leisurely lunch, taking advantage of the comfort, before the long stretch to the next town. As they left town, they passed by the Iglesia de San Juan, which is noteworthy because it is built in the German Gothic or Hallenkirche style. Once out of town and back into the countryside of the Meseta, mud brick or Adobe buildings become a common sight.

The pilgrims were next greeted by pine-scented forests after their climb into the Tierra de Campos, a region filled with nature and history. They entered the town of Boadilla del Camino and made their way to a stone column called the Rollo de Justicia. It is from the Renaissance period and sits beside the Iglesia de Santa Maria. The Rollo de Justicia was a gift from King Enrique IV to symbolize the independence of the region. It is Gothic in appearance, with various Camino-related symbols. It was the place where criminals were tied to allow them to be subjected to various cruel and unusual forms of public humiliation.

While in Boadilla, the pilgrims came to the imposing Iglesia de Santa Maria, a 16th century construction with a mix of architectural styles.

"This church has a baptismal font from the eighth century of note that I would like to see," Dean said.

Max and the pilgrims joined Dean and toured the church. Inside, there was also a tour group of Italian senior citizens. One of the women saw Max; she snapped her head back, stared wide-eyed, and gasped. Max turned and looked directly at her. He tightened and stiffened his posture. The woman gingerly walked over to greet Max.

With a tremble in her voice, she said, "Max, I'm surprised to see you here."

"Hello, Mrs. Martini. What brings you here to Spain?"

"The Basilica di San Marco has hosted this tour of the churches of the Camino de Santiago for the seniors of Naples. It was a once-in-a lifetime chance, so I had to come."

"So, will you be visiting many churches?"

"Yes, we will be visiting churches for two weeks."

"Enjoy your visit."

"What brings you here, Max?"

"I needed to get away from Naples and try to get over the death of my mother."

Mrs. Martini was still not convinced of Max's motive, but she just wanted to move on.

"I was sorry to hear of her death. You try to get over it. Goodbye."

I hope this woman won't be showing up and causing me trouble for the next two weeks. I don't need her blowing my cover.

"Goodbye, Mrs. Martini."

Max went back to his group.

"Who was that?" Eva asked.

"An old woman from my hometown. She is here with a church group tour of the churches of the Camino Francés."

"Small world," Eva said.

Yes, too small.

Between Boadilla and Frómista, the Camino and the pilgrims followed the Canal de Castilla.

"This was at one time part of a transport system, which is one of Spain's greatest engineering achievements. It took 70 years to complete, back in the mid-18th and early-19th centuries. It was used to transport grain, but with the arrival of the railway in the second half of the 19th century, it became obsolete," Ray said.

Sunni pointed at a couple of otters swimming in the canal and said, "It looks like it's still put to good use today."

Ray smiled and said, "That it is."

The pilgrims followed the towpath beside the canal all the way to Frómista. It was a pleasant walk, with the soft sounds of the water along with the elms rustling in the breeze.

When they reached the town, Dean said, "There is an interesting church just off of the Camino in the center of town. It is San Martin de Tours and is a good example of Spanish Romanesque construction. It was originally part of a monastery, which no longer exists. It has more than 300 human and animal faces carved in stone under its eaves. It is a national monument, and its main facade is framed by two round towers."

"It sounds like it is worth a look," Eva said.

As they reached the church, Vinny said, "That must be it, and it looks like it is half castle and half church."

A van of older tourists was loading after departing the church. Mrs. Martini was among them, but only Max noticed her.

How often am I going to see this woman? I don't need her talking to anyone.

The route out of Frómista leads to a path that parallels the road and is a flat walk that turns into a long, gradual incline all the way to the planned stop for the night, Carrión de los Condes.

The pilgrims entered the town of Carrión de los Condes and reached the Cuesta de la Mora, or Hill of the Mooress. Ray smiled and said to his fellow pilgrims, "There's a fountain on that hill, but you don't want to drink from it. It's cursed."

"How's it cursed?" Sunni asked.

Ray was waiting for such a question and told the story: "Back when King Alfonso was the ruler of this land, he had a Muslim lover. One time, she was late for a planned rendezvous at that fountain. The king was not accustomed to being treated in such a disrespectful manner, so he cursed the fountain. When his lover did show up, she drank from the fountain and died. Ever since, it has been Cuesta de la Mora."

"You are so knowledgeable and explain things so well; you should have been a teacher," Sunni said.

"I was, at one time, a social studies teacher. But after my divorce, I changed careers to make more money."

All along the Camino, the albergues are places of shelter and respite from the physical demands of the road, but every so often the pilgrim comes upon an albergue that becomes a special experience. The albergue of Santa Maria in Carrión de los Condes is one such place. This albergue is run by nuns, singing nuns, and not only do they sing, but they engage with the pilgrims and have them sing. It proves to be a moving and memorable highlight for all who are fortunate enough to choose this place for the night. It is a surreal experience that manifests itself as a spiritual epiphany that one can realize while making this pilgrimage. These nuns are another type of Camino Angel.

The group had chosen well this evening, even if only by chance. This place also provided Max with the opportunity to hear details about several other pilgrims as they described their homes, told their reasons for walking the Camino, and some even sang songs from their home countries. Max did not find any new candidates, but at least it was something different.

After a night of rejuvenation for body, mind, and soul, the pilgrims were up and on their way. This restful evening was fortuitous because when the temperatures are high, the next stretch of the Camino Francés can seem a desert-like environment. Pilgrims sometimes experience mirages in these conditions. Towards the end of this section, the pilgrims enter the small village of Lédigos.

"The church in this village, Iglesia de Santiago, is the only church on the entire Camino that has statues of Santiago depicting him in his three most common manifestations: the Apostle or Saint James the Greater, Santiago el Mayor; Saint James the Moor Slayer, Santiago Matamoros; and Saint James the Pilgrim, Santiago Peregrino," Ray said.

"Let's go take a look," Dean said.

The group approached the church doors and tried to open them, but they were locked.

"That's one of the sad things about the Camino; so many churches are locked," Mattia said.

Max noticed a group of seniors getting off of a tour bus across the road. It was Mrs. Martini's tour group.

"We have seen many churches; we don't need to visit them all," Max said.

"Wait, we might not have to go without seeing inside; there is a tour group coming over. And Max, your friend is with them," Eva said.

"She is more of an acquaintance; she is much older than me, and I never really spoke with her all that often."

The pilgrims were able to enter the church following the tour group, as they had arranged to be let into the church. Mrs. Martini waved to Max and said, "Hello Max, we meet again."

Mrs. Martini followed Max's group rather than her own as her natural curiosity and need for gossip abated any fear that she had.

"So, Max, has this trip helped you much in dealing with the loss of your mother? You never seemed like an emotional person to me. You and your friends are all such hard men."

"Yes, it is helping Mrs. Martini, and we are all humans with human feelings."

Mrs. Martini turned to Eva and said, "Are you enjoying your time with our Max?"

"We are all part of a Camino family and support each other and enjoy each other's company," Eva said.

"Max is used to being a part of a family of friends," Mrs. Martini said.

Max clenched his jaw and said while barely opening his mouth, "Your group may be preparing to leave; you should join them."

She's up to her old habits; she can be annoying and too nosey for her own good.

Mrs. Martini took the hint and went and joined her tour group.

Eva smiled and said, "What did she mean by that family of friends remark? Do you have a Camino family at home that you aren't telling us about?"

"She's just a lonely old woman who likes to talk too much," Max said.

"I know the type," Eva said.

The three depictions of Saint James did not disappoint.

"These statues of Saint James in the various settings show how much he meant to the Spanish people as an apostle, a warrior savior, and a pilgrim," Gina said.

"That is true, Gina," Ray said.

The pilgrims left the church, pressed on, and took advantage of the unseasonably cool weather this day. They made it all the way to the halfway point of the Camino Francés, Sahagún.

"I have read that there is also an albergue run by nuns in this town. The last one was so nice, we should stay there tonight. I liked staying with the nuns," Gina said.

The group agreed it was a good idea and proceeded to the convent albergue. They checked in and went about their daily routine. Max put his pack away while the others were taking their showers and slipped out to find a phone. He needed to call back to Naples to take care of a potential situation.

Max called his friend Sergio. "Sergio, it's Max; I need you to take care of something for me."

"Yes, Max, I haven't seen you for a while. What can I do for you?"

"I am in Spain on a job, and I need you to run some interference for me. I don't need any extra complications, and something has come up."

"What is it?" Sergio said.

"Do you remember Mrs. Martini? She likes to talk to everybody."

"You mean that she likes to get into everybody's business?"

"Right, that's her. Well, she is here and keeps showing up, and I don't need her talking with any of the people I am with. I need to keep a low profile and don't want anyone to become suspicious of me or my presence here. I need her to get called home," Max said.

"Her son works construction; those sites are dangerous," Sergio said.

"You're right about that. Dangerous, but not too dangerous."

"Got it, Ciao Max."

"Ciao Sergio."

Max went back to the albergue, and no one even noticed that he was gone.

After their showers, Vinnie and Mattia came out shivering.

"Man, that was cold. They have no hot water," Mattia said.

"Good call, Gina," Vinnie said with a mocking frown.

"It's just a reminder that we are on pilgrimage and not on vacation," Dean said.

"That is true," Mattia said, rubbing his arms as if to try to get warm.

Sahagún is a quiet town where the pilgrim can get a halfway certificate if they wish; most don't bother or even know about it. The big event of the evening in Sahagún is vespers at the church of San Lorenzo. It was a quiet night in a quiet town.

Along with the light from the sunrise came the songs of the birds and the smell of the morning dew. It was another glorious morning on the Camino, and the pilgrims all strolled along in the sunshine with their own thoughts. It was a typical Camino day, but then something was out of place. A foul scent caught Max's attention;

he hadn't come across it since he was last in Scampia. Definitely not on the Camino; it was skunk weed. It came from three young men who stood by the side of the trail, looked at the pilgrims as they walked by, and appeared to be discussing them. These young men were dressed in attire more appropriate for the street than the trail or a farm. They all wore jeans; none of them wore hiking shoes; and one of them even wore a leather jacket. They were not near any towns. Max looked them up and down as he passed.

They don't look like pilgrims or even locals. What are they up to?

Chapter Eleven

Max the Hero

Early the next morning, Mrs. Martini received a call from Naples. Her son had an accident on his job site. Some scaffolding had collapsed, and she was needed at the hospital. Her tour was cut short.

By midmorning this day, several kilometers had gone by when Max and company came upon a group of pilgrims who were gathered together, not walking or relaxing, but who appeared to be discussing things and pointing off in different directions. One woman in particular had reddened eyes and a shallow look about her face. Two men with sun-hardened skin and the rough hands of farm workers were talking with the pilgrims. After they reached the crowd, they learned that a young boy who was on the Camino with his family and who also had a tendency to walk far ahead of his parents was now missing. He was a ten-year-old Canadian boy named Teddy. The worried woman was his mother.

Dean, Ray, and the others decided they would spend the day trying to help find Teddy. The group discussed the search strategy with the others and planned to search both on the Camino and in the adjacent countryside and woodlands to try to locate the boy.

"Since we will be spending this time searching for the boy and we will be separated, we should plan to meet in a nearby town that is not too far ahead," Mattia said.

"Yes, that is a good idea. El Burgo Ranero is a nice town, and it is just a couple of hours ahead. There is also a nice albergue right on Calle Mayor called Domenico Laffi. It is built in the traditional style using clay and straw bricks and has a fireplace to get warm beside in the evening. It should prove very relaxing, and we will need to relax after spending the day searching for the lost boy," Ray said.

"Sounds good," Dean said.

The discussions ended, and the searchers decided to work in pairs. The local members of the search party, which had grown to twenty people, told the pilgrims that there were large, aggressive wild animals in the area they planned to explore. So, they should keep alert.

The search team now consisted of several pairs of pilgrims, including the boy's parents, plus two pairs of locals from the nearby farms.

Ray paired up with Pablo and planned to use the opportunity to have a heart-to-heart conversation with him. Pablo was becoming a little less disagreeable, so the time was right.

Vinny asked Orla to pair with him.

"If we must," Orla said.

Max wore a sly grin as his efforts to keep the group intact appeared to have worked.

Mattia and Gina paired up. Mattia was a natural conversationalist and decided to pair with Gina, who was not as talkative as the Italian girls he knew. He would use the one-on-one opportunity presented by the search for Teddy to try to help her feel more comfortable in the group.

Dean and Eva paired up, and Eva was interested not only in finding Teddy, but also in finding out more about Dean and how he decided to become a priest. Eva had a thirst for knowledge, loved people, and always wanted to learn more about them.

The final pair were Max and Sunni, two people who were naturally quiet but made an effort to be sociable while on this pilgrimage.

The search party progressed along, and each pair veered off into the woods on either side of the path at regular intervals.

The first pair to break off were Ray and Pablo, as they walked among the trees with the sounds of leaves beneath their feet and the chirping of birds. Pablo was inspired to open up and said to Ray, "Teddy's parents seem really upset."

Ray said, "You start to worry about your children from the day you learn they are to be born until the day that you die. You want to protect them from every potential danger, but it is just not possible."

Pablo asked his father, "Why did you and Mom divorce?"

"That's not an easy question to answer. I do know that I wish it didn't happen. As you get along in life and things don't always work out the way that you had wished, you look for people to blame. Too often, that is the person who is closest to you. It gets to a point where you just look for things to get angry about," Ray said.

"Was it me?" Pablo asked.

"No, you were the best thing we had going. The problems we were having came from the fact that we would bring the stresses of work and the outside world into our marriage, and that isn't good. Instead of supporting each other, we argued. One of our worst arguments could have been avoided if I had just taken a little joke that your mother played on me and seen it for the fun that it was."

"What was the joke?" Pablo asked.

"Well, your mother had a party at the apartment for many of her lady friends, and I stayed to help with the food and drinks. You spent the night at your friend Jorge's house. I enjoyed myself a little too much and fell asleep on the couch while many of her friends were still there. The next morning, when I woke up and went to the bathroom, I saw that all of her friends had signed their names on my backside. I was furious, and your mother just taunted me. I didn't say anything to her the entire day except when I lashed out at her. Just before you were to return home, she told me that she had been the one who signed all of the names. Her friends had already gone home, and it was just a joke. I didn't take it very well, but in hindsight, it was pretty funny, and I wish that I hadn't been so cross with her."

"That was funny, Dad," Pablo said.

"Yes, Pablo, I know, and I now regret many things I said to your mother during those troubled times of our marriage."

Pablo had not been giving his father a fair break. The divorce wasn't really all his fault, and he had been trying to be a good father the entire time since it happened; Pablo just wouldn't let him. Pablo had so much anger, and it had only intensified since he lost his mother. Ray then said, "We will search hard to find this boy because we know how much it hurts to lose someone." They continued their search for Teddy.

Vinny and Orla next broke from the road, entered the woods, and called out for Teddy. This went on for some time. Orla then decided that it was time for a chat.

"You know, I would like to have children, but they can add a lot of stress to your life."

"No wonder your boyfriend dumped you; you're not even married, and you are already talking about kids," Vinny said.

"No, you arse, women just like to say what we are thinking; it doesn't mean that we want it at the time, just maybe at some point. But you men, you never say what you're thinking."

"That's because when we do, we usually get slapped for it."

Orla smiled. "And you deserve it. While we're on the subject, are you telling me that you have never thought about having children one day?"

Vinny grinned and said, "Of course. Well, maybe not the whole day."

"You are an arse," Orla replied.

Vinny smiled and continued looking around, peering through the trees, and calling for Teddy. After talking about children, he was now biting his nails and turned to Orla and said, "I hope that we can find him. I was lost once when I was young, when we were on a trip to the city. I wasn't found for about an hour, but it seemed like forever, and I have never forgotten it."

"I never imagined you being frightened at any age."

I guess he has some compassion after all.

When Mattia and Gina entered the woods, he asked her why she was on the Camino de Santiago. "I needed a change." She said it in a soft and hesitant voice.

Mattia realized that he would most likely be doing the majority of the talking; he was not surprised at this. "Back home in Italy, I live in the land of Romeo and Juliet. I provide tours to people from all over who have romance in their hearts, and there is romance in the air. So many tourists only visit the large cities of Italy, but the countryside and the towns of northern Italy have so much more to offer."

Gina almost grins and then nods her head in tacit approval. She was content with listening; her only vocalizations were occasional calls for Teddy.

Gina finally opened up for a moment. "I hope that we find him; this could be devastating for his parents."

"Yes," Mattia said.

She is such a solemn person, and I hope that she gets what she needs out of her pilgrimage.

There was a faint, far-off rustling of leaves and a glimpse of a dark figure behind the trees.

"Did you see that?" Gina yelped.

"I thought that my eyes were playing tricks on me, but if you saw it too, then I think that I did as well. It was only an instant, but it looked like a giant, hairy man running through the woods," Mattia said.

"Did you also notice that awful smell?" Gina said.

"Yes, it was like a combination of terrible body odor and a wet dog."

"I don't know what it was, but let's get out of here!" Gina exclaimed.

"I hope that thing didn't get Teddy. We need to keep our wits about us and find the others," Mattia said.

The search continued.

As Dean and Eva moved to cover their patch of woods, Dean asked her how things were going in her medical career.

"Things are fine, but the area where I work can be very trying and present challenges that most people can't even imagine. I'm taking this break to heal myself so I can continue to heal others," Eva said.

"Where exactly do you work?" Dean asked.

"I work in a clinic in the Reeperbahn section of Hamburg. I primarily care for the women who work on die sündigste Meile, the most sinful mile."

"That doesn't sound like a very nice place," Dean said.

"It's not; it's basically a block-long brothel," Eva said.

"You just don't have a career; you have a vocation. God bless you."

How did this pleasant young woman end up in a world she seems to be so totally removed from? It just doesn't fit her personality.

"How did you decide on that specific career path?"

"Since you are a priest, I will tell you. The early parts of this story were told to me by my older sister, and the later parts I remember. When I was a toddler, my sister came home from school one day and found me strapped in a child seat on the floor with a note pinned to me. My mother had left us. She could no longer take the verbal and physical abuse that my father inflicted upon her. When my father got home and read the note, he screamed and punched a hole in the wall. He then held his face in his hands and cried for what my sister said seemed like hours. For the next several years, it was just the three of us. Eventually, my father started drinking heavily. When he drank, he would stare at my sister, who was now in her early teens. He called her awful names. Then he started taking her into his room. This went on for several years. Then one day, he called me a little whore. That's when my sister decided to take me and run away to Hamburg. She was not going to let happen to me what happened to her. She found us an apartment and worked on die sündigste Meile to support us. She even put me through school and got me started on my medical degree. For this, her reward was contracting HIV and eventually dying a horrible death. That is why I dedicate my life's work to helping the women of die sündigste Meile."

"You are both a phoenix and an angel," Dean said.

"Now tell me how such an athletic-looking man like you became a priest."

"My story, too, is a difficult one for me to tell. When I was a young man, I was a prize fighter. I never really considered becoming a priest, even though my family always attended mass together. Then one night, tragedy struck during one of my boxing matches. I was a powerful puncher and had a reputation as a knockout fighter. Unfortunately, I knocked out my final opponent permanently; the man died, and I never boxed again. I was a shambles; I never thought that I would ever kill someone, and I will never do it again. I can't even imagine raising my hand to someone ever again. After thinking over my life decisions and direction, I realized that I had the calling to serve God. I decided I would enter the seminary and become a priest. I don't really like to talk about this and would appreciate it if you didn't mention it to the others. I don't mind people knowing that I was a boxer; I just don't want them to know why I stopped."

Eva, who loved to learn about people, had learned that knowing someone's inner turmoil could also end up resting heavy on her soul. The search for Teddy continued.

Max and Sunni next took their turn entering the woods. They continued on, not saying much to each other, but they called out for Teddy at regular intervals. Max then decided to break the monotony and ask Sunni how someone from Korea ended up on the Camino de Santiago. Sunni told him, "Many people from Korea walk the Camino for different reasons, as hiking is very popular and there are many Catholics in Korea. At home, I have a very demanding job, and I am also caring for two elderly parents. I have much stress and little happiness in my life. I spoke with my sister, who lives in Japan, and she agreed to come to Korea and care for my parents while I make my Camino. My wish is to have my spirit replenished by the time that I return home."

What would he think of me if I told him that I screamed at my father when he soiled the rug, stood there, looked at it, and then looked at me as if he didn't know how it got there? He couldn't help it, but I could no longer handle the stress. Then, to make things worse, the next day at work, I chastised a subordinate in front of the entire staff for a minor mistake. I earned my office nickname that day.

"I hope you get what you need out of your Camino," Max softly said.

"How about you, Max? What do you hope to get out of the Camino de Santiago? Are you hoping to change your life in some way?" Sunni asked.

"Do you think that people can really change? Can they become better, or even different?" Max asked.

"The Chinese philosopher Confucius taught that by going about your daily life tasks in a simple but disciplined manner, you can realize tremendous growth and change," Sunni said.

"That sounds like Saint Therese, the Little Flower. She dedicated her life to God by always performing the most simple and mundane tasks to the best of her ability and with a happy heart," Max said.

"Well, see, you already had your answer."

"But she died at a very young age, so I don't know if that is the best answer."

"I hope that you will find what you need on this Camino de Santiago," Sunni said.

They were deep into the woods, and there was a hurried rustling of leaves and grunting noises that intensified with each second. Suddenly a wild pig appeared, and it was charging straight towards them. Max picked up a large tree branch, and as the pig neared him, he swung it and thumped the pig on its head. Sunni stood there frozen with fear, both mesmerized and terrified. The pig rounded back towards Sunni, and Max swung and walloped it again, but he fell to the ground due to the impact. The pig lowered its head and tore into Max's leg with its massive fangs. Max picked up a rock and bashed the pig in the face. The pig, discouraged, turned and ran away. Sunni giggled both in relief and at the thought of the strange battle that Max had just fought.

Sunni laughed and said, "You are my valiant knight; you have saved me."

Max was disheveled and out of breath as he replied, "There is a good reason that we eat pigs; they are a nuisance."

He then looked at his leg and saw that he had a large, bloody gash.

"It's my 'Red Badge of Courage', you know, like the book."

"I am not familiar with that book."

"It's American; the priests in my school used it to teach us English."

"You are well educated."

Max grinned and nodded in thanks.

I guess crime does pay a little, after all.

Max and Sunni were now looking around, pondering where they were and how they would find their own way—nevertheless, find Teddy. Then they noticed an opening in the distance. As they approached it, a wonderful aroma rode through the air and called to them, drawing their attention to a farm across the field from where they now stood. The people at the farm saw them and waved to signal that they should join them. Max and Sunni were still panting and shaking slightly when they reached the farm. They described their terrifying ordeal to the farmer and the others, who were setting up for what appeared to be a festive barbecue. A boy, who looked to be about ten years old, was playing on the lawn.

"You have survived a terrible ordeal, and now you celebrate with us. You see the boy; he is the lost pilgrim for whom you were searching. My wife found him wandering down one of the farm roads. He was looking from side to side, was all by himself, and appeared to be lost. She knew that he wasn't a local boy, so she approached him and saw the worried look on his face. She spoke with him, and as he was a lost pilgrim who needed help, she took him back to the farm and notified the local police. Now that he has been found, the authorities are looking for the remaining searchers and telling them to meet at the farm. The barbecue is to celebrate

Teddy's being found and to thank the searchers for their efforts in helping to find him," the farmer said.

"That's wonderful; we could use a good celebration," Max said.

"It is also good old Spanish hospitality; we welcome our pilgrims," the farmer said.

The good news spread by telephone, radio calls, and word of mouth that Teddy had been found and was waiting at the farm along with a barbecue picnic for the search team. The first search team members to arrive were Teddy's parents, who had been driven there by a local. The other search team members arrived at the farm shortly afterwards.

Mattia and Gina were the last to arrive. They ran to their friends and couldn't wait to tell them of their near encounter with a forest creature.

"We saw this giant hairy creature in the woods. It was very scary," Gina said.

"It was most likely a Basajuan. They are intelligent, docile creatures and you were in no danger," Max said with a smile.

"Very impressive. How does someone from Italy know so much about Basque lore?" Ray asked.

"On my first day walking in the Pyrenees mountains, I met a Basque man who was walking along the Camino, but he did not look like a pilgrim. I spoke with him, and he told me that he was not a pilgrim but that he was hunting for Basajuan. I didn't know what he was talking about, so he explained it to me," Max answered.

"I'm sure that he was joking," Ray said.

"I'm not so sure, but I am here to learn what I can about the people on the trail. Anyway, that food smells good," Max said.

"I'm sure that your eyes were just playing tricks on you since you were in strange woods with sights and sounds that excited your imaginations," Vinny said.

"I know what I saw, and even though it was just an instant, it was real," Gina said.

"People all over the world see Yetis, Sasquatches, Chupacabras, and the like, but no one ever gets a good picture or any other real evidence," Vinny answered.

"When we read Don Quixote, one of his quotes was, 'Don't think that all that you don't understand is impossible,'" Pablo said.

"Pablo has a point, Vinny; you just have to have faith," Mattia said.

"I think that it's time to eat," Vinny said.

Mattia smiled and said, "You are correct, sir."

Everyone was gathered at a ten-meter-long table adorned with a farm-fresh feast fit for a king and his court. The aromas emanating from the open-pit wood-burning barbecue topped with an entire roast lamb—Cordero Asado, a Spanish culinary delight—were intoxicating. All started their feast by pouring cups of ice-cold Sangria.

"Try these roasted peppers; they're fantastic," Vinny said.

"They're called pimientos de padrón, and you are correct; they are fantastic," Ray said.

"I quite like these courgettes stuffed with goat cheese," Eva said.

"I love potatoes, but this salad is nasty," Orla said.

"It is Russian potato salad and is very popular with Spanish people, but many foreigners do not care for it. It is an acquired taste," Ray said.

"I don't think that I will be acquiring it any time soon," Orla said.

The hosts took the cordero off of the grill, and Max said, "I know a pig that I would like to see roasting on that."

Sunni laughed, and she and Max then told the story of Max's battle with the pig to the others. A potentially bad event had turned into a good and memorable afternoon—another day on the Camino de Santiago.

The discussion then returned to the cuisine. Mattia raised his glass and toasted, "To the finest food outside of Italy."

Ray turned and looked at Mattia and said, "Your overindulgence on the Sangria has obviously clouded your judgement; Spanish cuisine is the finest in all of Europe, and that means in all of the world. Does anyone else disagree?"

Max could not let Italian food go undefended and said, "Every year I take my mother to Zi' Teresa ristorante on the waterfront in Naples for her birthday. Now, my mother's cooking is the most delicious in this world, but the food at Zi' Teresa is heavenly. They make their own pasta, as many fine Italian restaurants do, and their orecchiette with clams and mushrooms in a white wine and garlic sauce melts in your mouth and grabs hold of you like a loving woman's embrace. I dare to say that it is even better than what my mother could make or anyone else in the world."

Ray, not relenting but not prepared to counter this description, said, "We must all meet in Naples for dinner sometime and partake in this heavenly experience."

Vinny raised his glass and said, "That sounds like a plan."

Dean looked around at his fellow pilgrims and asked, "What are some of the best foods from your home countries and cities?"

"We like pizza, sausages, and all of the regular stuff," Vinny said.

Mattia smiled and said, "We too like Italian food; it's just a bit more elegant. What about you, Sunni?"

"Koreans also like barbecue, and bulgogi is one of our most popular beef dishes."

"I've had that, and it is delicious. What about you, Gina?" Dean said.

"Sandwiches are popular where I grew up—hot, cold, beef, or pork. If you can put it on a roll, someone will make a delicious sandwich out of it. How about you, Eva?"

Eva gave her patented grin and said, "Everyone knows that Germany is famous for our wurst, the finest sausages in the land. My favorite is curry wurst, but like Russian potato salad, it is an acquired taste."

Eva looked down to be coy and took notice of Max's leg. She then went and got her first-aid kit from her pack. She tended to his wounds, applied a bandage wrap, grinned, and told him, "You need to keep this clean and let me know if it bothers you. It is not a trivial wound. And stay away from wild pigs."

After Eva finished tending to Max, Gina said to her, "One of my biggest concerns about walking in these remote areas was the availability of health care if any new or past health issues would come up. We are all so lucky to have you with us, Eva."

Teddy and his parents then addressed the table, thanking the pilgrims and the farmers for their help in finding Teddy and the wonderful feast that followed.

With their bellies and hearts full, Max said to Mattia, "Ready to go, Paisano?"

"How much did you have to drink? I am Mattia."

Mattia has a funny accent, and he doesn't know what a Paisano is; he could be the guy.

The farmers wished them all a buen camino, and the pilgrims thanked their hosts and continued on their way. They were tired and walking along in their own thoughts, and the prevailing sound was that of the slow cadence of crunching gravel. Max was reminded of a not-too-distant memory.

This Camino life is so different from my other life in Naples. No fat-cat bureaucrats or dead-beat borrowers to deal with out here.

As a result of the delay from the search for Teddy and the celebratory barbecue at the farm afterwards, the group stopped short of the originally planned town for the evening, El Burgo Ranero, and stayed in a small, remote village that had a large albergue considering the size of the village, so all was well. They were settled in, well fed, relaxed, and waiting to go to bed when three new pilgrims checked in. It was much later than pilgrims normally arrive, especially for a small village that was far from any other town. They were the three men that Max had noticed early that morning. He still didn't like their looks. The life he has led has given him plenty of experience with the criminal element. Everyone went to bed, but even though he was exhausted, Max wasn't able to sleep. He was still hyped up from the pig battle, and these three characters didn't help.

At around three in the morning, Max lay in his bunk, still wide awake, staring at the upper bunk with the residue of adrenaline from the pig battle still coursing through his mind. The three late arrivals were going through the other pilgrims' belongings; their whispers caught Max's attention.

I knew they were going to be trouble. If I do something, it could draw attention to me or even bring the police here. I need to stay in the background, but I can't let these assholes steal from us.

Max got up and crept towards them, taking care to remain silent. He quietly confronted them, and they attempted to knock him out of their way. Max jabbed the first man in the nose with a rapid and powerful punch, knocking him to the ground. He then went for the other two, grabbing them both by the scruffs of their necks. They both swung hard, hitting Max on his shoulder and ribs, but they didn't appear to have much of an impact. Max had taken punches from men far stronger and more vicious than these two. The first man then jumped onto Max's back and wrapped his arms around Max's head and neck. Max pulled the other two towards him and then pushed them forward. He simultaneously flipped and tossed the man on his back through the air, who held onto Max's shirt, almost tearing it in half. The man plowed into the other two thieves and knocked them to the ground. They jumped up and rushed towards Max; he just stepped aside, and they fell over themselves. The first man grabbed Max from behind, and he once again flipped him onto his cohorts.

These clowns better cut it out before I hurt them, and then the cops will have to come here.

They continued for a short time, but the outcome was inevitable. Even though they had numbers, they were no match for someone as experienced and powerful as Max. By the time it was all over, the three would-be thieves were laying on the floor side by side. "Sit down and be quiet before you get hurt. Get up against the wall," Max said as he stared them down.

By this point, most of the others had awakened, seen their packs opened, and surmised what had happened. They saw Max standing there with his shirt torn, exposing his entire upper sculpted torso, which was rippled with muscle as he kept watch over the dejected thieves.

"What is going on?" Ray said.

"We should call the Guardia Civil," another pilgrim said.

"Who are they?" Max asked.

"The Guardia Civil is the police force that guards pilgrims along the Camino," Ray said.

Max pulled off what remained of his shirt and threw it to the first thief, who sat brooding with blood running from his nose. "Wipe off your face."

He then turned to the other pilgrims and said, "No need to call the police; they're just kids, and they have learned their lesson. They will now leave and not bother pilgrims again. Right boys?"

The three boys looked at the floor and mumbled.

"What was that?" Max asked.

"Yeah, we won't," the first boy said.

"Alright, get out of here and only take what you brought with you," Max said.

Max convinced the others that they were just kids, even though they weren't much younger than him, and they agreed to send them on their way without calling in the authorities. Max told the other pilgrims that he didn't want to ruin the lives of these young men; he actually did not want to speak with any police himself.

"Max, you really beat those three guys up and didn't even crash into any of the bunks. Where did you learn to fight like that?" Pablo said.

"It's no big deal. When I was a young boy, I was sent away to school, and the older boys bullied the younger boys. I got tired of getting picked on and beat up, so I fought back. In time, I learned to fight well, and they left me alone."

"That's cool," Pablo said.

I'm not going to tell them that the school was a reform school.

What a kind man he was. They then sent the would-be thieves on their way. Eva noticed that Max's leg was once again bleeding, got her medical kit, and tended to his wounds. Max had now gained some additional stature among the other pilgrims. He proved to be a compassionate protector and was held in high esteem, if they only knew.

The next morning, Max had intended to call Carlo, but the search for Teddy, along with everything else that had happened, distracted him, and he never made the call.

It's too late now; I'm not calling Carlo unless I have a good result to report. I don't want to be the next target.

Joaquin Colón, a reporter at the León del Mundo newspaper, heard from one of his sources that the Australian hiker who fell to his death was in financial dire straits and was on Camino, hiding from the people he owed. Joaquin liked the idea of a story with an international twist and asked his editor for permission to pursue the story. "Jeffe, let me look into it and see if it turns into anything. We don't want the Camino to get bad press when it might be something that has nothing to do with the safety of the trail," Joaquin said.

The editor glanced up at the excited look on Joaquin's face and said, "Look into it, but the police think that it is nothing. Don't spend too much time; give it a couple of days at the most."

"Thanks, Jeffe; I know just where to start." Joaquin's source told him that Grant had checked into the Saints Peter and Paul albergue in Pamplona with several other pilgrims, so he would start there.

As a result of the pig battle and the tussle with the three thieves, Max was now a bit hobbled. Not only did he have a slight limp, but his pack squeezed his ribs, which were sore from some of the punches that he had taken.

"Are you alright, Max?" Sunni asked. "You seem to be limping, and I noticed that you groaned when you put on your pack this morning."

"I'm fine; it's all part of the experience."

Actually, this leg is killing me. If it gets much worse, I might not be able to keep up with this group.

"You should have Eva give you a checkup tonight."

"I don't think that will be necessary."

"If you say so."

The pilgrims made their way to El Burgo Ranero, the village of the frogs. Clay and straw brick structures throughout meld into the background, as this town is at one with its surroundings. Frogs, songbirds, and waterfowl alike find this area of the Camino particularly inviting and inhabit it year-round.

The pilgrims continue on through miles of cornfields before arriving in Reliegos.

"Look at that; it's the shire from The Lord of the Rings," Pablo called out.

"It looks like it, but actually they are wine cellars," Ray told him.

"That's exactly what I was thinking when I saw them. They are built right into the sides of the hills, made of mortar and stone. They have lawns for roofs that even have a rounded shape. They sure look like Hobbit houses to me," Vinny said.

"Like much of the Camino Francés, this is wine country," Ray said.

The pilgrims passed through the village and continued on their way.

Joaquin Colón reached Pamplona and began his search in the streets of Old Pamplona. He spotted the large golden scallop shell hanging on the wall of the albergue and knew that he had found his destination. He entered through the castle-like doors and turned left into the reception area. "Hello, my name is Joaquin Colón, and I am a reporter from León. I would like to speak with someone regarding the Australian pilgrim who fell to his death about a week or two ago. Can you help me?"

"I don't know how I could be of any help; I just check in the pilgrims when they arrive each day," the hospitalero said.

"You could show me the registration book that would include the day that he arrived."

"I have the registration book, but I don't know if I should show it to you."

"I'm just trying to look into the last days of this pilgrim's life so I can answer any questions that his people might have. You know, to give them peace of mind. I know you are a charitable organization, and I would be happy to make a donation to help your cause."

"I guess I can help you. What was his name, and when was he here?"

"His name was Grant Flynn, and he was from Australia. He was here a couple of weeks ago."

The hospitalero paged through the registration book. "Here it is."

"Was he with any other pilgrims, or was he alone?"

"Well, when he registered, he was with several other pilgrims, but as I remember it, he didn't end up spending the night."

"So he checked out?"

"No, he didn't make it back by 2200. We lock our doors then, and no one gets in after that. The next morning, the other pilgrims all left, and a couple of hours later, the Australian man came by to get his gear. That's probably why I remember him."

"Did he say anything about what had happened?"

"No, but he wasn't in the best of moods. I just let him have his pack and go."

"Do you have the names of the other pilgrims who were with him?"

"Yes, I can let you look at this page of the registration book. It looks like he was with these eight other pilgrims when they checked in."

"This is a great help; thank you."

The reporter scribbled down the names of the eight pilgrims who were with Grant and then handed the hospitalero a fold of cash. "And thank you for your kind donation," the hospitalero said.

Chapter Twelve

The Holy Grail

The stretch of Camino leading to León is comprised of many miles of concrete and monotony. Ray decided to make this section a little more interesting by boasting about a recent source of pride for the Spanish people: the discovery of the Holy Grail in León.

"You should know that two Spanish historians from León University who had studied ancient Egyptian parchments found at the University of al-Azhar in Cairo discovered a description of a goblet in these parchments that exactly matched the Chalice of Doña Urraca that is kept in the Basilica of San Isidoro in León. It originally made its way to Spain as a peace offering to King Fernando by the Emir of Denia so that his city would be spared during the Reconquista. They determined that this chalice must be the Holy Grail."

Ray held his head high and said, "This is Spanish history."

"According to Italian history, the Holy Grail is in the cathedral of San Lorenzo in Genoa," Mattia said.

"Everyone is entitled to their own opinion, no matter how misinformed it may be," Ray said.

"Fortunately, we don't need to determine who is correct at this time," Dean said with a smile.

They continued on their way to León.

Meanwhile, back in Philadelphia, over two weeks had passed, and Enzo and the boys had not heard a word on the progress in the search for Joey and the money. So Enzo once again called his cousin in Naples. "Carlo, why haven't I heard anything from your boy?"

"He called me last week but didn't have anything to report," Carlo said.

"Well, call him back."

"He didn't bring a phone because he didn't want to be tracked or to have a digital record of his location so that he couldn't be tied to any unfortunate events."

"Well, that's just great. Let me know as soon as you hear something," Enzo said, and then hung up.

Not wanting to sit and wait any longer, Enzo decided to send Rocco and Louie over to Spain to look for Max and get a face-to-face update. He also wanted to make sure that Max had not found the money and taken off on his own. The city of León was selected for the intercept since it was a couple of days ahead of where Max was expected to be at the time. The plan was for Rocco and Louie to get there, learn the lay of the land, look for Joey, and wait to meet with Max.

Rocco and Louie arrived in León and got to work, or their version of it, which was looking around, finding some good food, and even more good wine. They did spot some people with backpacks and approached them. Louie held up the picture of Joey, and while walking toward them, Rocco called out, "Yo buddy, have you seen this guy?"

The peregrino looked up at him and said, "¿Qué?... No entiendo."

Rocco raised his hands in disgust and said, "Not K, what are you talking about? Don't you know English?" He then held the picture of Joey up to the man's face and said, "We're looking for Joey, this guy."

The peregrino shook his head and said, "No." And he walked away.

"How we gonna talk to these people if they don't know English?" Louie asked.

"I don't know; just keep tryin'," Rocco answered.

Rocco and Louie continued to explore the streets of León, and they couldn't help being impressed with its ancient charm and historic architecture. When they reached the Parador, Louie called out, "Hey Roc, it's that palace hotel from the movie."

"Yeah, I guess we should have stayed there," Rocco said.

They next made their way to the park that runs along the river and passed by a bridge with large statues of lions.

"Hey look, Rocco, it's León the lion and his buddy," Louie chuckled.

"Right, let's walk through this park and see what we find. Backpackers like parks," Rocco said.

As they proceeded along the river, they spotted a McDonald's in the middle of the park.

"Hey Roc, let's go eat there. I don't know if I'm going to like this foreign food," Louie said.

"Alright, I could go for a burger and fries, and this might be the nicest spot for a McDonald's that I have ever seen."

Inside McDonald's, they noticed a group of younger people and showed Joey's picture to them. "Did any of you see this guy? He probably had a backpack," Rocco said.

"If he's a pilgrim, you should try the area with the tapas bars; they like those places. You should go over to the Barrio Húmedo in Old Town. There are plenty of good places there," one of the young men said.

"Thanks, pal," Rocco said.

Rocco and Louie took a seat, and Rocco said, "That place is in this guidebook that I got, and it says that it has a lot of tapas bars. I didn't know what the hell they were; we should check them out."

"Good idea, Roc, but let's eat now," Louie said.

That evening, Rocco and Louie made it over to the Barrio Húmedo; it wasn't hard to find a lively tapas bar. They went in and walked up to the barra.

"What will you have?" the barra attendant asked.

"What do you recommend?" Rocco said.

"You should start off with some patatas bravas and beer; you can then try some other dishes as you go."

"Sounds good. We'll take two."

The server brought them their beer and tapas, and Rocco showed him the picture of Joey. "Have you seen this guy around? We heard that a lot of pilgrims like to come into these places."

"No, I don't recognize him, but I see hundreds of people in here—locals, pilgrims, and tourists. You could always visit other tapas bars and try a different dish at each one. You can show the picture and have a nice tapas run while doing it."

"That sounds like a plan to me; these are pretty good," Louie said.

"I guess that you like that foreign food after all," Rocco said.

"So far, so good," Louie replied.

Rocco and Louie made their tapas run but didn't have any luck finding anyone who had seen Joey.

The pilgrims progressed past the Roman city walls that surround León and made their way into the city via the Puerta Moneda, the Money Gate.

By the time pilgrims have reached León, they have seen many beautiful and magnificent churches and cathedrals. They didn't expect to see anything too different from what they had been experiencing in the many cathedrals they had visited in the past few weeks. Upon entering the cathedral in León, the pilgrims were struck by the WOW factor. "My God, look at that. That glorious rainbow-like display of colors streaming from the stained-glass windows encompasses the entire cathedral. It is breathtaking. The Camino does not disappoint," Gina said.

"Señor Madrazo," a young woman called out to Ray.

Ray turned to look at the woman and paused with narrowed eyes. The woman then said, "It's me, Blanca."

"Of course, I should have known you. You were one of my best students. What brings you to León?"

"I'm studying history at the university and work part time as a guide. I give tours of the cathedral and around the old city. I would like to provide a tour to you and your friends so that you can see how much I have learned."

"That would be much appreciated."

"We can start right now," Blanca said.

Ray turned and addressed the group. "This is Blanca; she is one of my former students, and she has offered to give us a tour of the cathedral and the old city."

The group gathered around Blanca, and the tour commenced.

"The Catedral de Santa María de León design was inspired by the cathedral of Reims in northern France. It was built beginning in the 13th century on top of the original Romanesque cathedral, which was built on a palace erected by King Ordoño II, which was in turn built on top of public baths from the Roman era. Its 1,800 m^2 of stained glass represents humankind's supremacy on earth, with depictions of paradise, flora and fauna, saints, biblical stories, hunting scenes, and more. The current stained-glass dates from many different periods, but the circular window on the main facade is originally from the 13th century," Blanca said.

After the cathedral portion of the tour was finished, they departed the cathedral and continued to the Renaissance cloister. "You can see its Gothic walls with Plateresque vaults decorated with Gothic frescoes."

The tour next moved to the Real Basílica de San Isidoro. "This basilica was completed in the 12th century and is Romanesque in style, with Gothic and Islamic influences. We will now walk over to a stairway that leads to El Panteón de los Reyes, the Pantheon of the Monarchs, where the remains of 23 Leonese monarchs are laid to rest, along with various other dignitaries. It is considered a fine example of early Romanesque art, with well-preserved 12th century murals depicting scenes from the New Testament as well as agricultural activities. Its two entrances have depictions of rams' heads and biblical scenes."

Mattia whispered to Max, "I didn't hear her say anything about the Holy Grail." Max smiled and nodded.

The tour continued to the bottom of Calle Ancha, to the modernist Casa Botines. "It was designed by Gaudí and built after the Episcopal Palace in Astorga. The exterior is Gothic, with a statue of St. George killing a dragon above the main door. To its right is the 16th century Renaissance Palacio de los Guzmanes, with towers in each corner and arranged around a central courtyard. It now serves as municipal offices. This is where my tour ends, but there is much more to see in León," Blanca said.

"Thank you, Blanca; you provided an interesting and engaging tour," Ray said, and the others agreed.

"I may be leaving you here, but there is more to see in León," Blanca said.

"You must visit the magnificent Monasterio, or Hostal de San Marcos, which is on the Camino, when leaving town. Its origins date back to the 12th century, when King Alfonso VII ordered the construction of a building outside the city limits, on the banks of the river, as an albergue for pilgrims. The present building was begun in the 16th century by the Order of St. James and not completed until the 18th. Its facade includes depictions of San Marcos, Santiago Matamoros at the Battle of Clavijo, El Cid, Alfonso II, the Catholic Monarchs, the coats of arms of Santiago, and the Kings of León."

"The Kings of León, I have their CD," Vinny said.

"I don't think that it is the same Kings of León," Ray said.

"Now to continue, underneath its windows are rows of sculpted heads intended to represent human virtue. The attached church has some shell designs similar to those on La Casa de las Conchas in Salamanca. It is considered to be one of Spain's finest examples of Renaissance Plateresque architecture. Today it is a luxury Parador Hotel," Blanca said.

"It would be nice to stay in that Parador," Orla said.

"Your treat," Vinny said.

"I don't think so," Orla replied.

Ray and the others thanked Blanca again and said their goodbyes.

After having their spirits lifted, the group was off to the albergue to check in and get ready for a nice meal out on the town.

Rocco and Louie spent two days searching for Joey while also enjoying the food and wine of León, without a result. Then, while walking through the Plaza Mayor, they spotted a man who looked just like the picture of Max. There was still no one who looked like Joey, but this was the next best thing.

Max and the others sat outside of a cafe at a large table covered with tapas, wine, and beer in the bustling plaza. As the pilgrims ate, drank, and laughed, taking full advantage of the fare offered by this wonderful city, Rocco and Louie loomed as they planned their next move.

Rocco and Louie decided to try to make small talk with the man that they believed was Max. They needed to get him away from the others so they could have a serious discussion. There was a good-sized crowd in the plaza that evening, and it proved difficult for Rocco and Louie to position themselves so they could talk with him. Rocco told Louie to walk over, accidentally bump into him, and spill his glass of wine on him. Louie put the plan into action.

"I'm sorry, pal. I didn't mean that."

Max dabbed the wine spot on his shirt with his napkin, turned to Louie, and said, "Watch where you are going."

"Let me make it up to you; go get cleaned up, and I'll buy you another drink."

Max got up and walked towards the cafe to use the restroom. When Max was far enough away from the others, Rocco grabbed him and said, "Max, we need to talk."

"Who are you, and how do you know my name?"

"We're the guys who hired you, and we want to know what the hell is going on."

"Get your hands off of me."

Max broke free from Rocco's grip, and then Louie grabbed him. "Listen up, Max; we saw the news, and they told us at the hotel that a backpacker was killed when we asked them if they had seen Joey. You found him, killed him, and kept the money. That's why you didn't call in when you were supposed to, you prick."

"I said get your hands off me; I didn't kill anyone, and I didn't find any money."

They started to struggle, which turned into a fight. Chairs and tables were knocked all over the place, and the three of them were wrestling and rolling around on the ground. Max was trying to hold his own with these two much larger Americans, giving them everything that they could handle, but they were much bigger and stronger than the thieves in the albergue. He could taste both sweat and blood in his mouth; this wasn't the first fight for any of these three. All three men threw punches wildly, with little regard for who was hit. They were kicking, clawing, and writhing on the plaza pavement. Dean and Vinny were about to grab hold of Rocco and Louie when half a dozen policemen arrived and put an end to the brawl. They told Dean and Vinny to back off, and they placed the three men in handcuffs.

Max, with his hands shackled behind his back, his head down, and his shoulders slumped, now had reason to be concerned.

Damn, I just blew this whole thing up. Who knows what these American clowns will say? I could end up in jail instead of finishing the job.

All three were placed in the backs of police cars. Ray tried to talk to one of the policemen and tell him that Max should not be arrested and that he did not do anything wrong. The policeman told him to go to the police station and tell his story there.

The pilgrims stood together, watching the police take Max and the other two brawlers away in separate cars.

Gina cleared her throat and said, "My god, I hope that Max is alright. Those guys looked like a couple of animals."

Why were they bothering Max?

"What happened? Why did they attack Max?" Sunni asked.

"Don't worry, we'll get this straightened out," Ray said.

"Max seems to get into a lot of scuffles for such a quiet guy, even with pigs. Is he really a pilgrim, or is he up to something?" Pablo said.

"Sometimes trouble finds good people, and Max has looked out for us. We need to help our friend when he is in need. Haven't you learned anything on this Camino?" Ray said.

"Let's go," Dean said.

Ray and Dean told the others that they were going to the police station to petition and plead for Max's release. On the way to the station, Dean said to Ray, "I didn't expect to be tried in this manner while on my pilgrimage; I had to fight some demons from my past I had thought were long gone."

"You never know what type of challenge the Camino will provide. The key is to overcome it and grow from it," Ray said.

"You are a wise man, Ray."

Rocco and Louie were placed in a cell together, and Max was in a separate cell with a local who was in custody on an unrelated matter. Max sat with his shoulders slumped and stared at the floor.

I have failed at a job for the first time. What will I do now?

Max's cellmate looked over at him and said, "You're a foreigner."

"So."

"They don't like foreigners coming here and starting trouble; they are going to throw the book at you. You could spend some time in jail."

"What happens, happens," Max answered.

This could really foul things up. How am I going to get out of this to finish the job and not get stuck here? I don't need this aggravation.

In their cell, Rocco and Louie discussed their predicament.

"Louie, you idiot, I had it under control; Enzo is gonna be pissed."

"You didn't have nothin' under control."

"Just shut up; either way, we didn't find out nothin'," Rocco said.

"We just gotta hope that we get outta here now; we don't know nobody here, and we can't call Enzo," Louie said.

"No shit," Rocco said.

Ray and Dean arrived at the police station, went in, and saw the desk sergeant sitting under a large police insignia behind a counter that spanned the width of the room.

"Señor, we are here to explain that an innocent man has been taken into custody," Ray said.

The sergeant looked up from the document that he was working on and put his pen down. "And just how did this great miscarriage of justice occur?"

"We are a group of pilgrims who have traveled together for more than two weeks—eight of us. We were just sitting there having a nice evening meal when a crazy American spilled wine on our friend Max. Max got up to go to the restroom to clean up when another American grabbed him and started a fight," Ray said.

"And your friend did nothing to instigate this fight?"

"No, he is a good man. During his time with us, he helped to find a lost boy and also stopped thieves from stealing from the pilgrims as they slept. My friend Dean here is an American priest, and he can vouch for Max."

"Yes, Señor, Max is not a criminal. He is a victim of an unprovoked assault by two drunk tourists," Dean said.

The sergeant was a church going man, and this made sense to him. He agreed to release Max without processing him.

Max was brought out of the cell, and the sergeant told him, "I am releasing you because of what your friends have told me. They are respectable people, and you should appreciate their support and not do anything else to disparage them."

Max held his head down and said, "Yes, sir, gracias."

The desk sergeant then looked Max up and down and said, "You should also see a doctor; you are a mess. Some of those cuts and bruises look pretty bad. They will need to be tended to before you continue your Camino."

You don't have to tell me; just as my leg was feeling better, these assholes banged it up again.

"That will not be a problem; we have a skilled doctor in our group. She has been taking care of us all along the way."

The sergeant pointed to the door and said, "Buen Camino."

After walking out of the police station, Max gave a wide smile along with a nod and shook the hands of both Ray and Dean with his right hand while grasping the back of their hands with his left. He now had reason to believe in these Camino miracles. The mission would continue.

Max's luck had held out for now.

I don't need clowns from America interfering with my work.

"Max, you handled those two much larger men pretty well; you looked like you had a surge of power when you tossed them around," Ray said.

"All Neapolitans have some Mount Vesuvius in our blood; it helps us to erupt in times of need," Max said with a sly grin.

"That must be it," Ray said as he smiled at Max.

When Max, Dean, and Ray got back to the albergue, the rest of the pilgrims greeted them with hugs and cheers. Gina went up to

Max and said, "I was so worried about you. Who were those guys, and why did they bother you?"

"I don't know, just a couple of drunk American tourists."

"We're not all like that," Vinny said.

"I know that every country has good and bad people."

"That was some fight you had. Those were big guys hitting you; did you see stars?" Vinny asked.

Max squinted his eyes, tilted his head, and asked, "No, why do you ask?"

"I once had a fight with a big guy like that, and when he hit me, I saw stars just like on the old Batman TV show. I always thought that was fake until it happened to me."

"I guess you were hit harder than me. This Camino is turning out to be a little bit rougher than I anticipated. I think that I would like to relax now," Max said.

"That's a good idea," Ray said.

With the recent turn of events, Max could no longer put off talking to Carlo. "I'm going for a walk to clear my mind and try to settle down. I'll see you all later." He excused himself and went off in search of a place to make his call.

He found a pay phone in a local bar. "Carlo, it's Max."

"What the hell took you so long to call?"

"I was working on finding the target and wanted to have a result before I called you again."

"So you found him?"

"No, but there was a problem."

"What problem?" Carlo said, emitting his controlled rage through the phone.

"Two of your primo's crew showed up, started a fight, and got us all taken to jail."

"What! How did you get out?"

"Two of the men who I'm walking with talked to the police and got them to let me go."

"Do the police know who you are or anything about you?"

"They have my name, but I don't think that they have done anything with it."

"What about the two Americans? Are they going to cause trouble for us?"

"I don't know what will happen to them; I was just glad to be let go myself."

"I don't care about the Americans; you better find this stronzo and get me that money. If you don't, your welcome home won't be a pleasant one."

"Alright, Carlo, whatever you say. Ciao." Max hung up the phone and stared at the ground as he walked back to the albergue.

I'm getting tired of all of this; I don't need Carlo threatening me. I don't even know if I want to do this. This is no kind of life.

Rocco and Louie didn't make out as well with the police as Max; after processing, their dubious pasts were discovered, and they were turned over to Interpol, who interrogated them and subsequently escorted them to the airport and sent them back to Philadelphia.

Rocco and Louie bickered for most of the eight-hour plane ride home; they had to report their failure to Enzo.

"We should go on the lam for a while until things cool off," Louie said.

"If we go on the lam, the only things that will cool off are our dead bodies. We got to man up and tell Enzo what happened," Rocco said.

They took the longest cab ride of their lives. It was only a few miles from Philadelphia International Airport to Hank's Hoagie Palace, but the world decided to move in slow motion. Then, all of a sudden, they were there.

"What do you have to tell me, boys?" Enzo said.

"It's not good," Rocco said.

"What's not good?"

Rocco looked at the floor and told him, "We got picked up by the cops and kicked out of Spain."

Enzo threw up his arms and yelled, "You morons. I could have sent my mother and aunt, and they would have done a better job than you two."

Rocco and Louie stood there like schoolchildren who had just been disciplined by their nun and mumbled, "Sorry, boss."

Louie smirked and said, "It's kinda funny, though; we got kicked out of a whole country."

Enzo waved them out with the back of his hand and yelled, "Get outta here; I gotta think what to do now."

Chapter Thirteen

The Iron Cross

It was a new day; the pilgrims were ready to get back to their Camino, and they were on their way out of León. Ray mentioned that somewhere between León and Astorga was where the peregrina disappeared, that the hospitalero told them about in Burgos. He said that he also recalled several news articles appearing after she first went missing, detailing other unpleasant encounters that peregrinas reported after the disappearance made the news. Some women were approached by men in cars, and others by men on bikes. One account even told of the section where false arrows were placed to cause pilgrims to become lost.

"I feel a little less safe on this part of the Camino knowing what has happened here," Sunni said.

"I feel the same," Gina said.

Ray tried to make the others feel comfortable while not making light of the situation and said, "I would imagine that report helped catch the woman's killer. Though it does appear from the multiple and varied reports that there are others who are still out there, we need to stick closely together during this section."

The others agreed; it was what a Camino family did.

After this talk of the tragedies that have happened to pilgrims over the years and discussing the closeness and bonding of the Camino family, Max walked along, looking down and wearing a deadpan face. There was something that bothered him, something that he rarely contemplated and didn't consider at all when on a job: guilt.

I have done so many terrible things in my life and have never given them a second thought. What kind of life have I been living? I have no wife, no children, and no family at all. The people who really know me either fear me or use me for their dirty business. These people in my Camino family don't know me; they know the person I am portraying to them. Who am I, and what kind of person am I?

As the pilgrims neared Hospital de Órbigo, Ray said, "We may have another battle on our hands."

"What are you talking about?" Pablo asked.

Ray then proceeded to tell the story of "El Paso Honoroso, the Honorable Pass."

"Back in the 15th century, a knight by the name of Suero de Quiñones made a promise to a lady for whom he had an unrequited love. He vowed to battle anyone who attempted to cross the bridge into Hospital de Órbigo. It is said that he fought 166 men and defeated them all. After this feat, he decided that he no longer needed the love of this woman. He then rode onto the cathedral in Santiago and made an offering of a jewel-encrusted neck band. Sadly, at a later time, he came across one of his foes in León, who was vengeful and struck him dead."

"I guess the moral of that story is that payback is a bitch," Vinny said.

"And so was that lady," Mattia added with a chuckle.

"We have learned of many legends during this journey through Spain," Sunni said.

"Some of the people of Spain say that there are more legends than there is history," Ray said.

"I understand why," Sunni said.

Next up for the group was Astorga, and then on to the Cruz de Ferro, one of the most important points on the Camino de Santiago.

In Astorga, the group decided to deviate slightly off of the Camino route so that they could take in some of the more historic sights in this important city on the Camino. As they approached the Episcopal Palace, Vinny exclaimed, "Now that is one fancy building; it looks like a cross between a castle and a high-end apartment complex."

Ray told him, "This is actually a more subdued example of an Antonio Gaudi building. If you visit Barcelona, you can experience creations of his that appear to be from another world, yet they are all part of everyday life for the people who live there. I believe that his creation, "Park Güell" must have been the inspiration for your country's Dr. Suess when he created his worlds of wonder."

Astorga also has a cathedral with beautiful stained-glass windows and ornate carvings adorning its walls and halls. Like most Spanish towns of note, Astorga has its Plaza Mayor and Town Hall, and it also has Roman Walls. Like much of the Camino, it is a fascinating trip through history.

About midway between Astorga and Foncebadón, the pilgrims came upon the small town of El Ganso, home of a famous Camino watering hole. It was still too early in the morning for drinks, but they couldn't pass by this well-known spot on the Camino without having a look inside. So they entered the Mesón Cowboy bar, the only wild west bar on the entire Camino Francés and possibly the only wild west bar in all of Spain. "I never expected to see a place like this on the Camino," Vinny said.

Dean laughed and said, "I guess it's a little taste of home here in Spain."

Thinking that Dean was serious, Sunni asked, "What are cowboys like?"

Dean just smiled and answered, "Tough; they're real tough."

Ray poked his head out of the door, stared at the dark clouds, and said, "That was fun, but the skies look ominous. We better get moving, as we still have a long way to go and there's not much between here and Foncebadón."

Not long after their departure from El Ganso, the skies opened up and a steady rain beat down as the pilgrims started their climb in this steep section of the Camino Francés. They entered Rabanal del Camino and didn't see a single soul. Like many small towns along the Camino, as well as in other parts of rural Spain, there are very few people who still live there. They're akin to ghost towns.

"I'm getting really hungry, but I don't want to eat outside today." Mattia said.

Neither did any of the others. "We just need to keep going until we can find an open cafe," Ray said.

While ascending a steep and steady incline with a harsh wind blowing the rain directly into their faces, Ray slipped in the mud and rolled back down the hill. Pablo laughed and said, "Nice move, Dad."

Ray looked up at him and, for the first time on the trip, yelled at Pablo, "I'm tired of your crap; try to start acting like a man."

Pablo didn't say a word, realizing that he went too far and that his father could have been injured.

Dean went to help him up, but Ray said, "I'm fine; I just need to get somewhere dry."

The group then continued all the way to albergue in Foncebadón, where they planned to spend the night before taking on the final climb to the Cruz de Ferro.

Foncebadón is another village brought back to life by the rebirth of the Camino. At the beginning of the 20th century, it had 215 inhabitants, but due to poverty, its population dropped to nothing by 1990, and much of the village was in ruins. As the last village before crossing the mountains into El Bierzo, which also marks the highest point on the Camino Francés, it has always been a popular stopping point.

After settling into the albergue, Mattia dropped his pack and said, "I don't ever want to leave. I just want to dry off, get warm, and live out the rest of my days here."

"That sounds good, but first, I want to eat. I'm wasting away to nothing," Vinny said.

Orla grinned and wryly said, "I think that we all second that, but you're not as thin as you think."

Vinny just smiled back at her.

"I think that might have been a worse day than the first day out of Saint Jean," Pablo said.

"It was definitely less pleasant. I now need a hot shower, a hearty meal, and a good night's sleep," Ray said.

"You've got that right," Dean said.

The pilgrims settled in and dried out, fed themselves, in preparation for the climb to the Cruz de Ferro.

The morning of the climb to the Cruz de Ferro arrived, and the pilgrims were dressed in their rain suits, ponchos, gloves, and buffs. The rain came hard, and the wind drove it and the pilgrims sideways. There was not much to see as the visibility was poor and the climb was as steep as it was long. Each step was an effort. The pilgrims struggled not only with the climb and the weather, but fatigue was taking its toll on all of them. Max was limping as his leg wound was slow to heal, and the weight of his pack and the length of the journey were wearing on him.

This is difficult. I need to continue; I don't want to stop now. I can't stop, but I am in constant pain. Why am I continuing? Is it the job, or is it the pilgrimage? I don't know.

The pilgrims earned their visit to the Cruz de Ferro that day. The effort was worth it, as it is a meaningful place for pilgrims and one of the most iconic of the Camino Francés.

Cruz de Ferro is where pilgrims leave their stones, which many have brought from their homes, in a symbolic lightening of their burdens. Max did not have a stone; his Camino was not intended for this purpose, or at least it hadn't been.

As each of the pilgrims scaled the pile of stones left by millions of pilgrims over the years, looking for the perfect spot to place their stones, Max walked around to the back, where he would be alone. He climbed a little and got down on his knees, looked to ensure that no one could see him, and then dug a deep hole in the stones. The other pilgrims allowed him his privacy to remember his mother. Max clenched his teeth, held the picture of Joey in his hand, crushed it into a ball, and buried it. Looking down, he held his face in his hands and was not sure if he would carry out his original mission. The Camino was having an impact on him, and his contribution to this pile may have been the greatest burden relief for any of the group. Once Max stood, Gina walked over and hugged him. This hug invoked memories of his mother, and he was happy; he felt a little less alone for the first time since his mother's death. *These people are all nice, virtuous, and honest.* He had not been around people like this, except for his mother, for a very long time. Max's metamorphosis into a pilgrim was almost complete.

I have killed many people in my day; it was my duty. I was just doing what I was told to do, and it didn't mean anything to me. After all, my father was killed. I needed him, and nobody cared.

Am I guilty of what I have done? Why should I care? Did they have children or family that loved them? What is going on?

The pilgrims were gathered on the west side of the hill of stones. Dean led them in a prayer, and then just when they were ready to continue on, a strange sound, at least for the Cruz de Ferro, approached from the east. They moved back around to the east side and could see the veteran with the prosthetic leg, whom they last saw in Pamplona, as he scaled the hill, and the pilgrims around him were all cheering and applauding his efforts. Max and his group of pilgrims joined in the applause; his was an inspirational pilgrimage, and his burden was likely a great one.

Dean approached the veteran and said to him, "You are a truly remarkable man; you make your country and your parents proud."

"Thank you for saying that, but it wasn't always the case."

"We all have our pasts; yours probably isn't so bad," Dean said.

"You can judge that for yourself. You see, I joined the Marines to avoid going to jail. I was a juvenile delinquent. I stole a car and crashed it while racing one of my friends. I caused my parents far too much heartache during my younger days. At one point, my mother was so frustrated with my bad behavior that she took me down to the youth detention center and asked them to put me in jail. They laughed at her and sent us home."

"Like I said, we all have pasts; hopefully we learn from them, and you have certainly paid your dues," Dean said.

Once all of the pilgrims had unloaded their burdens, they were not yet finished climbing for the day but eventually descended down the mountain.

When Joey left the Cruz de Ferro, he couldn't help but wonder if he'd made a mistake by giving up his life at home and searching for something that he may never attain.

By late afternoon, the pilgrims were drudging along, tired, and ready to spend the night in Molinaseca. "I know that we have all been unburdened, but I am wiped out," Mattia said.

"I agree; it was a very taxing day, both physically and mentally," Ray added.

At the evening meal, Dean asked, "Did you all get to unload the burdens you were carrying with you?"

"It is still a work in progress, but I have hope," Ray said.

"It is the same for me," Gina said.

"I'm getting there as well," said Orla.

"Just being here is a major part of my unburdening," Vinny said.

"I agree with that," Sunni said.

Max was looking at the floor and hoping not to be called upon to reveal his burden, and as this was obvious to the others, they respected his wish.

"What about you, Dean?" Pablo asked.

"I'm getting there and will know by the time I have completed my pilgrimage."

Enzo decided to act on his own clever idea and sent his mother, Aunt Millie, and Joey's mother to Spain to help Marie find her poor Joey. They had no background issues, were brighter than the last two guys that he sent, and a nice Italian boy like Enzo would treat his mother and her friends to a vacation. Armed with photos of Joey, they set off for Spain to begin the search.

Joaquin Colón returned to León with the information that he gathered in Pamplona and told his editor that he believed that the circumstances of the Australian's death warrant further investigation.

"What did you learn?"

"I found he checked into the albergue with a group of other pilgrims, but didn't return to the albergue with them that night. He did collect his pack later the next morning, but he was alone."

"Is that it?"

"No, I also have a list of the names of the pilgrims with whom he was traveling."

"Let's see it. Most of these don't mean anything, but this one name, Max Castello, is interesting," Joaquin's editor said.

"Why's that?" Joaquin asked.

The editor then told Joaquin, "There was a fight in the plaza between some tourists from America and an Italian pilgrim. His name was Max Castello. The two Americans were deported since they had criminal records and did not disclose this information when they entered Spain. They were brothers, and their names were Rocco and Luigi Rizzo. The police let the Italian go free since the other pilgrims vouched for him and said that he was assaulted and was completely innocent of any wrongdoing. Since they were upstanding citizens, the police had no reason not to believe them."

"I'll look into this further. The 'upstanding citizens' could be on this list. I also need to find out if this Max Castello is really the upstanding citizen that his friends think he is," Joaquin said.

"You do that. You should be able to determine approximately where they will be based on their last known location. You can then check the larger albergues in that area," the editor said.

"I've already been thinking about it; they should be in or around Sarria by now based on when they were in León," Joaquin said.

"Go see if you can find them."

Joaquin was off to Sarria to track down Max and company to try to dig up whatever dirt he could.

Chapter Fourteen

Only a Priest Can Say Mass

The Camino city of Ponferrada boasts an awe-inspiring Knights Templar castle. "Ponferrada Castle, El Castillo de Ponferrada, is a typical Templar castle similar to many others built around the time of the Crusades. A moat surrounded it on all sides except where it faced the river. At the height of its power, it functioned almost like a city in miniature, with shops, a bakery, accommodation for visitors, a permanent population of several hundred people, and even a prison."

This majestic castle lords over the town and inspires thoughts of knights, chivalry, and quests of a bygone time. These Knights Templar, these warrior-monks who resided within the confines of these walls, provided protection for pilgrims of old from the many bandits and ne'er-do-wells who preyed upon them. They are an integral part of Camino history.

Sofia and the other ladies arrived in Ponferrada to start their quest and their vacation.

As they unpacked their luggage, Sofia suggested, "We should walk around the town to stretch our legs. We don't want to go to sleep right away, or we will not adjust to the time zone."

"Good idea," Aunt Millie said, and Marie agreed.

The three ladies walked around the town, exchanging smiles and nods of hello with the townsfolk. "This reminds me of our hometown back in Italy," Aunt Millie said.

As they turn the corner, Sofia gasps and says, "Oh my. We didn't have a castle like that in our town."

"No, we didn't," Aunt Millie answered.

Marie pointed at a group of approaching pilgrims and said, "There are some backpackers. We should show them a picture of Joey and ask them if they saw him."

Marie greeted the pilgrims and asked them, "Have any of you seen this man while you have been backpacking?"

They each looked at the picture, shaking their heads, and one man said, "We haven't, but there are many pilgrims on the Camino; just ask them as you have asked us. Maybe you will get lucky."

Marie sighed, thanked them, slumped her shoulders, and turned to Sofia and Aunt Millie.

"It is only the first day, and they are the first people that we have asked. I'm sure that we will find him soon. We have an entire week," Sofia said.

"Let's explore this beautiful castle before we go for dinner," Aunt Millie said.

Max and his Camino family were still in the countryside, many kilometers from Ponferrada, and had no reason to overtax their bodies or their minds by hurrying to get there.

Mattia said to the others, "We are still really far from Ponferrada; I think that we should stay here tonight."

"That's a good idea; the guidebook lists a nice family albergue for this village," Sunni said.

The group spent the night in the small village. While they explored the village, they went into a little church, and Vinny joked, "Father Dean, are you ready to say mass?"

An elderly local woman who spoke some English immediately approached Dean.

"Father, please say mass for us; priests never visit us any longer, and we need mass."

Ray explained to Dean, "These small villages with small churches and dwindling populations rarely, if ever, get a visit from a priest. These residents will be very appreciative if you say mass for them." Dean could not deny these people, who have all but been forgotten by their church but who have not forgotten the church themselves. Dean was considering leaving the priesthood, had no intentions of saying mass, and decided to lighten his pack so he didn't bring his priest kit. "I will gladly say mass for you, but as I was not planning on saying mass and wanted to lighten my load, I do not have the required items.

"That is no problem, Padre; we have hosts and a large goblet that you can use as a chalice," the local woman said.

"That will do fine," Padre Dean said.

Dean said mass with local wine and stale hosts that must have been over a year old, but no one seemed to mind. Most of the village residents attended the mass, as did all of the pilgrims who were traveling with Dean and some other pilgrims as well. The locals prayed and sang loudly, with subdued smiles on their faces. They were happy to once again have mass in their village. Dean gave his homily on the Camino family and how it not only included the pilgrims who traveled together but also the local residents who lived along the Camino route and provided so much support for the pilgrims. As Max glanced around at the faithful faces in the church and his fellow pilgrims praying together, he couldn't help but feel that Catholics have a special bond with the Camino that the others don't get to fully appreciate.

What right do I have to feel this way? I am not a church regular, and I have not lived a good life, but I do feel like I belong to some extent.

After having witnessed Dean say mass, Max remained in the pew, staring towards the altar but not really seeing it.

Dean is a priest, and I have one less suspect. I will now focus on Vinny and Mattia, but I'm not too sure about them either.

The pilgrims stayed in a small, family-owned albergue on a farm this night. It was cozy, with soft couches, a spinet piano, and hammock chairs dangling from the ceiling. The menu del dia listed conejo as the featured dish. While exploring the grounds, the pilgrims couldn't help but notice there were lots of conejo, or rabbits, as they are called in English, around the property.

"There are many rabbits on your property; is that why you offer them on the menu?" Mattia asked.

"Yes, that is no coincidence. We bought two male rabbits as pets for our children, and it is either a miracle or they were not both males because we now have many, many rabbits. So now conejo is now the specialty of the house. Besides, it tastes like chicken, no?" the owner said.

After dinner, they sat around the table and chatted. A lone pilgrim who was also at the table noticed Orla slumped in her seat with her arms crossed and a grimacing far-off stare and innocently asked her, "Why the sour puss?"

She turned and shot darts at him with her eyes.

"I was just trying to make conversation," he said in an attempt to soften her ire.

Vinny lashed out, berated the man, and told him to mind his own business. The man just wanted to talk and realized that he didn't want to be part of whatever this was, so he just gave his apologies and left.

Orla jumped to her feet, leaned on the edge of the table with both hands, leered at Vinny, and balked, "You mind your own business; I can take care of myself!"

Vinny sniped back, "I was just trying to help."

"I don't need nor want your help." Orla sat down, and they continued to quarrel back and forth, albeit quietly, until Orla stopped talking and wore a taut face and glassy eyes, prompting

Vinny to say, "Stop pouting; when you pout, you win; when we fight, I win." Orla grinned at this statement. They were still talking, and Orla actually relaxed her pose, causing Vinny to do the same. They both tried to keep from smiling and were almost successful. It did resemble more of a family spat than anything else. After all, they were part of a Camino family.

Sunni decided to try to change the conversation to a more pleasant topic. She said to Eva, "When we were showering, I noticed that you have a pretty tattoo of a small butterfly on your lower back. It is not common for physicians to have tattoos in Korea."

"Well, it's actually on the top of my butt cheek, and it is not very common in Germany, either. My sister and I each got these butterflies at a tattoo parlor not too far from where I work in Hamburg. It brings me happy memories of her."

This triggered a memory for Mattia. "I was once in Hamburg for my older brother's stag party when I was just 18 years old."

It was not only Hamburg that brought back this memory, but also the fact that the working girl that he visited while there also had a tattoo of a small butterfly on her butt cheek. He kept this information to himself, but he couldn't help but think about that surreal night.

We traveled from Italy to Hamburg because one of my brother's friends was there when he was in the army. He said that it was the greatest place in the world to have a stag party, and that's why the Beatles loved it so much. We went to a club that was half discotheque and half strip club. The music pounded off of the walls, the lights flashed, and girls were dancing and twirling on poles. After we were thoroughly inebriated, we decided to explore the area. We walked around for ten minutes or so and stumbled upon a street that had eight-foot-high metal barriers and signs that read, "No women are permitted on this block." I could not believe that there could be a street with such a restriction in Europe. Then we walked beyond the barriers, and the entire block was lined with large windows that had women behind them. I understood why they had such a restriction. It was like a tiny version of Amsterdam. I'm not telling anyone about this. I still have trouble believing that it was real; why would they?

"I know that this might be old fashion, but in my opinion, putting a tattoo on a beautiful woman is like painting a moustache on the Mona Lisa," Ray said.

"What about you, Max? Do the young people of Italy have many tattoos?" Sunni asked.

"My mother always said, 'God gives you your body, and you shouldn't disrespect him by defacing it with tattoos,'" Max answered.

"Did you always listen to your mother?" Sunni asked.

"Whenever I could."

Eva, not wishing to stay on the subject of her tattoo, said to Gina, "I like that LOVE necklace that you have; it says it all."

"I have had this for years, but I have only recently started to wear it. It is the only piece of jewelry that I still own. It's just right for the Camino."

"I plan to buy a silver shell necklace when we get to Santiago," Eva said.

"That's the place to do it. I understand that there is a section near the cathedral that is known for its silversmiths," Gina said.

Many of the small villages along the Camino routes are very welcoming to pilgrims, as they are once again thriving, and the added commerce provided by the pilgrims is a prime reason. It is a symbiotic relationship, as pilgrims also need the care and supplies provided by these villages. This commerce does have its traffic jams, but not like those in the non-Camino world, which are a reason for strife and frustration. On the Camino de Santiago, they have just the opposite effect. Their traffic jams are typically caused by large flocks of sheep or herds of cattle being moved by local shepherds and farmers. It provides the opportunity to view the animals and talk with the locals, who provide much of the food that supplies the nourishment required to make this pilgrimage.

As the pilgrims proceeded along, basking in the joy and majesty of the great outdoors, they came upon a wonderful scene worthy of a Norman Rockwell painting. An elderly Spanish couple was working in their vegetable garden. The man with his hoe in hand was tilling the soil, and ten or twenty yards away, his wife was yelling something to him as she was waving her arms frantically. He kept his head down and worked the soil. You see, he had the gift—the one that you only have after many years of marital bliss. At least that was how it appeared—another nice scene along the Camino.

The three ladies from South Philadelphia spent their time in Ponferrada exploring the city and showing the picture of Joey to any and all pilgrims they came across. It was late in the afternoon of their second and final day there, and they noticed a trail of pilgrims strung out along the street heading into the town center. They managed to catch the attention of the last man in line. Marie showed him the picture of Joey and asked if he had seen him during his time hiking. He put his finger to his mouth; his posture stiffened, and his eyes widened. Max had recently buried a picture of the same man. "No, signora, I have not seen him. My friends and I have been walking for weeks, and we have not seen anyone who looks like this."

What is going on? Who are these ladies, and why are they looking for the target?

"Why are you looking for him?"

"He's my son, and I haven't seen him for nearly a year, and we think that he may be here."

"Buona fortuna. Arrivederci." Max left the three ladies at a brisk pace to catch the others.

Max caught up with the others, and as they walked through Ponferrada, he couldn't help but notice the many pilgrims and locals sitting outside of the cafes drinking coffee and chatting with their friends. It was such a simple and peaceful life.

This life I lead, some consider glamorous, if they only knew how stressed, unfulfilled, and lonely it has left me. Do I really want to continue living this way?

After admiring the castle, Vinny was struck by a strange sight.

He turned to Ray and asked, "Why do they have a statue of a KKK clansman here? I thought that they didn't like Catholics."

"No, no, no, that is not a KKK statue. It is a penitent. They are religious men who wear hoods and robes during Semana Santa processions to seek forgiveness for their sins," Ray said.

"Oh, why did they copy the KKK?" Vinny asked.

"They have been around for centuries, much longer than the American KKK. There are different brotherhoods that wear robes and hoods in purple, red, or white. They are good people and an Easter tradition here in Spain," Ray said.

"Holy week must really be something here in Spain," Vinny said.

"Yes, it is," Ray said.

Sofia, Aunt Millie, and Marie ended their time in Ponferrada without coming any closer to finding Joey. They next planned to visit Sarria, where they would continue their search and vacation.

Sofia, Aunt Millie, and Marie arrived in Sarria to spend a couple days searching for Joey and taking in the sights. Sofia got a town map and decided that she would lead the way to see the town and find likely sights where pilgrims might be. She held her map in front of her face and squinted her eyes as she attempted to execute her plan. Aunt Millie and Marie could see that she was holding the map upside-down but knew better than to correct her. It didn't really matter, anyway. The three ladies wandered around the town, occasionally showing Joey's picture to pilgrims, but with no luck. The evening had come, and they came upon a street of restaurants that had outdoor tables with various local dishes on display. The ladies settled in and had much of what was offered, including some pulpo Galician style, a favorite among locals and visitors alike. "This is so delicious; you don't get much octopus at home these days," Marie said.

"I haven't had it in years," Sofia said.

"Neither have I," added Aunt Millie as she wiped her face with a servilleta.

They also enjoyed much of the local wine and, of course, Sangria, as they were now in more of a vacation mode than a quest to find Joey. Then the music started, bagpipes and all. Traditional folk dancers performed the muiñeira and invited all, including the ladies, to join in. The ladies gave it their best shot and ended up spinning in circles and laughing uncontrollably. They provided more entertainment to the locals than the musicians and dancers.

For the next few days while in Sarria, the ladies continued to try to speak with pilgrims and show them Joey's picture, but pilgrims are less open to talking with people who approach them with pictures or clipboards when in and around Sarria, as the area is known for scam artists who prey on pilgrims. One pilgrim did take notice of the picture and told them, "I think that looks like the picture that two Americans were showing to pilgrims in León when I was there."

"That can't be right; who would be there that wanted to talk with my Joey?" Marie said.

Once their time in Sarria was over, they moved on to Santiago de Compostela.

The pilgrims continued on their way, passing through small towns and villages that provide respite and support for those making pilgrimage, and reached the goodly sized town of Villafranca del Bierzo.

They first passed the Iglesia de Santiago on their way into town.

"This church can be the end of the Camino for some pilgrims, or at least in the past, it could have been. I'm not sure if it is still the case," Ray said.

"What do you mean?" Sunni asked.

"Sometime back in the 11th or 12th century, the bishop of Astorga obtained a papal bull that would allow this church to grant an indulgence to any pilgrim who is unable, due to illness, to continue to Santiago. I'm not sure if this is still the case. I know that I have never heard of anyone who has received it here, but like the cathedral in Santiago, it has a door that is only opened during Holy Years," Ray said.

The pilgrims continued on. They came to a castle, Castillo de los Marqueses de Villafranca, which was built as a residence for local nobility. They proceeded along Calle del Agua, where the many traditional houses of the nobility are adorned with coats-of-arms and balconies overhanging the streets. Back in the early days of the Camino, the valley of the Valcarce River was notorious for thieves and the organized crime-like practices of some of the local residents, who extorted money from pilgrims in exchange for safe passage. Happily, these practices were ended by the Knights Templar, who took on the task of protecting pilgrims in the 11th century.

The group entered Galicia and embarked on the unrelenting climb to O'Cebreiro. Galicia, with its ample rainfall, is adorned with green, leafy foliage and effervescently colored green, blue, and yellow reptiles. They say that the human eye can distinguish between more shades of green than any other color, and that capability is exercised to the fullest in Galicia. Another feature that catches the eye of the pilgrim in the O'Cebreiro area is the Celtic-style thatched roof structures that are like no others on the Camino.

While making their way through an alley made of two short stone fences, Pablo spotted a large, bright blue lizard and tried to catch it, but it was too quick for him. After another fifty meters, he went for a florescent green lizard as it scurried up the side of the fence. It too was too quick for him.

"Did you see that green lizard? It had a pointed stump for a tail," Pablo exclaimed.

"That's because someone like you tried to catch it and got hold of its tail. Lizards can release their tails to escape predators, and that is most likely what happened. From now on, please just look at the lizards and leave them with their tails intact," Ray said.

"Okay, but they are pretty neat."

"This is such a quaint little town," Eva said.

"It is a quaint town, but also a significant town. O'Cebreiro is a town rich in the traditions of the Camino de Santiago, including a miracle. During a tremendous snowstorm sometime around the year 1300, a mass was said at what is now one of the oldest remaining churches on the entire Camino de Santiago, the Iglesia de Santa Maria la Real. This mass was attended by a lone farmer who made the arduous journey uphill and through the storm because of his devout beliefs. The priest, who said this mass and was questioning his own dedication, resented the farmer's strong faith and actually belittled the man, calling him a fool for traveling through the dangerous storm. The man was not deterred and stayed for mass, for which the priest was not prepared since he thought no one would brave the storm. The priest was reluctant and half-hearted when he said the mass. During the consecration of the bread and wine, the bread turned into flesh and the wine into blood. Some of this blood dripped onto the corporal, a linen cloth used during mass. The priest had instant regret for his lack of faith and fell to his knees, prayed for forgiveness, and professed his dedication to the Lord. This was the Miracle of O'Cebreiro. and in the church today, there is a shrine donated by Queen Isabella where the chalice, paten, and blood-stained corporal are all on display for the visiting pilgrim to view.

"In more modern times, a priest from this area played a large role in the revitalization of the Camino Francés because, in the 1970s and 1980s, he marked the road to Santiago with the yellow arrows that so many now depend upon to follow the way. Since then, many groups have joined in on marking the Camino, including the government, local organizations, and private individuals. They get very creative in their method of marking the trails, not only painting the yellow arrows and placing signposts, but also placing tiles on the sidewalks and paintings on walls. You will find them in cities, on trees, and in the most remote mountain areas, guiding the way. This is just another example of the love and support that the people of Spain provide for the Camino pilgrims," Ray said.

After dinner that night, the group's discussion turned to the story of the Miracle of O'Cebreiro.

"Is this miracle part of the Camino magic?" Sunni asked.

"That's a very good question. Miracles are very sacred things to the Catholic Church, but everything that adds to the wonder of the Camino experience could be considered part of the Camino magic," Dean said.

"Believing in and hoping for miracles is one of the things that keeps people going to church and walking the Camino," Mattia said.

"Some people just go to church so that they can look down on others," Orla said.

"Hopefully, that is a very small minority. Just think of all of the wonderful people we have met while walking this pilgrimage," Dean said.

"I guess that we are all a little bit crazy," Orla said.

"We need to be crazy sometimes; if we were always sensible, we'd never do anything," Eva said.

After a day of mostly descending from the heights of O'Cebreiro, the pilgrims arrived in Triacastela. Immediately after departing Triacastela, a decision must be made. The traditional route goes through San Xil, but when taking that route, the pilgrim misses the chance to see the monastery of Samos.

The history of Samos is representative of the history of monastic life in Galicia. The foundation of the monastery is attributed to San Martín Dumiense, sometime before the seventh century. It was abandoned for a time during the period of Muslim rule, reopened in the ninth century by a Mozarabic migrant from the south called Argericus, and has been in use as a monastery ever since.

The pilgrims next entered Sarria and passed by restaurants, cafes, banks, and pharmacies. There was also a train station and even a hiking shop; this town was no hamlet.

The Camino was a powerful motor of development for Sarria (even before it became the starting line for the 100 kilometer dash), with albergues, hermitages, bridges, inns, and other facilities developing to serve the needs of pilgrims. Raiding by both sides during the Reconquista, the decline in pilgrim numbers in the late middle ages and the ravages of the plague caused a corresponding decline in the fortunes of the town, from which it only began to recover in the 19th century when the arrival of the railway provided wider markets for local produce. King Alfonso XI died in Sarria in 1230, while en route to Santiago.

The number of pilgrims had also increased dramatically after they entered Sarria. All of a sudden, loads of pilgrims appeared donning backpacks with fresh faces and pressed clothes. The volume, if not congestion, along the Camino had grown, as it did with the increase in people. Even the most welcoming pilgrims who have walked since the early stages can't help but look at these new additions as a different kind of pilgrim.

"Where did all of these pilgrims come from?" asked Max.

"Many Spanish people start here when they only have a limited amount of time to spend on the Camino. It is the most convenient starting point that allows you to meet the minimum one-hundred-kilometer requirement for the Compestela," Ray said.

"They don't all look Spanish," Max said.

"They're not; many tour groups, the elderly, and even some people who are terminally ill start here so that they have a better chance to complete their pilgrimages," Ray said.

"This seems more like the boardwalk in the middle of summer rather than the Camino in the fall," Vinny said.

"Yes, you're right," Gina said.

"It will be a different experience than we have had so far," Dean said.

In his attempt at being the mellow tour guide, Mattia added, "It's all good."

The group continued walking through Sarria, as this was not their planned resting place for the evening. As they made their way through town, Max noticed an old, rugged-looking man who seemed familiar to him, but he could not place him.

Where do I know him from? He's old, but he looks like a street-tough Italian. Did I have dealings with him in the past? I don't remember who he is, and I don't like it.

They continued onto Barbadelo for the night, as they did not want to deal with the crowds that come with a stay in Sarria.

The evening in Barbadelo started out quietly and uneventfully for Max and his group of pilgrims, but then a visitor arrived who wanted to speak with them.

Joaquin Colón was ready to give up after checking every large albergue in Sarria when he decided to try the towns just past Sarria. His diligence paid off when he reached Barbadelo. He explained that he was following up on the death of a pilgrim and had some questions to ask. He showed his list to the hospitalero, and all of the pilgrims on the list were staying there that night. He escorted Joaquin in and gathered the group in the dining hall. "I am Joaquin Colón, a reporter from León, and I am looking into the death of Grant Flynn. I know that you were with him in Pamplona, and I would like to ask you some questions."

Ray, with raised eyebrows and a glassy stare, said to the reporter, "We did not know that the pilgrim who was found dead was Grant. We were concerned that it might have been him, but we did not know until you just confirmed it now. We were told that the police determined that it was an accident, so you seem to be trying to stir up a story that is not there."

"I have my own sources, and the information they provided leads me to believe there may be more to the story than the police have reported."

"We were not with him when it happened; why do you need to speak with us? We know nothing about it and do not wish to be part of your tabloid journalism. The police know how to do their jobs, and that is good enough for us," Ray staunchly said.

"Yes, the police have made their determinations, but I am following up on my information and would like to clear up a few items just to satisfy my reporter's curiosity."

"What is this additional information you have?" Ray asked.

"First, I have a couple of questions for you, and then I will tell you what I have learned. Back in Pamplona, all of you, including Mr. Flynn, checked into the albergue together. Is that correct?"

Most of them nodded their heads, and Ray answered, "Yes, that's correct."

"But he did not spend the night at the albergue, nor did he leave Pamplona with you the following morning, is that correct?"

"Yes, that's correct," Ray answered.

"Why is that?"

Ray tightened his face and said in a soft but harsh tone, "Because he was acting the fool, disrespecting the women and everyone else, so we decided to leave him on his own." The others nodded and mumbled in agreement.

"And that's the last that you saw of him?"

"Yes, it is a shame what happened to him, but we had nothing to do with it and know nothing more about it," Ray said.

"What about the fight in León?"

"What does that have to do with anything?" Ray said.

"Well, you see, Mr. Flynn was in Spain on Camino because he was having financial difficulties and was in debt to some dangerous people. He borrowed money from some acquaintances of a childhood friend named Vito Milanese. These people want their money and have the connections to track him down internationally and get it. I noticed that a number of you have Italian surnames such as Forziatti and Castello; how do I know that you are not affiliated with them?"

Max furrowed his brow and grasped his thighs with his hands. *What does this guy know? Is he going to blow this job for me? I need to get rid of him without blowing my cover.*

Max was not to worry. After hearing this comment, both Vinny and Mattia jumped to their feet, and Mattia yelled, "You asshole, take your bullshit prejudicial stereotype and get the hell out of here!"

Vinny then added, "People like you are always trying to blame everything on the Italians. If an Italian has a successful business, you say that it is mob-run. You are a moron and jealous of the success that Italians have had throughout the world and throughout time." He then flipped his fingers from under his chin at Joaquin and yelled, "You heard him. Get outta here!"

With that, the meeting was finished, and the pilgrims walked out of the dining hall.

This did not turn out as the reporter had planned. Max's Camino family helped to send Joaquin Colón on his way.

Max smiled as he returned to his bunk.

This is a good Camino family that I have. I'm not surprised at Vinny, but who knew that Mattia was such a badass? This clown should now go home with his tail between his legs, like a whipped puppy.

The next morning was a serene calm after the storm, and the pilgrims were once again on their way to Santiago. After a couple of hours of walking, the group passed through Brea and then came upon the 100 kilometer marker. This post indicates the minimum distance on the Camino Francés that a pilgrim must travel in order to qualify for the compostela. There were some pilgrims there taking pictures with the post, wearing freshly pressed outfits. Pablo blurted out, "Posers," as the group walked by the last-minute pilgrims.

Ray shook his head and said, "Even though you and even some others might think that, you don't need to say it."

"It doesn't matter if you walk 100 kilometers or 1000 kilometers; the Camino distance is the same for everyone—the 30-centimeters from your brain to your heart," Mattia said.

"100 kilometers to go; that's over sixty miles. A month ago, I would have thought that's an incredibly long distance to walk. Now it seems like this will be over all too soon," Vinny said.

Orla smiled and said, "That's because of the great company that you have been blessed with."

Vinny looked at her, smiled, and said, "That must be it."

After passing the 100 kilometer mark, pilgrims look forward to the completion of their journey and also start to think of their lives at home and what has led them to their Camino. Vinny, Mattia, and Max walked together, and Max took the opportunity to talk to them about their reactions to the reporter's questions.

"You two really put that reporter in his place last night," Max said.

"You know, you get tired of hearing that nonsense so often," Mattia said.

"That's true, but I do remember a funny story from my time working in construction where two nice old men benefited from that stereotype," Vinny said.

"What happened?" Mattia asked.

"There were these two little elderly men from the old country, Eduardo and Alphonso. They both stood about five feet nothing and were two of the nicest and happiest people that you could ever meet. They had a drywall business together. Considering their vertical challenge, it was kind of funny. Even with their drywall stilts on, they were about the size of an average guy. They were very good and never lacked for work. There was a time when the economy was slow, and some of the businesses that used them weren't paying them. Then one of them burned down. A rumor was spread that Eduardo and Alphonso were connected, and the mob had burned down the building to send a message. The debtors then lined up to pay their bills. Now Eduardo and Alphonso never had any connection to the mob, nor would they ever use illegal tactics to collect on a debt, but they did reap the benefits resulting from the negative stereotype," Vinny said.

"I'm glad that it worked out for them, but I'd rather that it didn't happen," Mattia said.

"You've got that right," Vinny said.

After a few more kilometers, Max's group stopped at an outdoor cafe for lunch. While eating, Max once again saw the Italian old man, who seemed familiar, walk by.

Has this old man been sent to take over the job? Carlo was pretty angry with me. Is he here to take me out? This is crazy; he wouldn't have a chance against me. I need to be done with all of this nonsense.

After they finished lunch, they reached the bridge that lies at the foot of Portomarin. As the pilgrims crossed the bridge, Pablo noticed the outline of several buildings underneath the water.

"Dad, look at that. There must have been a flood, and the whole village was drowned."

"Believe it or not, Pablo, that is intentional. They are just the foundations of some of the buildings that are now up the hill in town," Ray said.

"Yes, the story is in my guidebook. It is very interesting. I can read it to you," Sunni said.

"Please do," Ray said.

Sunni, with an ear-to-ear grin, reads from her guidebook, "Portomarin: In 1956, construction work began on the Belesar dam, whose reservoir now covers the original village. The village and bridge in use today were built from scratch. The churches of San Nicolás and San Pedro, an arch from the original bridge, and the Ayuntamiento were all painstakingly dismantled and reconstructed in the new village. In times of drought, especially in late summer when the water level in the reservoir is low, the ruins of the old village and the old bridge over the river Miño can be seen. Some remaining arches from the even older Roman bridge may also be visible. When the Church of San Nicolás was rebuilt on the village's central square, it was positioned at a different angle from the original, whose apse faced Jerusalem. The design of this church is sometimes attributed to Maestro Mateo (who designed much of the original cathedral in Santiago); however, there is no conclusive proof of this. It is a fortress-church dating from the 13th century and built by the Order of St. John of Jerusalem. It has some interesting sculptures: birds with human heads staring at some distant point, the Virgin Mary, and an angel with a plant with three leaves from which hang the pine cones of fertility and immortality. Opposite it on the square is the Casa del Conde, the Ayuntamiento. Because of the crossing points of the river in Portomarin, it became an important point on the Camino Francés. As a result, both the Knights Templar and the Knights of St. James had a presence here."

"Thank you, Sunni; that was very interesting," Ray said.

The pilgrims crossed the bridge into Portomarin; they came to the bottom of a large flight of stairs that sat right in the middle of the Camino.

"The hills are hard enough; now there are large flights of stairs. My body is already aching," Orla said.

"I know how you feel," Ray said.

The pilgrims climbed the steep set of stone stairs, all at their own pace. A couple of young men passed them by sprinting up the steps; even though they had packs on their backs, it didn't slow them down.

Orla yelled, "Show off," as they passed her.

They then chanted, "Show off," repeatedly while they laughed and mocked her.

The pilgrims made their way through Portomarin.

"This town has more modern buildings than many of the others on the Camino," Eva said.

"They did much rebuilding when they moved the town up the hill," Ray said.

At the end of town, the pilgrims crossed the bridge and made the climb to and through Gonzar, onto Castromaier, and into a small forest of eucalyptus trees. They continued up to the pass of Ligonde at the high point of 756 meters.

The pilgrims entered Melide, a town with a long Camino history, and its old town has an architectural heritage to match. The pilgrims were impressed by a collection of town houses built to accommodate the local glitterati.

"These townhouses must be like the brownstones in Brooklyn; they are full of rich people now," Vinny said.

"That's who lived in these houses as well. The Ayuntamiento, the town hall, with its 17th-century facade, is also nice," Ray said.

Next to the Ayuntamiento is the church of San Pedro; the pilgrims skipped it in favor of their final stop in Melide, the church of Santa Maria and its murals.

"The collection of liturgical murals is worthy of any museum," Dean said.

The pilgrims moved onto and through the town of San Marcos and crossed a creek, taking a footbridge made from sequentially placed stones of two meters in diameter. They arrived at 'Monte do Gozo', the Mountain of Joy. It is where pilgrims get their first views of the Santiago de Compostela Catedral.

While admiring the cathedral in the skyline, each of the pilgrims reflected on the impact that this journey has had on them. Max stared at the majestic sight.

I have not found the target, but I have come to terms with the loss of my mother, and I now have a Camino family.

Gina's lips curled into a slight smile.

This has been a wonderful journey. I am rejuvenated and may be ready to start my new life.

Dean held his chin high and took a deep breath.

I now understand my purpose in life.

Vinny looked up and scratched his head.

I don't know what I want to do for a living, but I know that it's not construction.

Orla focused on the cathedral in the distance with a face that seemed to shine.

Life goes on, and I'm better off without that arse after all.

Eva wanted to smile, but instead wore a deadpan expression.

I wish that my sister could have been with me for this.

Mattia stood solidly, with his jaw set.

I will come back next year to do this again.

Sunni planted her two hiking poles and gazed at the cathedral.

I miss my parents and look forward to getting back to them.

Ray smiled and exhaled while considering the future.

There is hope.

Pablo dipped his chin, slumped, and bit his lip.

My dad's not so bad; I should give him a break.

The pilgrims approached the city limits of Santiago; the journey had nearly ended, and Max had not completed his task. When he started this trip, he would have been devastated; at this point, he just walked along with a relaxed gait and appreciated both the city sights and his company.

My chances of finding the target aren't very good at this point. I don't care as much as I should, but how am I going to tell Carlo?

Chapter Fifteen

Santiago de Compostela

Sofia, Aunt Millie, and Marie reached Santiago, the final city of their vacation and search. The three ladies weren't able to book a hotel in Santiago, a town with not only many pilgrims but also a good supply of tourists. They settled on a room with three single beds and a bath in a private albergue. The hospitalero greeted them as they entered the albergue.

"Welcome, ladies; you must be the three Americans we are expecting."

"Yes, we are. We have booked a room for three with a private bath," Sofia said.

"We have it ready for you; it is on the first floor. Please show me your passports, and then you will be all set."

The three ladies handed him their passports.

"Will you be joining us for dinner tonight?" the hospitalero asked.

The ladies talked among themselves, and Sofia said, "Yes, we will; we are tired from our travels and could use a relaxing night in."

This worked out well for the trio, as they were now more focused on enjoying themselves and not so worried about finding Joey. They rested in their room until it was time for dinner. They would explore Santiago in the coming days.

At the communal meal, they showed the pilgrims they were dining with Joey's picture, but none of them had seen him. After dinner, they stayed and participated in some games. One of the games was Truth or Dare. When it was her turn, Aunt Millie would not be intimidated; she chose dare. Her task was to serenade one of the young peregrinos with a love song. As she belted out her song, the others winced as if in pain, as she was so out of key. They dared her, but she had the last laugh. The three ladies thanked the hosts and the pilgrims for making them part of their night and told them that they were "Gooda boys and girls." The ladies experienced a nice Camino night.

For the next few days, the ladies continued to tour and occasionally showed Joey's picture to a pilgrim. There were many pilgrims, but none had seen Joey.

Their trip was now over, and they left Spain and the Camino de Santiago with fond memories, but without finding Joey.

As the pilgrims reached Santiago and the well-known colorful sign made of metal block letters that read "SANTIAGO DE

COMPOSTELA" was in sight, their pace quickened, and chatter erupted.

"Look, Dad, we are there," Pablo shouted.

"Yes, son, we are almost finished."

"We should stop at the sign and get pictures of our group," Sunni said.

"Almost every pilgrim does; it is a well-earned rite of passage," Mattia said.

The pilgrims went to the sign where other pilgrims were already taking photos.

"Would you like me to take a photo of your entire group for you?" Dean asked the pilgrims, who were now at the sign.

"Yes, please, thank you. We can do the same for you," the pilgrim with the camera said.

Dean took the photo with the pilgrims' cameras and a couple of their phones as well.

Sunni and the others then handed their phones to the other pilgrims for their photos to be taken and gathered around the sign.

"When I started this journey, I never thought that I would be in a photo, especially with a group of people that I hadn't known before I started," Max said.

"We are now your Camino family, and it is only natural to have a commemorative photo of our time together," Eva said.

"Having another family is something else that I had never planned," Max said.

The pilgrims made their way through the streets of Santiago and towards the cathedral via the Rua de San Pedro. The yellow arrows that the pilgrim followed for much of the Camino have been replaced by golden scallop shells. Santiago, like many of the larger cities on the Camino, embeds these symbols into the sidewalks to enable the pilgrims to find their way. The increase in traffic and numerous stores and other businesses provide an initial indoctrination for the pilgrim back into their non-Camino lives. There is still the cathedral, compostela and other pilgrims to fend off total re-entry for now.

"How did this city of Santiago get selected as the place for the Camino to end?" Sunni asked.

Ray said, "There is a detailed history behind that. The legend of the discovery of St. James' tomb in this remote corner of Iberia dates from between 788 AD and 838 AD; the exact date is unknown. What is certain is that within a couple of generations, what had been a sleepy village with cows in the streets was transformed into one of the most important pilgrimage sites on earth. In 997, the Muslim leader Al-Mansur, as part of a general ravaging of the Christian north, came to Santiago bent on destruction. The story goes that he found the shrine deserted, except for a single monk, who, when asked what he was doing, replied that he was praying to St. James. Al-Mansur told him to continue praying and withdrew his troops.

"However, the following day, he had the shrine completely destroyed and parts of it, including the bells, taken away and used in the building of the Grand Mosque in Córdoba. But, whether out of respect or fear, he left the relics untouched. Thus destroying a symbol of Christian resistance to Muslim rule without desecrating sacred Christian relics. The story of the destruction of the Apostolic Shrine spread throughout Christendom. The rich and powerful rallied to the cause and sent money for its reconstruction, while the poor and humble came in person, by whatever means they could. The result was a frenzy of construction in Santiago and all along the Camino Francés, which was to last into the 13th century. It can be seen to this day in the many churches and monasteries from that period that are still standing. In 1236, following the recapture of Córdoba by Fernando III, the bells of the cathedral were returned and installed in the rebuilt cathedral, where space had been left for them.

"And so began a golden age of pilgrimage throughout western Europe. In the following centuries, pilgrims came despite plague and war. Santiago grew and flourished, flushed with the wealth and prestige the pilgrims brought. History was not on its side, though, and as the Reconquista pushed south, Spain's centers of political power followed. Until 1561, the newly reunited country established its capital in Madrid. Then in 1589, fearing a raid by the English privateer Sir Francis Drake, who had landed at A Coruña, the archbishop of Santiago, Juan San Clemente, had the sepulchre containing the relics in the crypt of the cathedral bricked up to keep them safe from the marauding Englishmen, and in time the secret of the hiding place of the relics was lost. The loss of the relics made little difference because the pilgrims still came. In the following century, King Felipe IV, a religious man and a patron of the arts and flush, for a time at least, with the spoils of Spain's expanding empire in the Americas, provided the funds necessary for a new program of construction, which began the transformation of the cathedral from its modest Romanesque origins to the magnificent Baroque construction that stands today. The fortunes of the Camino ebbed and flowed, as did the fortunes of the city.

"In 1879, the then Cardinal of Santiago, Miguel Payá, taking advantage of renovation works being carried out on the cathedral, set out to locate the relics. On the night of January 28, 1879, they were found behind a wall behind the main altar. The rest, as they say, is history. During the 20th century, the flow of pilgrims continued to arrive, thanks in part to the support of the Francoist regime, which made St. James the patron saint of Spain. Few arrived on foot during this period, and by the 1970s, their numbers had dwindled to fewer than a hundred each year. Then, from the 1970s onward, each new year saw more walking pilgrims; the pace of annual growth was only disturbed by the Holy Years, when generally more than twice as many made the trek."

"And now we are keeping this tradition alive," Sunni said.

The pilgrims approached the cathedral in Santiago from the east on the way to the Praza del Obradoiro. They passed through an archway as they were serenaded by a lone bagpipe player.

"That is harsh; I never expected to hear a bagpipe here in Spain," Vinny said.

"Some consider it beautiful music and others erratic noise, but all welcome these sounds as they indicate you are nearing the completion of your pilgrimage," Ray said.

"You're right about that," Vinny said.

Upon entering this magnificent square, pilgrims migrate to its center to gaze at the surrounding structures, particularly the cathedral. Pilgrims congregate around the zero-kilometer plaque, the official end of this pilgrimage route. All around the square, pilgrims are gathered in celebration of their accomplishments, paying little attention to the tourists mingling among them.

Standing in the center of the plaza, Mattia dropped his pack and turned to take in the entire view.

"Look at that magnificent Baroque facade of the cathedral, and to the left, the parador Reyes Católicos. I wish we could have gotten some of the pilgrim rate rooms there, but there are not many, and they go fast. And on the right is the San Xerome rectory of Santiago University, and behind us is the seat of the presidency of the Galician regional government and the Santiago city council."

"How do you know so much about this area?" Eva asked.

"I took a tour here after my last Camino," Mattia said.

After basking in the glory of their efforts, the pilgrims then proceeded to the pilgrim reception office in order to receive their compostelas. In addition to the pilgrims from the Camino Francés, there were pilgrims from the various other Camino routes that end in Santiago de Compostela, and all were waiting in line to receive their certificates of completion, their compostelas. It is here that the pilgrim not only sees many pilgrims for the first time, but also many of the pilgrims that they have met throughout their journey. It was a time to both rejoice and reminisce with the friends that have been gathered along the way.

The man who had walked after recovering from a heart attack stood in line with what appeared to be another hundred pilgrims. He waved to Max and walked over to him. "You made it," the man said with a smile.

"Yes, you too. By the way, I never got your name," Max said.

"That's because you figured there was a good chance you would never see me again. I am Don."

"Well, it's good to know you, Don. I am Max."

"You know, sometimes on the Camino you can make a connection with someone with whom you have only spent a brief amount of time; there are no strangers among pilgrims," Don said.

Max smiled and said, "I think that you are correct, my friend, Buen Camino."

They then took their places back in line. Max was next greeted by Lars, who said, "Good to see you, my friend. What an adventure we have had."

"Yes, we have," Max replied.

"Now that it is back to home and the real world, I will miss this place," Lars said.

"What's next?" Max said.

"I will go back to work at the dairy plant, and I would like to write a book of poetry, as the Camino has inspired me so much."

"That sounds good; myself, I'm not sure what I will do next."

"You can always try a pilgrimage in your home country of Italy."

Max was intrigued, and he asked, "What pilgrimage is in Italy?"

Lars told him, "The Via Francigena—for one, you can find pamphlets on it in the tourist office here in town."

"Maybe I will."

I know that I am in no hurry to go back and face Carlo after failing to complete the job.

The line progressed, and each pilgrim entered one by one as they were called to one of the many pilgrim processing stations. Here, the pilgrims were questioned about their journey, but they were first required to hand over their credentials so they could be inspected to ensure they had met the requirements for the compostela. There must be enough stamps in the proper order to show that the pilgrim has walked at least the minimum of 100 kilometers. This was not a problem for Max and his group of pilgrims, for they had walked the 800 kilometers from Saint Jean Pied de Port.

When the pilgrim's number is displayed, the pilgrim goes to the indicated station, and the questions begin. Most were simple, such as "Did you walk the entire Camino?" But one question in particular caused Max to pause: "For what purpose did you walk the Camino de Santiago?" Max tilted his head and grinned.

If I tell you that, you will never give me the certificate.

As he paused, the clerk made some suggestions: "Religious, spiritual, for your health."

Max answered, "Yes."

The clerk grinned and said, "OK, what name do you want on the compostela?"

"Massimo Giovanni Castello."

The clerk handed Max his compostela, and it read, "Maximum Iohannes Castello."

Max cocked his head slightly and stared back at the clerk.

"It is in Latin, as is the tradition for all pilgrims who have received their compostelas throughout time," the clerk said.

Max smiled, nodded, and said "Grazie" and walked out of the office.

As each of them received their compostelas, Max's Camino family gathered outside, waiting for the others to exit the pilgrim's reception office and show their hard-earned compostelas. There was both joy and sorrow, as the end of their time together was near, but not yet finished.

Joey had also finished his Camino Francés, but he was not ready to return home. He didn't know where he would go or what he was going to do with the rest of his life. He still needed time to figure that out.

It was now time for Max and his Camino family to drop off their packs at the albergue and visit the cathedral. On the way to the albergue, the group once again entered the Plaza del Obradoiro, filled with pilgrims and tourists alike. Suddenly it started pouring rain; the tourists ran for cover, but most of the pilgrims in the square reacted differently. Nothing was going to dampen their spirits; they kicked off their shoes and danced in celebration. It was as if the heavens were cleansing and celebrating with the pilgrims. Then, as suddenly as it started, the rain stopped, and our pilgrims were back on their way to the albergue. Camino magic?

In addition to the pilgrim's mass, there are a few other traditions in which the pilgrim partakes while at the Santiago de Compostela Cathedral. Among these are the embrace of the Statue of Saint

James, accessed via a stairway from the side of the high altar, and saying a prayer of thanks at the crypt containing the remains of Saint James. Max, who had now been in more churches this past month than the rest of his adult life combined, took the opportunity, kneeled at the crypt, and prayed for Saint James to guide his mother into heaven. He knew that she belonged there, but hoped that his life's deeds had not made it more difficult for her.

The cathedral visit ended. The group exited through the Portico de la Gloria and walked down the front steps. Max noticed a small group making hurried gestures and conversing rapidly. They were gathered around someone lying on the steps. Max glanced down and saw the somewhat familiar old Italian man. He walked over, looked at the man lying on the steps, and gazed into two dark pits in the place of his eyes. Max jolted his head back. These were the cold, empty eyes that reflected the black heart of the man who had killed his father.

With his identity revealed, Max went back to the time when he had first encountered this soulless devil.

It was one of the most wonderful times of the year in Naples, the San Gennaro festival. Max and his family, like most everyone else in Naples, would partake in this celebration. The cobblestone streets were alive with laughter and traditional folk songs of Naples that had become known the world over, such as Tarantella, O Sole Mio, and Santa Lucia. Max's mother, wearing her glowing smile, kept hold of Max's hand as they navigated this wondrous display of colorful stands and stalls lined with twinkling lights and adorned with flowers and bunting. Max's eyes were wide with anticipation as he marveled at the toys and games that lined the street. Max's father attempted to walk with his arm around Max's mother, but it proved nearly impossible as he was continually greeted by well-wishers wanting to shake his hand, give him thanks, and show him respect. He was well known to the people of his community. Max's father joyfully pointed out the fire jugglers, festive dancers, and minstrels with their tambourines and drums, making the most of his time with his family.

Max's mother couldn't help but reminisce about her childhood when she attended the San Gennaro festival with her parents. It has always been a joyous occasion and a sense of community, of belonging to something larger than oneself.

The aroma of the food stands floated through the air and called to Max and his family. His father would treat them to arancini, Italian rice balls, pizza, and, best of all, as far as Max was concerned, zeppole with powdered sugar. With their bellies full and hearts content, they continued to explore the festival, taking in the lively street performers and upbeat music. Max even joined in on the dancing.

Sundown, with its vibrant canvas of pink, blue, orange, and yellow sky, was the cue that the procession was about to begin. Max and his family had positioned themselves in front of the cathedral along with multitudes of others, with their hearts filled with reverence, ready to witness the procession of San Gennaro illuminated by candlelight.

The procession ended, and Max and his family strolled through the back streets of Naples in an attempt to make it home while they avoided the crowds. On one empty and dark street that was little more than an alley, a dark figure stepped out from the shadows and pointed his Beretta M9 with silencer at Max's father, and with three quick shots to his chest, sent him to the ground. Max stared into the eyes of this devil and saw nothing but black. Max's mother hugged him, and the killer was gone in an instant. Max's father lay there bleeding and still, very still. His mother tried to wake him, but he was gone.

Max's heart pumped furiously, his face reddened, and sweat gathered on his brow. With his fists and jaw clenched, he stared into the face of the man who had killed his father as he lay on the steps. Max was in a trance. Then this devil's pits sealed themselves, his head turned into the step, his body went limp, and he was no more. One of the bystanders put his hand on Max's arm.

"Are you alright, sir?" the man asked.

This broke Max's trance, and he said, "I'm fine."

Well, whatever he is here for, it is no longer a concern of mine, unless this is a glimpse into my future.

"What happened to him?" Max then asked the man.

He said, "He told us that he had terminal cancer and walked the Camino to atone for his sinful life by completing the pilgrimage before he died."

I would have killed him if I recognized him, but now I cannot. Maybe it is a sign, I can now start my new life.

Max joined his friends again, and Mattia asked him, "What was going on over there?"

"An old man who had cancer walked the Camino in a last attempt to be forgiven for his lifetime of sins. He died on the steps before he was able to enter the cathedral."

Ray made the sign of the cross and said, "It is not uncommon for people who are ill to walk the Camino for such reasons. They sometimes die just after making it to the cathedral. It is their internal drive and willpower that keep them alive long enough to finish."

"That's what helps all of us complete the Camino. Fortunately, most of us live to reap the benefits," Mattia said.

The group would have one last dinner together, and Mattia had heard of a hidden treasure of a restaurant just off of Plaza de Cervantes. While they walked to the restaurant, Max decided to test Mattia and asked him, "Did one of your Paisanos tell you about this restaurant?"

Mattia once again looked confused, and Dean said, "Paisanos are from the south of Italy and the big east coast cities in the US; a northerner like Mattia doesn't know what you mean."

Mèrda! I thought that I had found him.

Vinny then joked, "In my old neighborhood, he would have been considered almost a Frenchman coming from way up there."

They laughed and kept walking towards Plaza de Cervantes until they reached their destination, Damajuana. The menu del dia there offered several options for each of the three courses, with wine included, of course. All of the pilgrims were extremely pleased with their meals. Vinny, who had the razor clams in garlic, mixed seafood grill in gulas, a fish-based pasta that looks like baby eels, and a cheese torte, was overwhelmed by the deliciousness of his meal. He could not believe that something could be so good that his mother did not cook. When the chef came into the dining room to speak to a guest at another table, Vinny got up, gestured to his plate, and then hugged her. She was all smiles as the entire dining room clapped for her. It was a feast fitting of the Camino de Santiago and one that the pilgrims would not soon forget.

Max now knew that his suspicions over Mattia's accent were unwarranted. He will take one last stab at Vinny. He asked him, "It sounds like that in your neighborhood there are many Italians; where is that?"

Vinny said, "Bensonhurst, you know, Brooklyn, New York." Max was still not having much luck in his search, but he didn't really find it as troubling as he would have at the start of his Camino.

After dinner, during coffee, the topic turned to what they got out of their Caminos and what was next for each of the pilgrims. Ray said, "I wanted to heal my relationship with my son, and I believe that I have made great strides in achieving that.

Pablo squirmed in his seat and said, "What my dad said, but for me."

Ray added, "We are getting along and now realize that we need each other and that life will be easier as long as we try to understand each other and get along."

Sunni said, "I just want to be less tense and go back to Korea and try not to live up to my office nickname, The Bitch."

"I'm so surprised to hear that; you are so sweet and congenial," Ray said.

The others nodded and remarked in agreement.

"That's because I am not in the office, and I have been on my Camino away from the stress of daily life."

Gina looked up with an expression that simultaneously reflected both contentedness and sadness and said, "I wanted to make my life better, and the Camino has been part of my effort to make that happen. Although I did lose my LOVE necklace, maybe it is just a sign that I am shedding the constraints of my old life as I enter my new life."

"I was all alone in the world with no family after my mother died, and now I have a Camino family," Max said.

"Yes, you do," Gina said.

Mattia said, "I just wanted to go for a long walk and be with some good people, and I have done that. I will now go back to my job as a tour guide because I love people and always enjoy meeting them."

Ray said, "You have the personality to be a success in the hospitality and tourism worlds."

Dean said, "I needed to decide how I could continue to serve God with all of the external challenges and contradictions that being a priest in these times presents. I now have a clear understanding of how I will live my life. I plan to enter a monastery. When I said mass in that small village last week, I knew that I still had the calling. I must now focus on my faith and not the actions of those I cannot control." None of the others were surprised at this.

"You have found your Personal Legend," Gina said.

Dean shrugged in tacit agreement just to be polite; he didn't fully understand what she meant but appreciated the sentiment.

Ray, sensing that Dean had no idea what Gina meant, told him that "finding your Personal Legend means that you have found your true purpose in life. It is from the book 'The Alchemist' by the Brazilian writer Paulo Coelho, which has inspired many people to go on the Camino de Santiago."

"Somehow, I never got around to reading that book," Dean said.

Eva said, "I needed a break from the sadness that I feel for my patients. I also wanted to once again have happy memories of my sister. I've accomplished that, and now I will go back to work in my clinic refreshed and ready to help those who need it."

Ray said, "You are a fine doctor; we may not have made it without your care and advice," and they all agreed.

Orla said, "I needed to rid myself of the hangover of a bad relationship and to feel better about myself. I have done that with your help, and especially Vinny's help."

Mattia said to Max, "I thought that they hated each other."

Max replied with a Cheshire Cat grin, "Camino magic."

Vinny said, "I needed to get away from a job that was killing my spirit and decide how I wanted to go on with my life. I'm not exactly sure how I will do that, but I do know that a fiery Irish girl is part of the solution."

Orla, with the biggest smile that she has had her entire Camino, tilted her head, pushed up her shoulders, and said, "Vinny will be traveling to Ireland with me so we can spend some time together."

"That is Camino magic!" Mattia exclaimed.

"I suspected as much with the way that their arguing turned into bickering. I'm sure that there was always an attraction there. They just needed some time to come to terms with it," Eva said.

"I, too, was not surprised; I did notice the changes in their behavior towards each other as we progressed along the Camino," Sunni said.

"It was kind of obvious if you paid attention to their mannerisms while they were bickering and not just their words," Gina said.

Gina then told them all that she planned to continue on to Finisterre. She then said, "If anyone would like to join me, you are welcome."

Max welcomed a reason not to return to Naples immediately and report his failure. "I'd like to go along with you; I'm in no hurry to get home."

She hasn't said much during this trip, but when she did talk, she was kind and insightful. She should be good company.

Gina said, "Good, it makes me happy that part of our group will continue."

The group was to become a duo.

Max then raised his glass to toast, "Alla mia famiglia Camino."

Glasses clicked, and chatter of agreement filled the air.

Dean rose and provided a blessing for all and then added, "All of us have shown the reason you undertake this holy pilgrimage has a great bearing on what changes you experience as a result of completing this Camino de Santiago."

At this time, after all of the walking was done, a sadness set in with the pilgrims, as this wonderful and meaningful adventure had come to an end. They had all suffered many bumps, bruises, blisters, and sleepless nights, and many of them couldn't wait to do it again. The Camino de Santiago is far more than just a long hike.

"Remember that the Camino is always there for you; if you need to, you can always return, and you will always have your Camino family," Ray said.

Chapter Sixteen

The End of the World

On their last morning together, the pilgrims got up early to wish Max and Gina a Buen Camino and say their goodbyes to each other. They were heading to different parts of the world but would bring a part of the Camino, which is now part of them, with them.

"I did not know any of you just a little more than a month ago, and now it pains me that I will not be with you for these coming days," Sunni said with tears in her eyes. Eva then hugged her.

"It is difficult to leave your Camino family. We have a special bond," Mattia said.

"Remember, as I told you at dinner last night, Spain always welcomes you to come back to the Camino," Ray said.

"It is good that some of our family will remain together for now: Ray and Pablo, Orla and Vinny, and Gina and Max. And may God bless you all on your life's journey," Dean said.

They hugged and finished saying their goodbyes to each other.

Max and Gina began their journey to Finisterre.

They spent the past month together, but they didn't really know much about each other.

Max started his Camino focused on identifying his target. He primarily talked with someone to gain information. As time went on, this changed, but not much.

Gina spoke frequently enough to be sociable but stayed reserved when compared to the other pilgrims. She enjoyed listening to them talk. So they continued on and would get to know each other a little better over the next few days.

As the two were now together and there was no one else to talk with, Gina decided to try to connect with Max.

"Early on, when we were all explaining our reasons for going on Camino, you mentioned that you were trying to cope with the death of your mother; I assume you were very close with her," Gina said.

"She was the only real family that I had for most of my life. I lost my father when I was very young. It brought me great pain to lose her, and it left me lost."

"I, too, am very close with my mother; I miss her and hope to see her again soon, if I can."

"Why can't you?"

"It's complicated. I will see her when I can."

"Take it from me; see her as soon as you can. You never know when it will be the last time."

"You are probably right; I need to think about it. One thing that I have figured out on this Camino is that life is a tragedy, and you need to enjoy what you can of it while you can," Gina answered.

"There aren't many other pilgrims on this section of the trail; we need to pay close attention to the markers," Gina said.

"The only problem with that is that there aren't as many markers on this section as there are on the Camino Francés," Max said.

As they searched the roadway to spot markers along the way, Gina commented, "We made it this far without getting lost; I think that we will be OK."

"I'm sure that you are right," Max said.

Gina then said, "You said that you are from Naples; I bet that you eat a lot of good pizza."

"Yes, we made it first, and we make it best."

Max then asked, "Do you have good pizza where you come from in America?"

"Yes, we have many people from Italy, and the Italian food is all very good."

Max then asked, "Where is that?"

"The east coast," Gina answered.

She doesn't like to talk much about herself.

He then jokingly asked, "Are you a millionaire, like most Americans?"

Gina laughed and said, "No, I once had a lot of money, but I have spent it all bettering myself; I am now a pauper and happy to be one."

Max grinned as he looked at her, not knowing exactly what she meant. He could tell that she didn't want to talk about it at the time. He chalked it up to his difficulty understanding women.

Max and Gina walked along in the sunshine and a pleasant breeze, enjoying the sights and sounds of Galicia on the road to Finisterre.

"Galicia is some of God's most beautiful work," Gina said.

"I think that woman is the most beautiful thing that God has ever created. Don't you agree?" Max said.

"That may be so, but some women get help from modern medicine," Gina said.

"I guess so. You mentioned that you are considering becoming a nun; is that still the case?"

Gina looked at the ground as she walked and answered, "Probably not; I don't think that they would take someone like me, anyway."

Max looked at Gina with a puzzled gaze on his face. He was once again confused, but didn't pursue the subject. He just put his hand gently on her shoulder and said, "I understand; I bet that is a difficult life to lead." He didn't really understand; he was just trying to be supportive.

They continued on quietly, and Gina stared off in the distance and began to reflect on how she had gotten to this wonderful point in her life. She fondly remembered her parents, but also the unhappiness that prompted her to make the changes that she thought she needed in her life. She left her home and came to Europe to have the surgery that helped her become the woman that she is today. She started as an unattractive gawky guy with a big nose and is now a fine-looking woman ready to move on with her life.

If Max and the others only knew, they wouldn't believe it.

At the end of the day's walking, Max and Gina reached their planned stop for the night, the town of Negreira, the largest town, before reaching the coast.

"Over there are some remains of old foundations. Maybe it was some type of little village," Gina said.

"Look, there's a sign. It might explain it," Max said.

"It's in Spanish, but I think that I can translate it," Gina said.

"It says that these are remnants of castros and are evidence of the town's long existence. They can be found throughout this area," Gina said.

Max and Gina spent the night in Negreira. They next planned to move on to Olveiroa.

The following day's journey took our remaining pilgrims to their first brief glimpse of the Atlantic Ocean when they reached the Alto Cruceiro da Armada.

"There's our objective; we should be there tomorrow," Gina said.

"It's much easier to spot than a yellow arrow," Max said with a grin.

They then made the steep ascent to work their way around the bay through the town of Cée and on to Corcubión to spend their last night before reaching Finisterre and ending their journey together.

"Since this is our last day of this wonderful journey, I will fill in for Ray and tell you the story of Santiago in this part of the world that I found while doing the research for this trip," Gina said.

"Please do; I would love to hear it," Max said.

"The legend tells how Santiago came to Galicia during his lifetime to try to spread Christianity, but having had little success among the heathen inhabitants, he fell into a great depression and despondency. One day he was sitting on a beach north of Finisterre near Muxía contemplating giving up and returning home to Palestine when, in the distance, he spotted a strange boat, which, when it approached the shore, he saw to be made of stone and to be piloted by no other than the Virgin Mary herself. Having made landfall, she immediately set about consoling and comforting him, reassuring him that both she and her son were by his side while he went about his work. Whereupon she disappeared, leaving the stone boat on the shore, where it remains to this day in a place called Pedra dos Cadrises. Reinvigorated by this apparition, Santiago continued with his work. Although he didn't meet with any great success among the Pagans, he subsequently returned to Jerusalem, where he met a grisly end."

As the coast grew closer and the journey to Finisterre was measured in hours and then minutes, the aroma turned from pine trees to the smell of the ocean, which filled the air even before it could be seen. This added to the anticipation and provided an extra bit of excitement for the finale.

Gina lifted her head, sniffed the air, and said, "You can smell the ocean; it's just like being down the shore!"

Max asked, "What is this down the shore?"

Gina shrugged and said, "Oh, it's just a Philly term for being at the ocean."

Max involuntarily jerked his head and shoulders. This statement hit him harder than the thump that he received from the mule.

Down the shore, a Philly term: I once had a lot of money but used it to better myself; the nuns wouldn't take someone like me. Is Gina Joey? Is Gina the target? Joey has had much more than a nose job; he has had a full-on sex change, and a convincing one at that. That's what he spent all of the money on.

Max turned and looked into her eyes. They were Joey's eyes. He had stared at Joey's picture for weeks. He couldn't believe it, but it was right in front of him. There was no denying it.

Max's mind raced, then his face went pale and his eyes glazed over.

What is going on here? I didn't find Joey, and that was OK. I was going to explain it to Carlo. I met his mother, and she cared for him enough to come over here to search for him. Gina was so kind to me. I even began to feel like a true pilgrim. We had become a Camino family that had built a bond of trust with each other. Now I don't know what to think. Am I angry and betrayed, or disappointed and sad? What was the purpose of my Camino?

Max remained silent for the rest of the walk to the beach. He knew what he was supposed to do, but he didn't know if he wanted to or even could.

The seagulls soared high above, calling out to their new visitors. "The sky is so blue, and the birds are so lovely. I can already taste the ocean and hear its roar," Gina said.

Max remained silent, looked at the birds in the sky, and shook his head in disgust.

Seagulls are filthy animals that eat garbage and shit all over the place, and the wind is blowing sand in our ears. I'll be glad to get out of here."

They reached the beach at Finisterre, walked towards the water, put down their packs, and moved to the water's edge. Gina inhaled the sea air and said, "My mother is a few thousand miles that way."

Max tersely said, "I know."

Gina stared off into the distance.

If she could see me now, she wouldn't believe it.

Gina turned to Max and said, "It's tradition to go in and wash away the dust and sweat of the Camino.

Max nodded, and they both went into the water. "This is so refreshing; it makes me feel so alive," Gina said.

That's good; enjoy it while you can.

Gina stood in the water and stared at the horizon.

I've done so much and made so many big changes, but I'm not really sure if I am any happier. Will it ever be safe to see my mother again? What am I going to do now? I do not believe that I have found my 'Personal Legend.' Was it all worth it?

"It does wake you up and let you know who you are," Max said.

Without any conscious effort, Max's heart rate increased rapidly, his senses became focused, the only sound, his pulse throbbing in his ears, the only sight, his friend Gina standing in the sea, staring off into the distance. After some time, Max exited the water alone and was off to the bus stop and into town. Max had realized his Personal Legend.

The following morning, Max was on a pay phone at the bus station in Santiago. He reported that there was no money left, and the job was done. He told Carlo that the money was all spent on a sex change operation. Carlo yelled, "What the hell are you talking about?"

Max heard the last call for his bus and blurted out, "I gotta go, Carlo," and hung up.

He hurried to the bus, the first of three on his way back to Italy. A man seated in front of him was reading the local paper. Max noticed the headline, which read "Peregrina se ahoga tras completar una 900 kilometros," which means a female pilgrim drowns after completing a 900-kilometer pilgrimage.

Max stared at a Via Francigena pamphlet in his hand.

Everyone knows the story of "The Scorpion and the Frog."

Epilogue

Max returned to Naples and reported the details of the job to Carlo. He told him that Joey had spent all of the money on a complete sex change operation, acted alone, and was now heading home in a bag like one of the bags of cash that he had stolen.

"Honest to God, Carlo, I never suspected that it was Joey until the very end, when I pieced together some of the details from the conversations that we had on our way to Finisterre. If I hadn't gone on the last part of the trek, I would have failed."

"You got the target, but the money would have been better," Carlo said.

"I did find out that Italy also has a pilgrimage like this one in Spain; it is called the Via Francigena," Max said.

"I know that, Max. I have also found out that the Via Francigena is where the government hides many of the rats that turn on this thing of ours. They set them up with new identities and gave them jobs and even businesses along that route, all for ratting us out.

Since you made it through this last job, I have another for you on the Via Francigena. You will go this spring when things open up there," Carlo said.

"Yes, boss." *I wanted to walk the Via Francigena at some point, anyway; I didn't think that it would be so soon, especially not for a job.*

"Who knows? You might even run into one of your father's old friends."

What does he mean by that? No one ever told me why my father was killed and I know that I can't ask Carlo. He just gives orders, not information.

A reporter in León reads an article off of the wire: "Peregrina se ahoga tras completar una 900 kilometros."

"Jefe, this girl was in the group that Grant Flynn was with before he died."

Glossary

Albergue - Spanish hostel typically used by pilgrims.

Arrivederci - Italian word meaning "Goodbye."

Arse - Slang term used in Ireland and the U.K. meaning "ass."

Bandito - Spanish for bandit or criminal.

Barra - Tapas counter.

Bastardo - Italian for "bastard."

Benvenuto - Italian for "welcome."

Bodega - term used in Spain a wine cellar, in the U.S. it means a small market.

Bon chemin - French for "Good Way", common greeting on the Camino de Santiago.

Buona fortuna - Italian for "good luck."

Buen camino - Spanish for "Good Way", common greeting on the Camino de Santiago.

Conejo - Spanish for rabbit.

Capo - The head of a branch of an organized crime syndicate.

Cazzate - Italian for "bullshit."

Dago red - Italian American slang term for red table wine.

Donativo - An albergue that accepts donations in lieu of set prices.

Gabagool - Italian American term for capocolla, an Italian spiced pork cold cut.

Gaguzz - Italian American slang term for idiot.

Gîte - French hostel typically used by pilgrims.

Grazie - Italian for thanks or thank you.

Hospitalero - Albergue host or worker.

Idioti - Italian for idiots.

Marone - Italian American slang used to express frustration.

Medigan - Italian American term slang referring to non-Italian people.

Mèrda - Italian for shit.

Mi scusi - Italian meaning "excuse me."

Melanzane - Italian American slang term referring to African American people.

Mulligan - Term used in golf meaning to ignore a bad shot and shoot again.

Oi - Australian slang used as a greeting or expression of shock.

Paisano - Term used in southern Italy and the United States, meaning friend.

Pazzo - Italian for "crazy."

Pfennig - German copper coin predating the Euro one cent coin.

Retablé - An ornate structure behind the altar in a church with depictions of Christian figures.

Schweinehund - German slang used similarly to bastard.

Stronzo - Italian slang for "asshole."

Stunad - Italian American slang for a "stupid person."

"To get straightened out" - To be made an official member in organized crime.

Acknowledgements

Much of the history, lore, and locale descriptions were developed using "Walking Guide to the Camino de Santiago: History, Culture, Architecture" by Gerald Kelly. His websites are www.CaminoGuide.net and www.caminoapp.net.

I would like to thank the beta readers who provided invaluable feedback: Mary Shaw, Ethan Shaw, Maureen O'Brien, Steve Dunham, Dean Mancini, and Craig Elicker.

The Legend of San Virila: The great siesta of the abbot of the Monastery of Leyre, La Voz de Galacia S.A., was inspired by a story from the Viva El Camino website, https://vivecamino.com.

The story of the Holy Grail in Leon is based on information included in articles on the Guardian website dated March 31, 2014, www.guardian.com, and the Aleteia website dated June 1, 2022, https://aleteia.org.

The story of the lost peregrina is based on information taken from an article on the Guardian website by Ashifa Kassam dated May 27, 2015, www.guardian.com.

During my Caminos and research trips, I used the Camino Guide App by Gerald Kelly, the Wise Pilgrim-Camino Francés App, and the Camino de Santiago guide book by Sergio Ramos. These all helped guide me through my Caminos, and I recommend them to anyone who wishes to walk the Camino de Santiago.

I would like to thank my editor Louise Morris.

I greatly appreciate Erica and Ricky from Camino Tellers for reviewing my book. They can be found on Youtube, Facebook and at www.caminotellers.com.

About the Author

Peter Shaw grew up in Philadelphia, Pennsylvania, and now lives in San Diego, California, with his family. This is his first work of fiction. He spent most of his life working as an engineer in the research and development of integrated navigation systems and sonar signal processing algorithms. His other publications are all related to that work. He has walked the Camino de Santiago with his wife, with his eldest son, and alone.

Printed in Great Britain
by Amazon